Smith's

I0554009

MONTHLY

Every Month Original
Novels, Stories, and Articles

USA Today Bestselling Writer
Dean Wesley Smith

TABLE OF CONTENTS

Short Stories

Always a Way
    A Marble Grant Story   6

Another Damn Deal   16

A Reason to Play a Hunch
    A Poker Boy Story   44

Hidden Canyon
    A Thunder Mountain Story   52

Full Novel

The Adventures of Hawk   62

Nonfiction

Introduction:
    Finally, An Ending...   3

Killing the Top 10 Sacred Cows of Indie Publishing
    A WMG Writer's Guide
                    Part 1 of 2   20

Introduction
Finally, An Ending…

Way back over three years ago, in issue #1 of this magazine, I started a book serial called "The Adventures of Hawk." It ran for over thirty-five thousand words in the first twelve issues and then I stopped.

The reason I stopped was pretty simple. I had Danny Hawk and his four friends in a world of problems and darned if I could figure out a way to get them out and wrap up the novel.

So this is my magazine and I had the option of just stopping and I did. I figured that when the solution occurred to me I would bring the serial back and end Hawk's first story.

A few readers asked about what happened and I told them, but as another year went by, and then a third year, Danny Hawk and his friends sort of got forgotten.

Then as I was looking at writing novels for this fourth year of the magazine, I remembered Hawk and I instantly knew how to end the story of Hawk's search for his father.

It seems my creative voice had finally figured out the problem. Took it long enough.

So you could say it took me over three years to write this novel, but the truth is, the length is closer to fourteen years.

You see, I initially came up with Hawk (only he had a different name) when I wrote a few short stories in this saga in 2004 for a company that went out of business. The stories were never published and I got the rights to the stories back.

I had liked what I had done with those short stories, but not enough to send them out anywhere. So for eleven years the stories sat in a file until this magazine idea came along.

I figured back when I started the magazine, it would be fun to serialize Hawk's story and do it the way I wanted to do it. So each month I fixed the older story, adding to it, and then for the last six issues of that first year I wrote new Danny Hawk chapters before I got stuck.

Thanks for the Support

Dean Wesley Smith

So now, in this issue, after almost fourteen years since I first created him, Hawk's first novel is finally done and in print.

Also note, the number for this issue is one of those special round numbers.

This is Issue #40.

I have filled my own magazine with short stories, novels and other stuff for forty issues now. If that doesn't make your head shake, I don't know what will.

Mine is shaking at the craziness of doing this, to be honest.

But I'm still having fun and I sure hope you are having fun reading each issue.

Thanks for sticking with me for all this time.

And Danny Hawk and his friends thank you as well.

—Dean Wesley Smith
June 6th, 2017

Coming Next Issue in *Smith's Monthly*

TOMBSTONE CANYON
A Thunder Mountain Novel

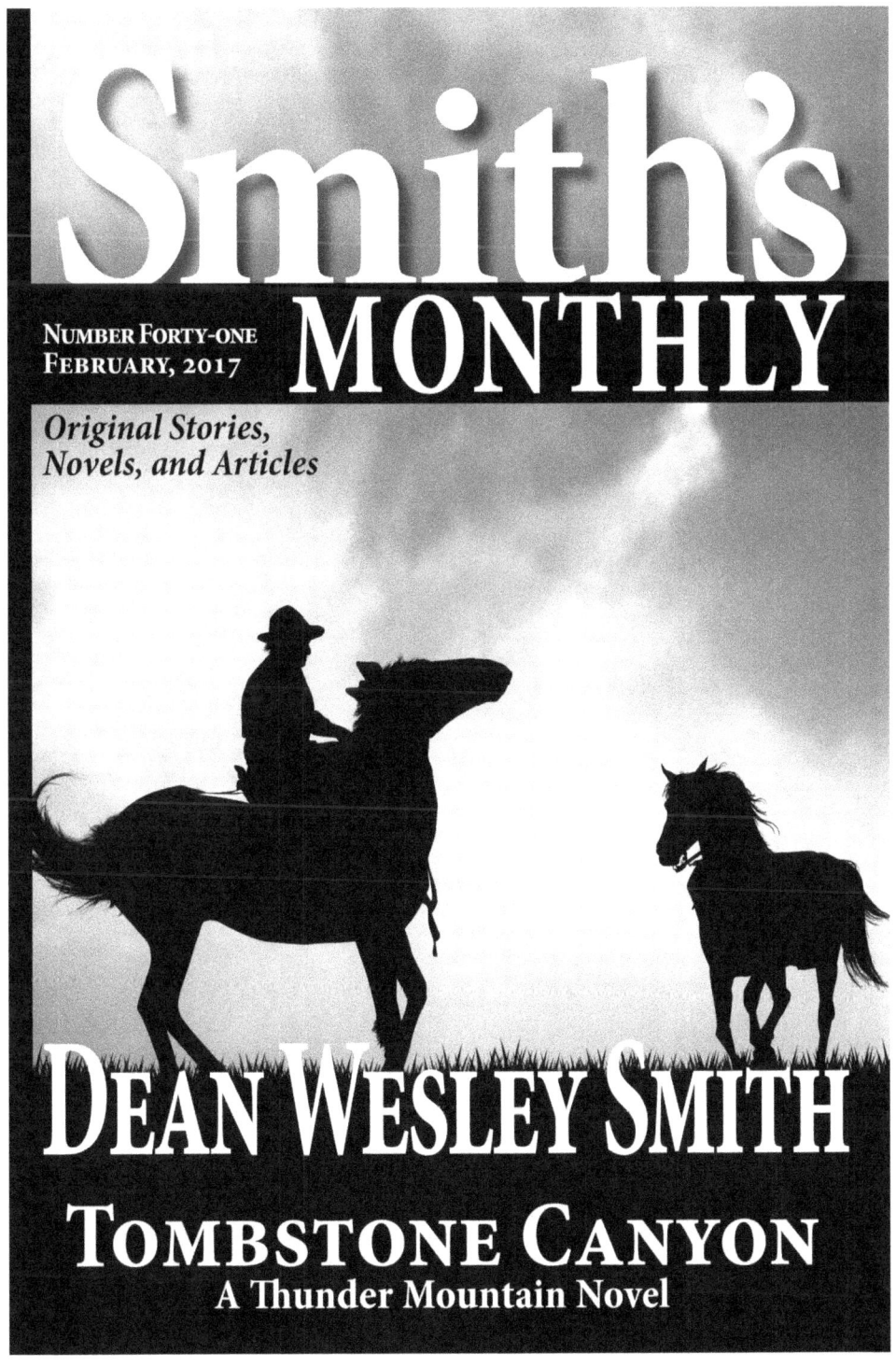

Smith's
MONTHLY

NUMBER FORTY-ONE
FEBRUARY, 2017

*Original Stories,
Novels, and Articles*

DEAN WESLEY SMITH

TOMBSTONE CANYON
A Thunder Mountain Novel

Marble Grant and her partner Sim stumble on one of the darkest secrets of human nature.

Can two former superheroes now turned brand new, but very dead, Ghost Agents figure out how to save hundreds of lives in their first large case together?

And stop the evil at the same time?

The third story in the growing Marble Grant saga.

Always a Way
A Marble Grant Story

One

I LOVED WHAT I called mornings. Actually, my morning was what most people call noon, but I'm far from most people.

Besides, being dead brought all sorts of privileges.

Right around noon I usually managed to stumble naked to the kitchen, get a cup of coffee from the pot my wonderful Sim, roommate and partner, had started before she left.

Every day I would take a sip, sigh heavily, then stagger with the cup back to the bathroom trying my best to not spill anything, even though it would never make a mess for long on the tile since it was ghost coffee.

By the time I got done in the bathroom and with that first cup of coffee, I was almost human.

Almost.

At least I could be talked to safely at that point.

Since being dead, I had taken to wearing mostly comfortable clothes. Expensive silk blouses, sports bra, jeans that fit my frame, as Sim said, like a stretch glove, and running shoes.

Sim and I put on our "get screwed" dresses once a week and went out on the town to dance and drink. But the rest of the time I could see no reason not to be comfortable.

I got back to the modern, spotless kitchen with white quartz counter, took a wonderful-tasting fresh bagel that Sim had picked up earlier this morning, spread some cream cheese on it, and went to the patio to sit at the glass table there with a second cup of coffee. I would usually just sit there for about a half hour and stare out over Las Vegas.

After that I was really human and completely safe to talk to.

Honest. No matter what anyone said.

Those mornings on the balcony were so special, I couldn't imagine not doing them. Our two-bedroom condo in the Ogden building in downtown Las Vegas had a view to die for, if I wasn't already dead. I could see all the way out the Strip toward the airport as well as the mountains beyond.

At night the lights of the Strip were just dazzling.

This morning the air had a crisp bite to it, which sort of surprised me considering the day was supposed to be a hot one. But the coffee kept me warm enough.

Sim would still be training with Jewel and Tommy this morning. All three of them were morning people. I was a night person, which Sim and I decided would work out great.

She would get up, have time in the condo without me, get out and do some work. We could work together in the afternoon and then we could share the evening together and after she went to bed I would head out to do what we Ghost Agents did.

Our jobs, it seemed, were to help people. Since we could be inside of people's minds and thoughts and control their actions while in there, we knew who was in trouble and who wasn't.

Most of the time we could even figure out fixes or at least help the person some.

And to me, honestly, that felt damn great. I had been a superhero working in real estate and hotels for the last hundred years before I got that bullet in the forehead. Now, as a Ghost Agent, I was managing in a month to do more good than I did in a year as a superhero.

Every day I felt lucky. I know. Sort of bug-crazy. Most people say they are lucky to be alive.

I'm damn lucky to be dead.

Go figure.

And I am even luckier to have met Sim. We just fit together completely and, as she said after two months together, she

---

More Marble Grant Now Available from all your favorite booksellers.

couldn't imagine how she lived without us together.

I felt the same way exactly.

Plus she was a tiger in bed and every morning she made me coffee and brought me fresh bagels. What more could a dead girl ask for?

Really?

Two

I WAS JUST finishing up my coffee and rinsing out my cup in the sink when Sim appeared beside me.

She kissed me on the cheek.

"Marble, you know you don't have to do that?" she asked, pointing to the cup I had just rinsed and put in the dishwasher.

A ghost element of a glass or dish just vanished in a few hours if we were not touching it. The real cup I had used was still sitting on the shelf.

So there was no need to wash anything. And we had never once started the dishwasher.

I noticed her morning dishes were still in the dishwasher as well as I put my coffee cup in there.

"I know," I said, smiling and pointing at her dishes. "Old habits die harder than we did."

She laughed, then she got that serious look on her face I had come to love.

Sim was a natural blonde and seemed to have almost no eyebrows. Her long blonde hair was thin and fine and felt wonderful to run my fingers through. And her large blue eyes could pin me to a wall with just a look and take my breath away.

I was starting to realize she might be one of the smartest people I had ever

met as well. And devious at times, which matched right into my attitude perfectly. It was a hell of a lot more fun to be devious when the situation warranted.

"Got us a wife beater this morning," she said. "It was his fetish, to beat on women."

I shook my head. "What did you do to the bastard?"

She laughed and grinned. "He thinks of hitting his wife or any woman again, he will automatically punch himself in the nuts."

"Oh, my," I managed to say after I caught my breath from laughing. "Was that fun to watch?"

Sim just smiled and nodded. "He was having breakfast at a café off the Strip, suddenly stood up and punched himself in the nuts. He was still screaming in pain, but starting to recover, when the paramedics got there. One of them was a pretty young woman and our pervert punched himself in the nuts again before they could restrain him."

It took me a full minute to stop laughing. "Damn, wish I could have seen that. We do that a few more times and they might start thinking it is a disease."

"Ball-punchers syndrome," she said.

"A rare but painful disease you can't get shots for."

She laughed at that, then got serious again.

"There's more."

I nodded.

"He was part of a pretty active dark web group that believed all women should be subjects and beaten regularly. Sims voice was soft and angry.

I had already learned in our few months together that making Sim angry was never a good plan. She was sweet and gentle almost all the time, but had a core anger that could level a building. Luckily, that anger had not been aimed at me so far. I hoped to avoid that at all costs.

Now I moved over and held her.

I knew that about ninety years ago she had ended up marrying an abuser, so finding an entire network of them that talked about it must have dug up those old memories in a horrific manner.

After a moment I asked, "You had lunch yet?"

She shook her head.

"How about we jump to the Golden Nugget Buffet and figure out a plan on how we're going to take down that group?"

Sim nodded. "Think we can do it? We're just new Ghost Agents and those creeps are spread all over the world."

"We might need some computer help," I said. "There is always a way."

"I hope you are right," she said.

"We'll figure it out," I said, "and then a plague of the puzzling crotch-punching disease will spread over the world."

She laughed and hugged me.

"Just think," I said, pretending to look serious. "The companies that makes ice bags to take down swelling are going to make a fortune."

We were both still laughing when we arrived at the buffet to plan.

Three

TURNS OUT SIM'S worry about taking down this group being difficult was justified.

We started off in the hospital with the original crotch-puncher Sim had run across this morning. His hands were both strapped to the bed and his normally pasty face was red.

He looked like he was drugged a little and was just staring at the tile ceiling.

What looked like ice bags were strapped over his crotch. If we could pull this off, my joke about the ice bag makers might actually be right. Who knew?

Crotch-puncher's wife, a woman who looked like she had been beautiful once, twenty years before, sat beside his bed silently. Now she had her mousy brown hair pulled back off her face and wore clothing that clearly hid her arms and neck. She seemed almost shrunken in on herself.

"We've got to do something to help her," I said as we arrived.

Sim nodded. Then she said, pointing at crotch-puncher, "You ready? It's not pretty in there."

I could tell the woman I was completely in love with was having issues.

"As much as I will ever be," I said. "And you know you don't need to go back in that creep's head again. I can get what we are looking for just fine. Why don't you help the wife?"

Sim nodded, looking relieved. "Thanks."

"That's what partners are for," I said.

Then I turned and went inside crotch-puncher's body.

Sim had been right. This guy was a bastard at all levels. Hated at work, hated in his neighborhood, hated by his wife. And all caused by his anger. I could see his computer setup in a book-lined study in his home in Los Angeles.

His wife, from his memories, had clearly been beautiful when they met. But he had started hitting her about five years into the relationship and then basically made her a prisoner to his money and anger.

I dug back and got exactly how he logged into the dark web, the group he went to, and so on.

A group of women-haters like I never knew existed. I knew some men hated women, feared women, thought of women as property even in this modern age. I just had never imagined a group that bragged to each other about the violence they had done to their wives.

And not just a few, but from what I could tell the group consisted of hundreds and hundreds just as screwed up as this guy.

We were going to need massive computer help, of that I had no doubt.

I got all the information I could get, then planted a clear command that he would allow his wife to leave him and not contest any divorce.

I saw where Sim had planted the punch-in-the-balls command at the thought of hitting a woman and made it stronger and deeper, a trick that Jewel had shown me how to do.

This guy would never get that command out of his system, no matter how much counseling he took or medical help he got. He would suffer the rest of his life, just as his wife would suffer from what he did to her the rest of her life.

I climbed out of the guy's mind and then did a trick Jewel had taught me to remember the information I needed to remember and let the rest of the memories of that sick mind fade.

A moment later Sim appeared beside the wife.

"I tried to help her," Sim said. "But she is pretty broken. She is going to go find help at a woman's shelter here in Vegas and divorce the bastard."

"I made sure he wouldn't fight the divorce and give her the settlement she asks for," I said, hugging my partner.

At that moment the wife stood, life back in her eyes again. She looked at her husband strapped to the hospital bed.

"No one will ever hit me again," she said to crotch-puncher.

With that, she turned and walked out.

I was cheering and Sim was crying.

Crotch-puncher was trying to get his hands free so he could hit himself again.

Four

TURNS OUT THAT two Ghost Agents that lived and worked together in Portland, Oregon, were experts in computers.

And hot? Wow, were they hot. The Sunset Kid and Gail, his partner, were the most striking couple I had ever had the chance to meet.

The first time we met them, Sim took my hand and squeezed it.

Then she sighed and I barely could keep from laughing.

Both Gail and Sunset looked like they could have stepped out of a fashion magazine. They dressed much nicer than Sim and I did, with Sunset actually in a silk suit without a tie and Gail in designer clothes.

And they were clearly very in love.

Later that night at home in Las Vegas, Sim and I talked about how much fun it would be to join the two of them for a romp in a very large bed. And that got us both hot thinking about it, even though we both knew that would never happen.

Still, a fun night of thinking about it. Put it this way, we messed up our own bed pretty well that night.

Both Gail and Sunset wanted to help the moment they heard what we were trying to do. And said they would also help in setting the crotch-punching command as well once we figured out how to get to the bastards.

Jewel and Tommy were also going to help.

So we had six Ghost Agents on this. All we had to do was figure out how to track all these sick men through their computers.

I was hopeful, Sim doubtful.

Gail and Sunset said it would take them some time to figure it out. They actually went to the crotch-puncher's house in LA and used his own computer and log-in information to get into the group.

Sim and I stayed to our routine, with Sim training with Jewel and Tommy in the mornings while I was still asleep and then I would go out with her and we would see who we could help around Vegas.

There was never a shortage.

At night, after Sim toddled off to bed, I went out on my own to see who I could help as well.

Four days after we had talked with Gail and Sunset, they appeared on our balcony with Jewel and Tommy.

Sim and I had been sitting together, planning our day.

Sim got them all some coffee and I got them bagels and the six of us sat on the balcony on a warm Las Vegas afternoon planning.

Gail and Sunset had figured out how to get through the group and they had all the names and address of the over seven hundred signed-in users to the sick place.

I suppose it shouldn't have surprised me there were that many members, but it did. For some reason I thought the simple fact of getting onto the dark web would stop most, and then not wanting to brag about being a monster would stop others.

Then I realized that chances were I was right. We were only going to hit the tip of an iceberg.

And that just made me angry.

We all decided we couldn't wait one minute longer because women were in danger out there. It would take us late into the night, but we could get it done.

So we divided the list into three parts and decided we would go in as teams. One person would set the crotch-punching command so deep it would last the rest of the bastard's life.

The other partner would stay out and be there for support. Then at the next bastard they would switch.

We all decided we would also help the wife clean out some of the damage and get to help. And we would make sure that the husband would allow them to leave and not fight the divorce.

It was the least we could do for those poor women.

I liked that plan, but hoped to change it a little once Sim and I got going. I didn't have a history of abuse in my past. The only man who had hit me, I had killed.

Pretty simple solution. He never hit me again, or any woman for that matter.

More Marble Grant Now Available from all your favorite booksellers.

And no one ever found his body either.

It was 1921, a damn easy time to hide a body.

But Sim had gotten stuck for a time in an abusive relationship early on and it still haunted her. So I planned on doing the most climbing in bastards' heads.

But I knew she would want to do some just to help clear out some of her past.

And I would be there to support her when she came out of each one of those monsters.

I had no doubt that today might end up being one of the longest days in either one of our long lives.

Five

SINCE WE WERE the youngest team, we got to stick closer to home in the western part of the US and Canada.

We had done thirty-six of the bastards, then met everyone back in Vegas for dinner and planning. Then we had all gone back out.

It seems our plan was working fine.

But then on number forty-nine, Sim and I ran into a problem.

The moment I went inside the guy's head as he sat at his desk in his office in San Francisco, I knew I wasn't in one of the regular angry wife-beaters.

This guy killed women.

Lots and lots of women and only beat his wife as a hobby, for the most part.

The most evil person I had ever touched.

And I knew where he had buried every one of the poor souls.

I implanted the punch-in-the-balls command deeply and added another so if he even thought of killing a woman, he would also kick a wall as hard as he could for as often as he could until the thought ended.

Then I climbed out and went to find my partner, who had just finished with the wife in their home in the hills of Berkeley.

"She thinks he is a serial killer," Sim said, her face white with shock.

I nodded. "He is. I know where all of them are buried."

"How many?" Sim asked.

"Fifteen here in San Francisco. Another five in college back east."

"I think I'm going to be sick," Sim said.

I agreed with her completely.

We stood there, holding each other.

I have no idea at all how I could have done this job without her beside me.

After a minute we jumped back to the serial killer's office. He lay on the floor behind his desk screaming at his broken ankle and the damage he had done to his groin.

"We need help," I finally said after we stood there for another minute, hand-in-hand, watching the killer roll on the floor in pain. "I honestly have no idea what to do."

Sim nodded.

"Jewel, Tommy, some help?"

A few moments later Jewel and Tommy both appeared next to us. The serial killer was now whimpering on the floor behind his desk, alternating between holding his crotch and his broken foot.

"A serial killer," I said, pointing at the bastard. "Killed twenty. We have no idea what to do."

Jewel and Tommy both nodded.

"We've run into this a few times," Jewel said.

"And you will too, sadly," Tommy said.

"Take a deep breath, brace yourself, and follow me in there," Tommy said.

I took Sim's hand and we went into the serial killer's body once again.

Tommy quickly showed us how to set a command that for the rest of his life, at any chance, this guy would confess about his crimes and tell anyone who would listen where he buried the bodies.

And in great detail.

It was such an easy solution, I couldn't believe I hadn't thought of it. But I had been so shocked climbing inside the cesspool of serial killer's mind, I just hadn't.

Tommy removed the kicking the wall command I had set and the punching himself in the balls command and replaced them with a command that at any thought of killing or hitting a woman, he would feel extreme remorse. Remorse so intense he would have to tell anyone who would listen what he was feeling and how sorry he was for even thinking it.

And then confess every crime he ever did all over again.

Finally, Tommy planted a command that the killer call the police and report himself and tell them where the bodies were buried.

Then the three of us got out of the sewer of the killer's mind.

It never felt so good to be back in the air.

The killer climbed back into his chair and called the police. As he was saying he had killed some women, he started crying.

Then he started bawling and sobbing like a baby, trying to keep confessing.

"He will not do well in prison," Sim said, shaking her head.

"Exactly," Tommy said, smiling.

With that, Tommy and Jewel left, going back to their list.

I figured that the best thing Sim and I could do was keep going as well and she agreed.

It took us until four in the morning before we finished our list and told Jewel and Tommy and Gail and Sunset.

They were almost done as well. Just a few more each.

All of us looked wiped out.

I felt like I had been dragged through a garbage dump, but I also knew we had saved a lot of lives and punished a lot of abusers in ways the law of live society could never do.

Sim and I got a glass of wine and went out to our deck looking over the lights of Las Vegas.

We sat in silence, sipping the wine as the cool evening air around us took away some of the memories.

"That was a good day," I said after a few minutes. "I feel like shit, but it was a hell of a good day."

Sim nodded. "Have I ever said how I love how you look at the world?"

"No," I said, smiling at her. "But I'm glad you do because I sure love that wonderful smile and perfect body of yours."

She laughed. "Good, because I was hoping you would be up for scrubbing my back in the shower."

"I would love that," I said. "But only if we can crawl in bed together afterward and just hold each other."

"I'll drink to that," she said, smiling.

We sat drinking for a few more minutes, letting the memories of the monsters we had visited slip from our minds to be replaced by the beautiful view of the lights of the Strip.

Then Sim stood, took my hand, and led me toward the bedroom and a wonderful warm shower that would wash away even more memories of what we had seen in those heads.

We had been faced with a horrid problem. We had found a way to solve it and saved a lot of people in the process.

Ghosts saving lives.

And that felt good, almost as good as getting my back washed by a beautiful woman after a long day.

Almost.

~

Can't Get Enough of Ghost of a Chance?
These novels are available at your favorite booksellers in trade paper and electronic editions.

USA Today bestselling writer, Dean Wesley Smith takes a stab at why so many "Deal with the Devil" stories get published.

And what it feels like to be a writer at times.

First published in 1994 in Deals With The Devil *from DAW Books edited by Mike Resnick, Martin H. Greenberg, and Loren D. Estleman.*

Another Damn Deal

FAMED SHORT STORY writer Walter Kennedy Nurnberg had never written a "Deal with the Devil" story. He'd read thousands of them over his fifty years and thought them stupid and dull, with few exceptions. But on one Tuesday afternoon, without a story idea at hand, he decided to try one.

He rolled a blank piece of paper into the old manual Royal sitting on his huge oak desk, typed his name at the top, spaced down the page, and then paused to think of a title. The moment he touched the keys an explosion shook his chair. His ears rang and the room filled with the smell of brimstone and burning wood.

Walter spun around. There, standing on the third shelf of his built-in polished oak book case, next to his favorite copy of MOBY DICK, was the Devil.

The Devil had the standard pointed ears and barbed tail, but he stood no more than five inches tall and wore knickers with red- patterned, knee-high socks and white golf shoes. Instead of the pitchfork he carried a tiny little five iron.

Now Walter was surprised, even though he shouldn't have been. If he'd have thought about it he might have expected the Devil to appear right at that moment. It was the standard occurrence in most of the stories he'd read. But a five-inch tall Devil with a five iron shocked him.

"Why?" the Devil demanded, his voice high-pitched and squeaky.

"Why what?" Walter managed to say without laughing. He didn't know if he should laugh or be scared, but at the moment, with the Devil's tiny voice, laughing was winning.

"Why write another *Let's Make a Deal* story? Don't you think there are enough of them around?"

Walter shrugged. "I felt like it." Walter didn't want to mention that he didn't have any other idea at that moment.

The little Devil shook the five iron at the next shelf up. "Damn you!" he shouted.

It took a huge amount of will power for Walter to not laugh at that one.

"Who are you swearing at?" Walter finally managed to get out.

"Him," the Devil said, pointing up. "You know. God. He's the one responsible for all these '*Deal*' stories. And I'm tired of it. Makes me look bad every damn time."

"So," Walter said, "I'll write a good one, showing you to be the nice guy. How about that?"

"Would you really?" the Devil squeaked, striding over to the edge of the shelf and looking at Walter closely.

Walter thought for a moment, then said, "No. Probably not. It would never sell and no one would believe it. My stories are known for their verisimilitude, you know."

The Devil stamped his little golf-shod foot, then started pacing up and down past the Encyclopedia Britannia. Walter was sure there would be spike marks in the polished wood shelf and he was about to say something when the Devil again spoke. "How about if you don't write one at all?" The devil stopped in front of Walter's unabridged Shakespeare and leaned on the five iron.

Walter again thought, then shook his head. "It seems logical to me that if the man in charge upstairs makes writers do these stories, then it would also make sense that he would help them sell. That would explain why there were so many bad ones. Besides, I could use the money. You know how writers are about money."

The little Devil let out a deep sigh. "I can't believe this." He paced up and down in front of the Shakespeare and the encyclopedia, then stopped and squinted at Walter. "All right, what is it you want? We might as well get this part over with."

Walter laughed. "You mean you want my soul?"

"Why the hell would I want your crummy soul?" the Devil said. "Just tell me what you want for not writing the story and let me get back to the course. I'm two up after seven holes and I hate getting called away for these stupid PR problems."

For a moment Walter was tempted to ask who the Devil had been playing against, then decided not to and turned his attention to what he really wanted. The answer was clear. Money. "I want you to guarantee that this story will sell for over a thousand dollars."

"Excuse me?" the Devil squeaked.

Walter just smiled.

"Let me see if I understand this. For you to *not* write a "Deal" story, I must promise you that the story will sell?"

"Not quite. Your promise in exchange for me not writing a hundred "Deal" stories."

"Now wait just a damn minute!" Little wisps of smoke were coming from the edges of the Devil's knickers.

"Let me explain," Walter said. "Seems only logical that if the man upstairs," Walter pointed at the ceiling, "wants us writers to bang out these stories about you, then I could sure write a few hundred of them. In fact, it might be nice to be known as the best "Deal-with-the-Devil" story writer. Just imagine, my stories in every book, every magazine. Movie options. Maybe even a television mini-series." Walter smiled a dream-like smile.

Now the little guy was really mad. Blue smoke filled the air around him. "So, if I guarantee that you'll sell this one, you'll promise to never write another one? Is that it?"

"Bingo," Walter said.

The Devil shook his head. "How did I ever get into this? I should've stayed on the golf course." He sizzled and smoked for a few more moments, then reluctantly said, "Deal."

There was an explosion and a cloud of smoke and the Devil was gone.

Walter quickly went over to the bookcase and inspected the fire and spike-mark damage in the wood. He'd have to replace the entire shelf. But for a thousand bucks, it was worth it. He went back to his typewriter. Now all he had to do was come up with a story. He had a sure sale.

He looked at the white paper and the place where he should put the title.

Nothing came to mind.

Not one word.

The white paper, stark against the black metal of the typewriter seemed to laugh at him. All he had to do was think of a story, but somehow, nothing would come. He couldn't even remember the idea he'd first had.

He went into the kitchen to get something to drink, then came back and stared at the white paper the rest of the afternoon.

And then again the next day.

And the next.

And the next.

It was so simple. A guaranteed sale. All he had to do was write the story.

If he could just think of one.

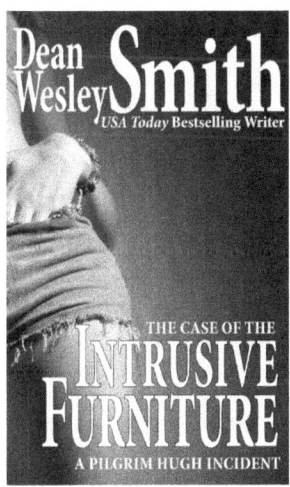

Three Pilgrim Hugh Incidents
Available at your favorite booksellers.

DEAN WESLEY SMITH

KILLING

THE TOP 10

Sacred Cows

OF Indie PUBLISHING

As indie publishing flourishes, many, many myths form around this new booming area of publishing. USA Today *bestselling author and major indie blogger Dean Wesley Smith takes a cut at killing some of the myths before they can take root.*

From the myth that indie writers can't get books into bookstores (they can) to the idea that indie publishing must be easy (it is and it isn't), Dean knocks ten myths down one after another and might just save you years of wasted time.

Author of the acclaimed Killing the Top Ten Sacred Cows of Publishing, *this companion WMG Writer's Guide for indie writers and publishers will become a necessity for your reference shelf.*

Killing the Top Ten Sacred Cows of Indie Publishing
A WMG Writer's Guide

Part 1 of 2

For all the brave writers out there who are going it alone.
Have fun.

Introduction

Welcome to the second book in the Killing the Sacred Cows series. The first book was called simply, *Killing the Top Ten Sacred Cows of Publishing*.

Both books are about the myths, which I call "Sacred Cows," that infest the publishing industry. I've been writing about these myths, killing one sacred cow after another, on my web site for years now.

Finally, last year, some of the readers convinced me I needed to put the Sacred Cows into a book. So I took what I thought were the top ten myths about publishing in general and created the first book.

But then, as the indie publishing world started to grow and gain traction, it became clear to me that the writers thinking of indie publishing were getting pounded with a lot of myths as well.

So thus this second book.

All the chapters in the two books were blog posts on my website and have some wonderful comments and questions attached. So feel free to go follow the discussions and ask questions.

There is a tab at the top of my website called Killing Sacred Cows that links to all the different chapters in a rougher form.

Why I Can Write About This Stuff

I sold my first short story in 1975, and have been pushing and working at writing ever since. I went through many of the general myths from the first book and survived them and finally started making a living in publishing in 1987, the same year I sold my first novel.

Also that year, Kristine Kathryn Rusch and I started a publishing company called Pulphouse Publishing, which quickly grew to be the fifth largest publisher of science fiction, fantasy, and horror in the nation.

I was the publisher and sometimes editor on some projects.

We shut the business down in 1996, but I kept editing at times, first for a magazine, then for Pocket Books in the *Star Trek* department. Also, during that time and up until around 2008, I sold over one hundred novels under various names to traditional publishers.

So sitting in the writer desk, the editor desk, and the publisher desk allowed me to see all sides of this business. And working for such a long time writing many, many novels, helped me clear out the last of the myths for myself.

Then the indie revolution started and I loved it right off.

I loved the freedom and the fact that I didn't have to spend so much time dealing with editors and such in New York.

So in 2009, Kris and I once again started up a publishing company called WMG Publishing Inc. to work on our indie titles and get our backlist out.

Now, as I write this in 2014, WMG Publishing Inc. has seven employees and three more coming on in the fall. It has over 400 titles in print and is publishing not only Kris's work and my work, but work by a lot of other writers as well.

So I know the indie side as well as the traditional side.

And both Kris and I have been voices in the indie growth on our blogs since it started.

The Goal of This Book

Writers hold onto myths like lifelines that are keeping them from drowning in a raging river of information. Sometimes sane people in the normal world will follow a publishing myth that makes no sense at all.

And they follow the myth, the sacred cow, without thought.

So this new series is an attempt to help the new world of indie publishing with the growing list of myths that plague it.

My goal is simply to show other sides of myths, to help writers become grounded in good business decisions.

Writing fiction is a business. Indie publishing your fiction is a business.

This indie publishing business can be fantastic fun and very profitable if you can make clear business decisions that are right for you.

My goal is to not show you the right way, or the only way, or any other such nonsense.

My goal is to help you push aside the myths that are swirling around publishing and make good decisions for yourself.

Thanks for reading. I hope this book helps your writing and publishing dreams in some fashion or another.

Dean Wesley Smith
June 9th, 2014
Lincoln City, Oregon

Sacred Cow #1
You Can't Get Your Books Into Bookstores

Or put more clearly,
indie writers can't get their books into bookstores

FACT: OF COURSE indie writers/publishers can. But some things must be done correctly and the bookstore owners or buyers must know your book is there. And it also must be something that fits what they are selling.

I'll lay it out below and in even more detail in a lecture that is now available under the lecture tab called "How to Get Your Books into Bookstores."

But let me say this here. Traditional publishers don't have magic wands that ship their books into bookstores. They simply know how to do it and indie publishers have yet to learn. Or at least some indie publishers. Some of us already know how and are making great money on paper books.

First Some History

As with all these publishing myths, to really grasp the myth and get past it, an indie publisher must know where the myth came from and why there used to be a little truth to the myth. Not much, but a little. Myths in publishing are often formed from half-truths of the past. But just as if you don't need a buggy whip to start your car, you don't need an agent to sell a book, or a traditional publisher to make a living at fiction writing.

And traditional publishers can't magically block you from going into bookstores. They can't even try, to be honest.

So where did this myth start? Most of it came from the old days of warehouse publishing and vanity press publishing. Writers (often horrid writers, but not all) would spend thousands and thousands of dollars through a scam vanity press to get a garage full of really ugly books. Then these poor writers would wander the roads and the streets peddling their books to any unsuspecting store who let them in the door.

Store owners hated these vanity-press people almost as much as they hated a young traditionally published writer with a handful of bookmarks. Sometimes a vanity press book had a local interest and the bookstore owner would take a few. (Young writers with bookmarks who demanded to have a signing were just flat annoying.)

Also, in those vanity press days, traditional publishers seemed to have a stranglehold on the book distribution network.

Of course, that wasn't true either, but it seemed that way.

In 1987, Kris and I started an indie publisher (called a small press back then) named Pulphouse Publishing. We got our books and magazines into traditional distribution systems just fine. Our magazines were on newsstands. And the company lasted for nine years selling to bookstores. Go figure.

Why could we do it? Simple, actually. We spent the little bit of time and energy to learn how to slot our books into what are called "the trade distribution systems." No one in the distribution system seemed to care that Pulphouse wasn't in New York City. Or that when we started we only had two books our first year.

Some Terms Before Moving Forward

POD means Print on Demand printing. CreateSpace, LightningSource, and others are *printers*, not publishers. You (your publishing business name) is the publisher.

DISTRIBUTORS are the companies that take your book from one place and sell them to another place. Baker & Taylor and Ingrams are two of the biggest distributors. There are thousands of smaller distributors that function in many areas, from regional to gift shops to books only on a certain topic. You name it, there's a distributor for it.

BOOKSTORES are places that sell your books to readers. Susy's Local Gift and Bookshop is a bookstore. Amazon is a bookstore. Kobo is a bookstore.

INDIE BOOKSTORE is a bookstore that is not associated with a chain store, or Amazon. Indie bookstores can be a chain, so the line is pretty vague most

of the time. Powell's Bookstore based in Portland is considered an indie store, but it is owned by a corporation and has many stores and a major online web selling site. Go figure.

ABA is the American Booksellers Association, a group made up of bookstores and publishers. (Yes, you can join as a publisher for around $300 bucks, give or take.) Their focus is to help bookstores learn new methods of selling and be a connection between publishers and bookstores. The ABA has many, many programs that help bookstores discover new books coming out. Some indie publishers can get into the programs, some a new indie publisher can't get into.

INDIE PUBLISHER. A writer or group of writers who have a real publishing name and imprint and act like a business using a business imprint name such as Teddy Press or CAT Publishing.

SELF-PUBLISHED WRITER. A writer who publishes under his or her own name, with no business publishing name. This will block you from most bookstores I'm afraid. (If you don't know how to get a business name, read my "Think Like a Publisher" articles under the tab above. It's scary simple.)

**So What Has Changed
in the Last Ten Years?**

When looked at in cold, hard terms, not much I'm afraid. I know those of you with no sense of history in publishing will scream at that, but sadly, it's the truth.

The real question, as Passive Guy has continually pointed out, is what will the disruptive technology hitting publishing change in the future. The big change has yet to come. And from what I can see, legacy (or big traditional) publishing is not reacting well so far.

So what hasn't changed? Let's look at history.

Pulp magazines came in around the last part of the 1800s and changed distribution of novels and stories to readers.

Then in the late 1930s, but mostly into the late 1940s, mass market paperbacks came in and changed distribution of novels and stories to readers.

And electronic books have now done exactly the same thing once again starting in 2009.

Nothing new, just the standard cycle of a new form of distribution of novels and stories to readers coming in. These changes tend to happen to allow over-priced books to find a less-expensive way to the general public. Pulps did that around 1900 and paperbacks did that in 1950 and now, sixty years later, history repeats yet again.

For those of you who are history challenged, the articles you see about what electronic books are doing are almost word-for-word from articles done about the advent of pulps. And word-for-word about the advent of the mass market paperback.

And those of you who don't like Amazon, they own very, very little of the sales market compared to the old *American News Company*, that basically controlled all magazine, most comics, and most book distribution in this country in the first half of last century. Then one day in 1957 they just shut their doors.

By the height of the pulps in 1940, about 50% of all novels published were only published in the pulps. In the height of the mass market paperbacks, around

2005, about 50% of all novels published were only published in mass market paperbacks. It's a safe bet that will be the number for electronic novels as well in a decade or so.

History can teach us a lot in publishing.

But how about indie publishing? That's new, right? We're all out in the great unknown, right?

Uhhh, no. Writers were publishing their own books for a very long time before "Vanity Press" scams made it a bad thing in the 1950s. Before the 1950s, publishing your own work or starting your own press was an accepted part of publishing. And the list of authors from that century who self-published their own books could fill a large book in very tiny print. It was perfectly accepted, as it is becoming yet again.

Nothing new. Goes around, comes around, and all that.

Let me give you just one minor example. Arkham House, run by August Derelith, the writer, started to reprint a few Lovecraft works. But almost half of all Arkham House books for the first thirty years were Derelith books. You really would have fun studying the real history behind some of the major traditional presses now and how they got started and why. Like Simon and Sons.

And folks, if you really go back and look at old books from a hundred years ago, you will see almost no sign, if any, of the publishers of today. The publishers you all think of as huge now were small press or solo shops, indie presses, back 50 or 100 years ago. The indie presses grew up to replace the old, slow legacy publishers of that day. And that's what is happening now as well.

In 1987, Kris and I started an indie press. And many small indie presses came and went while we were in business, and I still collect books from some indie presses in the 1950s and 1960s. (Arkham House shut down in 2005, lasting from 1938.)

In other words, there is nothing new happening.

Except... No, let me make that EXCEPT!!!!!!

—More people now think they can do it, and thus more people are starting their own publishing companies.

That will have an impact. The full type of impact is yet to be known. Too early.

But with more people doing this, discoverability is a growing problem area that Kris is talking about now in her great blog.

Is this discoverability problem actually new? No, not really once again. The results of books not easily found is that this trend is returning publishing to a time where blockbusters didn't exist. (Yes, I know... but the modern "blockbuster novel" that supports most of traditional publishing didn't really come around until the late 1960s and early 1970s and didn't become part of the traditional publishing business plan until the 1980s.)

So even this flattening of sales across more products has happened before.

I personally think it's a healthy correction, but I haven't been getting millions per book in advances.

So more writers jumping into the mix as indie publishers is the one thing that is different from any time in history. At no time in history have so many writers in such a concerted form, moved to indie publish as a mass.

My honest opinion... For a time that might have some interesting consequences, but I kind of doubt any consequence will be very long term, since most indie publishers will drop away given time, leaving, as

normal, only the survivors who can adapt and hold on through the technological-impact changes that are coming.

It's Easy, But It's Not

In the second Killing the Sacred Cows of Indie Publishing, I'm going to deal with the fact that so many people call this indie publishing "easy." I'll deal with that next chapter. It is, but it isn't.

But for the moment, I want to stay focused on the subject of this chapter.

Getting Your Books into Bookstores.

It's easy, but it's not.

Remember that.

What Does It Mean in 2014 to Have Your Book in a Bookstore?

Way back, again looking at history, bookstores were often the publishers as well. (Yeah, I know, publishers have been talking about vertical structures for some time, looking to see if it is possible to produce books and sell to readers at the

More WMG Writers' Guides
from all your favorite booksellers
in trade paper and electronic editions.

same time. Harlequin springs to mind.) And Amazon is playing in that area and Barnes & Noble has had their own publishing arm now for decades (I wrote a bunch of books and stories for B&N).

But back then, way back, before this modern era, bookstore catalogs consisted of what books the bookstore itself had printed, what books they were going to print, and what books they had in stock in their store, and maybe a few other books from a few other bookstore/publishers.

(And by the way, Print on Demand (POD) is also not new…it was being done in the 1800s in the backs of bookstores. We did it in 1987 at Pulphouse because we owned our own press. We printed to order, as did old stores a hundred years ahead of us.)

So what about today?

In today's modern bookstores, a book is considered to be "in the store" when…

1) it is on the shelves, or

2) in the bookstore catalog.

So to get your book into a bookstore, it needs to make it to a bookstore catalog or onto a shelf.

If you are dreaming of having a shelf full of just your book or books in a bookstore (like used to happen ten years ago), you need to change that thinking.

Most bookstores don't operate that way anymore.

Ten years ago, a bookstore would order ten copies of a book to sell five. The other five would get destroyed and credited by the publisher to the bookstore. So a publisher would have to print ten copies to sell five, so the five sold had to carry the weight of the costs of the extra books. That was called "Ordering to Stock" among other terms.

Today, smart bookstores "Order to Replace."

Distribution systems have gotten fast, so a bookstore owner will often take only one or two copies of a book, then when one sells, they order to replace it quickly. No returns and a ton safer.

ABA has been teaching bookstores this method for six years now, plus cash register systems and website book-selling design. That's why, for the last five years, there have been more bookstores than the year before. I know, another myth shot about bookstores going away. Head out of the sand, folks. Numbers of bookstores are increasing. Fact.

Using Ordering to Replace system, bookstore owners who are smart can get more titles in the same shelf area.

Think about that…

THIS IS A GOOD THING for all authors, because more authors actually have books in physical form in bookstores for readers to find. Instead of ten of the last Patterson, there are two of the Patterson and eight other authors' books in the same shelf space.

That is a good thing for all readers and writers.

Traditional bestselling mega-authors hate this new practice, however, because so much of the old system was based on books shipped, not books sold. That's right, big advances were based on having 100,000 books shipped, even if only 30,000 sold. That second number wasn't seen for months and months. The first number caused books to be on major bestseller lists.

But bookstores don't "Order to Stock," they now "Order to Replace." That's a HUGE CHANGE. (Nothing really new, just back to the pre-return system days of book selling.)

That's why you hear idiots like Scott Turow going on about how bad this new world is. He would rather return to the old returns system that destroyed five-out-of-ten books produced so his books-shipped numbers could be high. (And it was that old system that caused bookstores to collapse for eleven straight years of fewer and fewer stores, which is where the fewer bookstore myth comes from. Under the new Order to Replace system, bookstores are increasing every year and becoming stable.)

Today, in this new system, the returns system is drifting away and is now under 18% standard and still dropping. (Returns hovered between 50% and 55% at one point.) Many large publishers are even offering no-return choices for higher discounts and bookstores are learning to order smarter.

Give us five more years and the returns system will be around 10%, if that. Nothing more than a sales tool as it started off to be in the depression.

So How Do You Get Your Book Into a Bookstore?

Some basics first. All are critical, but most of you will just glaze over these looking for the secret, and these basics are the secret.

So let me be clear here. The Secret to Getting Your Books into Bookstores is:

1… Great cover, branded to genre.

2… Great sales blurbs. (Not your plot, sales blurb…if you don't know sales copy writing, learn it.)

3… A publisher name. (Can't be your writer name as publisher. Bookstores will shy away from that just as they were afraid of those authors with a fist-full of bookmarks coming through the door.)

4… A publisher web site. You also need an author web site. Treat your publisher web site like it is Bantam Books.

5… A major dealer/bookstore discount schedule on your publisher web site. You can copy the WMG Publishing discount schedule if you like.

6… Your paper books need to be priced correctly. Easiest way to figure this is go on CreateSpace to their price calculator, put in your trim size, your page count, and then experiment with prices. When the amount you make in the "extended distribution" program is above $2.00, your book is priced correctly.

From the Bookstore Side

So back in Spring of 2013, things changed in the two major distribution companies and most small distributors are following slowly. Ingrams and Baker & Taylor, for the longest time, had code in their monthly catalogs on the books that were produced with a POD printer. And they limited the discounts bookstores could get on POD books.

Then very silently in March and April of 2013, that code vanished.

The reason is simple. POD books have reached a level of quality that is often above a web press printed book quality. POD books could be done faster. And most importantly, major traditional publishers were using POD for short-run books, for second printings, and so on. So by having the code on there, the distributors were hurting their main clients.

So the code vanished. Poof.

What does that mean? Now your paper book, with your publisher imprint on it, is in the same catalog right beside any of the books from the hundreds of imprints from Random/Penguin. And since readers don't buy for publisher, but for author, any indie book was suddenly sitting beside any traditional book in the big discount catalogs.

And playing with the same tools. And the same field of sale.

So bookstores could order your book if they wanted… if the book looked good… if they knew about it… and if the indie publisher had set the price correctly to allow for enough discounts through the chain of custody for a book.

The key, of course, is that the bookstore owner must learn about your book through the normal trade channels. Granted, some store owners are on Goodreads and watch other reader review sites, but most still find their information through the trade channels.

Can an indie publisher get a book into a trade channel?

Of course. No magic keeping you out, honest there isn't.

A trade channel is simply letting the bookstore know the book is coming. For example, the major trade review magazine for bookstores is *Publisher's Weekly*. All bookstores look at it every week and get it for free. So send your books to *Publisher's Weekly* for review. (Act like a publisher. Don't use the paid side of PW and never buy a review anywhere.)

(I talk about all this over six weeks in the Promotions workshop. Both how to sell to readers and how to sell in the trades, and how to do your catalog copy. And more.)

The ABA has a bunch of fairly inexpensive programs so that you can let a thousand bookstores know your book is coming.

You can send things (not bookmarks), AS A PUBLISHER, directly to the bookstore. Bookstore mailing lists are free on the ABA web site.

Does this all take some time and learning? Yes.

As I said. It's easy, but it's not.

But chances are if your book has a good cover, a publisher name, a decent price, and is being carried by any standard entry distributor, it's already making its way to bookstores. The owner might not have a copy on the shelf yet, but it might be in the bookstore online catalog.

CreateSpace extended distribution is a service they provide as an entry point distributor. LightningSource (caution with their terms of service) is not only a printer, but can provide standard entry point to distribution channels.

Or you can have your book printed in any number of POD printers, or small presses in your local area and make a deal with an entry-point distributor and get your books out there.

There are hundreds and hundreds of entry point distributors. As a publisher, you will need to figure out what works for you and what is easiest.

It's easy, but it's not.

More WMG Writers' Guides
from all your favorite booksellers
in trade paper and electronic editions.

If you want really easy, just use CreateSpace and their extended distribution. Scary easy. But they are not the only way into the distribution system by a long, long ways. And with any printer and with any entry distributor, they have their drawbacks.

Make decisions as a publisher for yourself. Think like a business person.

I had my own printer in Pulphouse for most projects, for others I used a press only an hour away and a bindery only an hour away. My distribution was also fairly close when we jumped products into the channels. I found being local and close helped me work tighter with the printer and binder.

But the discount the bookstore is getting is wrong...

Sigh... I have to talk about this just to head off the thousand comments and questions on this one topic.

When a bookstore, and indie bookstore, gets books from distributors, the store tends to have only one or two or three major distributors it uses. This is normal. Think about how they only want to pay three bills per month instead of a dozen and you'll understand.

A distributor (both large and regional distributors) sets a basic discount for a bookstore on a number of factors.

1... How much the bookstore orders from the distributor.

2... The bookstore's credit rating.

3... How fast, over time, the bookstore pays its bills.

So a bookstore who only orders a few books from say Baker & Taylor per month, or who doesn't have a good credit rating, or who often pays late, will be sent the bottom (library) catalog.

If you, the indie author, go in there and convince them to try to order your book and they can only get a 20% discount, then chances are that store doesn't order much from that distributor. Or has credit issues. Or pays bills late.

NOT YOUR FAULT, NOTHING YOU CAN DO. WALK AWAY.

Or offer to sell them copies at your publisher discount.

Let me say this again to be clear... All those factors of bookstore discounts, once your book is priced correctly, are out of your control in almost all distribution channels and through all distributors.

And remember, if you have a good publisher web site, bookstores can order from you for up to 50% free shipping on ten assorted books. If you are thinking you don't want to pack books, you need to really think it through. You don't have to. Duh. You drop-ship the books direct from your printer to the store, just as any traditional publisher drop-ships books to bookstores from their printers. (I used to do this with some Pulphouse magazines from my printer in 1990. Nothing new.)

SUMMARY

You must do some things correctly to get bookstores to order your books. Covers, blurbs, correct pricing, and so on. Those are the secrets.

And as a publisher, you must have enough product to make it worth a bookstore's while to order from you.

But even more important, a bookstore needs to know your book exists. And that's the tough part.

Getting your books into bookstores is easy, but it's not.

But you, as an indie publisher, can absolutely get your books sitting right beside any book from any traditional publisher in a bookstore if you want.

There is no magic roadblock.

If you want, and are crazy enough, you can even get your books to Costco. (Go in there next time and notice how many books in Costco are regional presses. If they can do it, so can you, but I'm not talking about how to do it here. If you have to ask, you aren't ready.)

One of the keys is that you, as the publisher of your own indie books, must decide if paper books are worth it, if having your books in store catalogs and on bookstore shelves are worth it.

And that's a business decision only you can make.

WMG Publishing has books in bookstores and has over 200 titles in paper. For example, take a look at a simple search I did for Kristine Kathryn Rusch at Powell's Books, an indie bookstore. http://www.powells.com/s?kw=Kristine+Kathryn+Rusch&class=

More WMG Writers' Guides
from all your favorite booksellers
in trade paper and electronic editions.

Or a simple search of Kristine Kathryn Rusch books in Mysterious Galaxy Bookstore. http://www.mystgalaxy.com/search/apachesolr_search/Kristine%20Kathryn%20Rusch

We didn't approach either store. Yet WMG books are right there with Kris's traditionally published books just fine. We put the books into the system and let the system take care of itself and we are now working slowly to let bookstores know the books are out.

You know the decision we made three years ago. It's clear.

Getting books into bookstores is easy, but it's not.

But it can clearly be done, and anyone who tells you it can't be is just spouting a myth.

Have fun.

Sacred Cow #2
Self-Publishing and Indie Publishing is Easy

TRUTH: IT ISN'T. But it can be done.

It's easier by factors of thousands of headaches in working with agents and publishers. Sure. But it isn't easy when it comes to the amount of work indie and self-published writers have to do to get their books to readers.

But you hear this insulting and often dismissive comment from people everywhere. "Oh, you should indie (self) publish your work."

They say it as if you could indie publish your book in five minutes.

This comment comes from traditional publishers, editors, agents, and traditional writers who have zero idea what an indie (self) publisher does. Or how much work it is to indie publish a book.

These uninformed people say that statement as a toss-off for all kinds of various reasons, often meant to be insulting or dismissive.

And folks, it's about time to kill this myth that indie publishing is easy.

Reality: Here's what these dismissive people are saying. "Oh, you're out of shape…you should run a marathon."

So this second myth is going to be short because, to be honest, it's just so damn silly. But it needs to be addressed up front in this book.

A Quick Look At Both Major Routes for a Novel to Get to Readers

Writer finishes book.

Traditional writer mails book to agent. Nothing happens for six months, or a year if writer is lucky to have something happen that soon other than numbers of rewrites.

Indie writer gives book to a proofreader and must pay the proofreader real money or trade time and energy for services.

Indie book comes back from proofreader in a month. Indie writer must now either design a cover, or hire the cover done, write blurbs for the novel, set up accounts with different stores and printers and distributors. And then do the layout and learn programs to help with that, or hire it all done. And that's after they have at least set up a publishing name and business.

Usually, since most writers are broke, most of this work is done by the writer.

Book comes out to readers in three or four months. Traditional writer is still hoping for a response from an agent, or working on a rewrite for the agent,

months (if ever) from the book even making it to an editor's desk.

BUT… I hear people say, traditional writers can be writing while waiting.

And my response is yes, they can, but for what reason? All but romance publishers hate more than two books a year from any writer. Indie writers can write and publish more books in a year (even with all the extra work) than almost all traditional writers can.

So sure, while indie writers are doing all the work to get their books to readers, traditional writers could be waiting or writing, but for no reason. Even if the traditional writer is fast, eventually the traditional publisher will slow them down and their agent will drop them for not writing the correct book, or something even uglier will happen.

That's the nature of the traditional publishing world I'm afraid.

Why is this "Indie is Easy" Myth Dangerous?

When I hear some agent or editor or traditional writer tell a new writer "Oh, you should self-publish that," I get worried for newer writers.

Or I hear New York people going on and on about how threatened they are by all the writers indie publishing, I get worried for newer writers.

That indie publishing is easy is a myth. NEW WRITERS SUCK UP MYTHS like a sponge sucks up water.

Since New York people have no idea how hard all the indie writers are working, spending their own time, energy, and capital to get their books directly to readers, a writer told that it is easy, or led to believe it is easy, will quickly get discouraged when they try it.

I am already seeing this happen a lot to younger writers, actually.

Not only is the writer giving up the false dream of being stamped with approval from Simon and Schuster, but they are discovering that indie publishing is a lot of work, or very expensive. Or both.

And that turns many people away from writing and their dreams of being a writer. All because they heard people say that indie publishing was easy and it really isn't.

INDIE PUBLISHING CAN BE DONE, but it's not easy. It takes work and learning.

To learn how to indie publish, you must do the following things to start.

1… Follow the steps I lay out in the first and second chapter under the tab above called "Think Like a Publisher" to get your business going. It's simple and easy and cheap.

2… Learn how to do covers well enough to either do them yourself, or know what you are hiring.

3… Learn how to write good sales copy for your books. Not plot, sales copy.

4… Set up all the accounts needed to get your eBooks into as many online stores as you can, which means learning how to do clean ePub files these days.

5… Launch your book to all sites and fight through all that.

6… Learn how to do paper books, or hire it done.

7… And then the promotion starts, which will depend on the amount depending on the book. You have to constantly be learning about promotion and discoverability.

And you have to keep working on being a better storyteller, which is actually what sells books.

Yes, that's a lot of work.

But it can be done. And it can be learned slowly, just as training for a marathon is slow.

So, next time some idiot says to you in some flippant manner, "You should self publish your novel," tell them they should run a marathon in the same tone they used with you.

They could run a marathon, but it won't be easy.

Maybe they will stop saying something so stupid, and by you stopping just one person from passing something so false and misleading, you might save a new writer who will learn that indie publishing is work. And go into it with their eyes open.

Indie (self) publishing can be done. Just as running a marathon can be done.

It's not easy, but it is a ton of fun.

Sacred Cow #3
No One Will Pay Good Money for an Unknown Writer's Work

(So a new writer should make his or her work cheaper because it's worth less)

THANKFULLY, JUST A tiny bit of thought will kill this silliness for most people. But it is one of the most repeated myths young writers have.

Some History

Fact: Every writer started off as a new writer. (I know, shock.)

Fact: Every new writer who sold to traditional publishing for the first time in the last hundred years was paid decent, good, or fantastic money. Why? Because the gate-keepers thought they could sell a lot of copies of (you guessed it) an Unknown Writer.

Fact: A 100,000 word mystery from an Unknown Writer, when traditional publishing sells it, is priced EXACTLY at the same price as similar-sized novel from a bestselling writer. Price in old traditional publishing was based on printing and shipping costs and the size of the book and how many would fit in a sales and a bunch of other factors, including shipping cartons.

Fact: Not once in the last one hundred years did any traditional publisher price a new writer's book lower because the writer was unknown. (Nope, they priced it because of printing costs.)

Fact: All writers are insecure.

So in 2009 or so, here comes a workable electronic publishing that allowed writers in the door to set their own publishing businesses and thus, their own prices. And since all writers are insecure, beginning writers decided their books were worth less and thus, because they were suddenly given the control, priced their books less.

Talk about a wild and crazy time. While traditional publishers were fighting and breaking laws to not allow Amazon to lower e-book prices to $9.99 because it was *shockingly* too low, new indie writers were pricing their brand new novels at 99 cents because it couldn't be any good since they were new writers.

And thus this myth got started.

A bunch of us were fighting the trend and getting kicked for it by shouting to indie publishing writers to not cheapen their own books, just price slightly less than traditional.

And since a lot of us saw electronic books replacing mass market paperbacks, our suggestions were to price novels and collections in the same price range as mass market paperbacks. $4.99 to $7.99. Far under what New York traditional publishers thought was too low (back then and still in most cases).

But insecure writers (given price control) just won't believe that anyone will pay a decent amount of money for their book. So the novels they spent a long time writing go into the 99 cent discount bin, the perma-free bin, or the $2.99 price.

And they always have what they think are good reasons for doing so.

Insecurity is a bitch to fight in fiction writing.

BUT NO ONE KNOWS MY NAME... (add whining here...)

Really. Go ahead, ask anyone on any street if they know my name and they will look at you puzzled. Fact: No one (but a bunch of writers who seldom buy books) knows my name either.

And they certainly didn't know all the pen names I sold books under. Every time I sold a book under a pen name, I became a new writer. Duh.

Only difference was, I have been learning and practicing my storytelling skills for decades, so with a new name, my books still entertained people.

Since my wife has some open pen names, I'm going to mention her name here. She writes romance under the names Kristine Grayson and Kris DeLake. She writes mystery under Kristine Kathryn Rusch, Kris Rusch, and Kris Nelscott. All her science fiction is under Kristine Kathryn Rusch. With me, she wrote five media novels under Sandy Schofield. With me, she did a bunch of movie tie-in novels under the name Kathryn Wesley. And there are others.

All of those pen names won or were nominated for awards and sold thousands and thousands of copies per book.

So she was a new writer with all those names at one point or another.

AND NOT ONE OF THOSE BOOKS WAS DISCOUNTED OR SOLD CHEAPLY BECAUSE SHE WAS A NEW WRITER WITH A NAME NO ONE RECOGNIZED. Yet, she was exactly that because no one knew her pen name.

She sold all those books and started all those brand new names because she's a great storyteller and liked to write across genres.

I had one writer become rude and downright nasty with me recently, and from what people tell me, this writer is still badmouthing me every chance the person gets. Why? Because I had the gall to tell this person that the reason the person had good sales was because the person was a great storyteller, not because the person had discounted books.

This person's insecurity would not allow the compliment in. Ah, well. I hit a personal button with that one I guess.

But most new writers won't be angry at me with this. They will just not believe me because, you know, I don't *understand* what they are going through. (Add sarcasm snort right here.)

As a New Writer, What Do I Do?

There are a number of things you can do, but first off, you need to understand some really basic principles of publishing.

Principle #1… Your story has to be good. I didn't say well-written, I said you have to tell a good story. This takes years to learn, but is fun to learn. And you never get to the top of the skills of storytelling. And you, as the artist, never know when you hit on a good story or missed, so you put them all out.

Principle #2… You have to have more than a few products. When a reader, through promotion or word of mouth, finds your book and reads it and likes it, they want more instantly. If you only have one or two, they will move on and forget your name. Nature of the new world.

Principle #3… A writing profession is a long-term thing. It has always been that way, but this new world has allowed writers to get in a hurry, so many get discouraged easily without a lot of sales early on. To fight this, think in chunks of five and ten years ahead, not a week or month ahead.

So understanding those principles, what can a new writer do in this modern world?

The answer is simple… TAKE CONTROL

And when I mean take control, I mean take control of EVERYTHING. And part of that will be taking control of the three principles of publishing above.

—So first, make it a focus to keep learning how to be a great storyteller. This can be learned in books, online, in workshops, and a thousand places in this modern world. But you have to develop a quick filter to ignore all the stuff that doesn't make sense to you and work for you as an artist. And make this learning a focus that will never end.

—Second, make more time to sit in the writing chair and produce product. Even an extra fifteen or thirty minutes per day will do wonders. Every writer is different and every writer has different methods to get to producing fiction that readers enjoy. At first you may not be good enough to control the quality of your stories, but you can control how many hours you spend writing original words. (Rewriting and researching are not writing.)

—Third, set up your publishing press (basics are under Think Like a Publisher under the tab above), then learn to do covers, learn to do blurbs, learn to do paper books, learn how to upload your work. Even if you end up not doing it, you need to know how to do it to take control of everything.

—Fourth, start learning copyright. And read blogs and other factors about the good and the bad of traditional publishing so you are informed if and when you are approached.

All of the above are long term and you need to plan long term. Five and ten-year chunks, remember.

For example, ask yourself this: If you are giving over cover control to someone you hire, are you going to still want to be paying that money out in five years just because you are afraid to learn how to do your own covers? Think ahead. Learning is tough, but this is an international profession. And it can be learned.

Take everything you can under your own control. Learning, production, money, everything. Give no control away because you are afraid or lazy. That way lies disaster.

The Big Things You Need to Do

These will be the hardest two things you ever have to do in this business.

#1… Believe in your own art.

#2… Be patient with sales.

To believe in your own art, you need an ego. All successful artists have egos. We protect our work and do our best with everything we do and hold pride in our work. You have to believe in yourself and your own ability to keep learning to stand any chance at all in this business.

And there will be those around you and online who have a huge desire to pull you down. Ignore them, ignore reviews, do your own work from your own heart.

And that especially means don't discount your books unless for a special sale. For example, for twenty days, people can buy one of my books right now, as I write this, for less than $1.00 electronically because it's combined in a book bundle with other novels. But on all the major sites, it's still priced as a standard novel at $6.99.

You must learn how to be patient with sales. If you use sales as a self-worth measuring stick, you are turning over to others something you can't control. And the moment you turn over to others your own self-worth, you are doomed. Write and put books and stories up for only you. The fact that some people buy them, fantastic.

More WMG Writers' Guides
**from all your favorite booksellers
in trade paper and electronic editions.**

And yes, if you keep doing that, at some point you will make your entire living off of what you enjoy doing. It is very possible and likely if you believe in your own art and keep producing new work and learning.

Very likely.

But it's not easy. Nothing about what I have said here is easy.

You must keep learning and keep the value on your own work. If you don't value your own work, if you don't believe in your own work, even as a new writer, no one ever will.

Every professional writer started off as a new writer. All of us took years and years to get to making a living. But the one thing we all had in common right from the start?

We all believed in our own work, protected it, and never undervalued it in any fashion.

Sacred Cow #4
You Must Have an Agent to Sell a Book in Translation Overseas

This myth is based out of newer writers just not knowing facts and agents trying to stay relevant in a changing world.

Some History

More than fifteen to twenty years ago, it was difficult, at best, to sell many translation rights overseas for your books that were published here in the States. It took connections and even knowing who the overseas publishers were.

Then came along this funny little invention called e-mail. And the internet.

You all know what that is, I'm sure.

And overseas publishers could get directly in contact with writers. And with the increase in writer web sites, that's how overseas publishers got hold of writers, who then in the early days, not knowing any better, (and I was no exception) just sent the overseas publisher on to my agent.

And that's just the way it was done back in those dark days where we all had to walk both ways, uphill, in the snow, just to get a book published. It was horrid, I tell you. Horrid.

But Things Have Changed

I know a lot of people, a vast number of people in agent-land and traditional publishing, don't want newer professional writers to know things have changed. They want the old system to continue. But sadly for them, and great for the rest of us, things have changed a great deal.

Some general facts:

—In general, publishing contract with any publisher outside of North America is simpler by factors and factors. And easy to read.

—In general, publishing contracts from publishers outside of North America are clear to what the translation publisher is buying.

—In general, publishing contracts from publishers outside of North America have clear termination and reversion dates in them. And often limitations on print runs without a renewal.

—In general, after the first contract or two, you can do your own and negotiating is not often done. A small fee to an intellectual property attorney will often be enough on the first one or two.

—In general, most overseas contracts, (now all translation sales) are small unless your book is really taking off. Nature of smaller markets. Modern agents often don't feel it is worth their time to do a short-term $500 contract and get $50. (Their overseas agent will take the other $50 in fee.) So they often don't bother for their clients. Far too much work for them to deal with, they feel. (I personally like a $500 sales to a translation company.)

—In general, agents HATE contracts that have limited press runs, one fee, and no royalties because that means once they have the contract done, they get no more money and have no more hold on the book. So agents will try to make an overseas contract far, far more complex and add royalties.

—In general, the biggest area for agent embezzlement is from overseas book royalties. Authors don't know they are owed money because seldom do overseas agents forward the paperwork or the money from the overseas publisher, and if they do, the money often gets stopped or "forgotten" in the states agency. Hard for an author to actually get regular overseas royalty payments.

But How Do I Sell a Book Overseas Without An Agent?

This is the area that just stunned me when I learned it about agents. About one third of all agencies in the United States farm out their overseas sales to another agency here in the States that does nothing but sell books overseas. The second agency does massive lists with hundreds and hundreds of authors' names and books on it. (Nothing more.) And they regularly ship these gigantic lists to overseas agents to try to pitch to translation companies through overseas agents.

So, the flat honest truth is that unless you are a major bestseller, your book is ignored. When you have all the writers from twenty or thirty agencies on a huge list the size of a small town phone book, trust me, only the top even get looked at. And there are no covers or blurbs. Just title and author name, and sometimes genre.

That's another ugly truth about how most agents "respect" your work and try to sell it overseas. They will flat tell you they are trying to sell your book overseas, then give the name and author name to another agency, who will add it on a list to go along with thousands of others.

So you are an indie writer. Right? How do you get your books noticed overseas?

Let me think…

Oh, yeah, you publish the thing in all markets. Duh.

Amazon, B&N, Kobo, iTunes, Smashwords, CreateSpace, and so on down through the smaller electronic distributors and international stores. And when you do, you click all the overseas channels.

And boom, your book is available in English worldwide.

Last month alone, Kris and I sold English language books in 26 different countries. That's so normal, we seldom notice that now, where ten years ago, that would have been a major deal.

If you have your book available worldwide in English, people all around the world will have a chance to see your book, (with cover and blurb). If editor or someone at an overseas translation house reads your book and likes it (called a submission in the old world, but today they buy it instead), and the editor thinks your book will fit their translation line, the editor will contact you directly through your own publisher web site.

Or your author web site. (You do have "contact me" tabs, don't you?)

So it goes like this so this is clear:

Step one… You publish your book through all electronic and paper outlets available. (Not just Kindle.)

Step two… Your book is available with your great cover and blurb, worldwide, for anyone to buy in English.

Step three… An editor of a translation line at a publisher in an overseas company is looking for books for his line that will fit his topic. He finds and buys your book and reads it and likes it and thinks it will fit his line of books.

Step four… The editor contacts you by e-mail.

Step five… The editor will often ask for who your representative is. You write them back and say simply. "My attorney and I handle all translation sales."

Step six… The editor will make an offer directly to you. You say you are interested depending on the terms.

Step seven… The editor e-mails you a contract, you check it for rights grabs, sign it and e-mail it back.

Step eight… The translation publisher will send you the money by Paypal, wire, or direct transfer into your bank account. Done.

The translation publisher will send you a copy of your book in French or German or whatever when the book hits print.

It really is that simple.

Scary simple.

Since I got rid of my agent, and Kris got rid of her agent, we get many more offers from overseas publishers. The agents we had were blocking the small offers, while we take them, for the most part.

And the overseas translation publishers are finding our books because we are publishing them in English all over the world. In every format through every store. And keeping them in print all over the world.

As I said, things have changed.

So Why Is This Myth Still So Strong?

Actually, in this new world, it's logical why this myth that needing an agent to sell overseas is still strong.

1… Generally, newer professionals just feel this is scary. (It's not, if you don't panic and give it to an agent.)

2… Generally, newer professionals do not know copyright, which means they do not understand that all contracts must be done in the language of the author. (Berne Convention) They think they are going to get something in Chinese or something. Learn copyright, people.

3… Generally, agents are losing income and power by the day, so they promote this to get young, unwary professionals on board to sign their agency agreements. And many agency agreements are rights grabs of authors' works. Yet authors sign them all the time and discover the hard way they are trapped and have signed away percentages of their book for life of the copyright.

4… Generally, this area is a large money-maker for agencies because authors allow agents to have all the money and all the paperwork with that money, so overseas sales are easy to just leave in the agency accounts and misplace the paperwork. (All unintentional, of course… cough) So agents really, really push this to unwary newer professional writers and older professionals too busy to think it through.

5… Generally, authors feel that selling overseas in translation means they must send out stories into slush piles or something like that to get an overseas publisher to look at their work. So they think agents have the contacts, and agents pretend they do have the contacts. (Their contact is another agency here in the States.)

Authors don't realize that if they indie publish (not traditional), their books go out across the world to be seen.

And that's all there is to it.

Summary

There is no reason at all in this modern world to have an agent on an overseas translation sale. None.

—Contracts are simple and you can spend a few bucks to have an IP rights attorney look at the first two or so until you feel comfortable with what you are reading.

—Contracts are in your language and the money comes directly to you.

—Translation publishers see your book if you are publishing it in English around the world. There is no such thing as "selling" done by an agent. Your book sells itself and they find it because it's out there. (And if agent tries to convince you they can "sell your book overseas" ask them for a list of their overseas partner agencies, or ask if they go through a "specialty agency" here in the states. Either way, the agent who is telling you he will sell the book is lying, flat out. They will not. Period. They will simply hand off your book to someone else and do NO work.)

—The agent ship is going down quickly. Don't have your books trapped in their agency agreements because you are afraid of something that might take you all of thirty minutes to do.

Holding a copy of your book in translation in your hand is great fun. You might not be able to read it, but it sure feels neat.

Avoid this huge pitfall that agents are trying to sell you in desperation.

Sacred Cow #5
Printers are Distributors

LET ME PUT this in a different light to be clear.

Indie Publishers believe there are basically only two places to take their books to be printed and distributed to bookstores. CreateSpace and LightningSource.

This myth is logical because of how indie publishing came about with the ebook revolution and then slowly indie publishers (writers) started understanding that with a little extra work, they could do a paper book. But the myth that has indie writers believing they have to go to New York to get into bookstores has slowed the growth of this side of indie publishing.

Too bad.

Some Basics on Who Is Who

LightningSource is owned by Ingrams (and has such a bad terms of service, no one who actually reads terms of service would go with them.)

CreateSpace is owned by Amazon.

They are both what is commonly called POD printers. In other words, they have a printing structure that will print small quantities of your book for cheap as you need them. Print On Demand.

There are a lot of other POD service printers. But CreateSpace and

LightningSource get most of the press in this myth. Any Staples or Kinkos works as a POD printer as well, but prices are much higher in places like that.

You can Google and get all sorts of listings for POD printing prices and such, which vary all over the place. Wow. So caution. So far that I have found, CreateSpace is the cheapest by far for printing any perfect bound book unless you pay ahead or are up to using web presses (see below) at runs of ten thousand copies.

Some More Basics

—Printers print your books. Printers can be POD (copy machines), offset (high level color), or web press (newspaper and pulp paper). Publisher's choice.

—Distributors distribute your book. A distributor can distribute your book in limited ways, or into the big trade publishing channels. That will depend totally on how you want your book distributed. As a publisher, you have control of that.

Printers charge by a per page or per copy price.

Distributors usually take a cut of any books sold. Often to get good placement, the publisher pays a distributor some fees as well. All depends on the contract the publisher (you) negotiated with the distributor. The more books you want them to distribute, the better your deal.

The Problem With This Myth

Printers such as CreateSpace, LightningSource, and others, such as Lulu, have a part of their business where they will distribute the book into the trade channels. For writers who don't understand there is a difference between a printer and a distributor, this seems like a logical connection.

In fact, most POD printers I saw will sell your book on their own web site and into

More WMG Writers' Guides
from all your favorite booksellers
in trade paper and electronic editions.

basic channels such as Ingrams and Baker and Taylor, two of the major distributors.

And honestly, the distribution services offered by CreateSpace have been wonderful for the indie publishers to get paper books out into bookstores. (See early myth on this topic as to how easy that has become.)

But just lately, WMG Publishing was planning on doing some hardbacks on a few special projects. So we were going to go easy and go with LightningSource until we read the terms of service and decided we didn't want to give them copyrights to our books. So I shrugged and said that when we are ready, we'll just use a binder in Portland, Oregon, or maybe one near Seattle. There are, to my knowledge, without really looking that hard, almost ten quality binders in the Portland/Seattle area.

And I found two that were cheaper than LightningSource.

So it would work this way. We would have CreateSpace print the books, ship them directly to the bindery, and have a local hardback bindery bind the books into hard cases.

So besides selling them ourselves off our own web site or putting them on Amazon (which you can do), if we wanted to get these hardbacks we had bound locally into national distribution, what would we do?

Simple: We would go to a distributor and set up a deal to work with them to get the book into the trade book channels. (Meaning into the major distributors and to the major stores such as B&N and other stores.) And for those of you wondering, hardbacks are full copy returnable, and many distributors have no-returns programs you can get into.

(I can now hear the question… But where would we find a distributor? I didn't even know they existed.)

For a start, and only a start, the *Independent Book Publishers Association* has a pretty good list of book distributors. (Bet most of you indie publishers out there didn't even know the IBPA even existed, did you? (grin)) Now EXTREME caution with this organization and joining it because, to be honest, they haven't moved into this century yet. If they do, it might be something worthwhile to join. So caution, eyes open, I am not recommending them at this point.

But they do have a good list of distributors. Go look at that at least.

http://www.ibpa-online.org/resources/distributor-wholesalers/

Now I need to be very, very clear here. If you are not acting in your business completely like a publisher, this won't work. And if you do not have a pretty good list of books and have a schedule ahead of upcoming books, chances are most of these distributors will not work with you. They might work with someone who calls themselves a self-published author, but it would be tougher. (But I expect everyone reading this to be acting like a publisher, have a publishing imprint on their books, and a growing book list.)

Why Printer as Distributor Myth Damages Writers and Indie Publishers

Simple, really. This belief system that CreateSpace or LighteningSource or Lulu are the only way to print or distribute often forces writers and indie publishers into bad decisions. Granted, at the moment, it is a cheap and easy way to print and get into the system. But there are drawbacks to this cheap and easy system.

Running through an established distributor and into the trade system will get your books into better discount ranges to bookstores. You can get out of some of the lower level book catalogs on Ingrams and B&T. And often a good distributor will help in marketing and getting the word to their bookstore customers that they have a new book from you.

That might be worth it to some of you out there.

To work with these distribution people, you have to be doing a lot of things correctly, including pricing. And acting as a publisher as I said.

I understand that most reading this, including WMG Publishing, will be content to ride the horse we are on at the moment, which is CreateSpace.

But we know the options, we know that if something suddenly happened to CreateSpace, we would just continue right on publishing paper books and getting our books into stores.

Summary

Printers are very, very different from distributors. You have different printers in your own local town that can print books. Maybe not cheaply, but they can do it.

Distributors are companies that can get your printed books into the trade system (exactly the same as traditional publishers) and get your books to the same places.

CreateSpace and the other POD printers have a distribution arm. But here at WMG Publishing we often click off all distribution and just buy our books direct from CreateSpace. They are just a printer at that point. For example, we do that when we are doing a large order of ARCs.

Printers are not distributors. Some printers have a distribution side, but you do not have to use it.

So keep your mind open and the two forms of business apart in thinking and you, as an indie publisher, will make better decisions.

Part 2 of 2 will appear in the next issue of Smith's Monthly.

Poker Boy knows that sometimes you just wait for good hands. Patience, a hard skill to learn. A critical skill for a poker player and a superhero.

Poker Boy knows how to be patient.

But when a man appears in the Golden Nugget Poker room looking not only out of place, but out of time, Poker Boy moves to help.

And in the process learns the true meaning of patience and waiting for the right time to make a move.

A Reason to Play a Hunch
A Poker Boy Story

Chapter One

THE GOLDEN NUGGET Casino poker room in Vegas felt a little tight for space, but the players were friendly and staff and dealers tended to smile more than normal around Las Vegas. That made up for a lot.

The entire room was decorated in soft brown and wood tones, with polished brass everywhere. It had over twenty tables with black padded rails and nine padded brown-leather chairs per table. Almost all of the chairs were full at the moment and there was a waiting list to get into some of the games.

In the back corner of the room, the remains of the afternoon tournament were still going. At time cheers or moans would fill the room from there. A good ten people stood around that table watching intently at every hand.

And even with all the people in the pretty small space, the air was moving well and it wasn't even warm. That showed that the casino valued this poker room more than most casinos valued their poker rooms. They kept it updated, clean, staffed, and friendly. The perfect recipe for a successful room.

I normally didn't spend much time here at the Golden Nugget, but after working with my friends in the Ghost of a Chance agency on a problem we just wrapped up, I figured I would give the poker room a try.

The Ghost of a Chance agents tended to meet in the Golden Nugget Buffet up one floor from here and I had come to realize it was one of the top buffets in all of Las Vegas.

I also hadn't realized how much all the remodeling had done for the hotel and casino. It was as good as, if not better than, most hotels and casinos out on the Strip.

So in the last few days my girlfriend Patty, aka Front Desk Girl, and I had tried the buffet twice. And each time we had come down the escalator and gone to look at the poker room, Patty humoring me as we did.

After all, I was Poker Boy. Poker was what I did.

So now I was giving the poker room a try.

And so far I sure hadn't been disappointed. I was in a good five-ten no-limit game with only one local pro who didn't know me and six tourists bent on having a good time. Just about as perfect as it got.

It was interesting that when I had first become a superhero, when I was in Las Vegas, I always spent all my time at Binion's Casino across Fremont Street. I had met Patty there when she worked at the front desk of Binion's Hotel. And

Madge's diner, where the team used to meet in before we built my floating office, was only a block or so from here.

But I had never walked the fifty steps across Fremont Street to play here.

Now I wondered why I hadn't. Not only did this room feel like old times, but playing downtown felt like I had come home again. I liked that feeling.

I still had three hours left until Patty got off work at the MGM Grand and I was a good thousand up, just taking my time and enjoying the play.

The other pro at the table was about fifty years old, had a balding head, a wide grin, and a fun personality that hid his poker ability. After the first thirty minutes, we both just avoided each other where we could. There was more than enough to go around with the group at this table. Three men from Boise, two middle-aged women from somewhere in the Midwest, and one elderly man from Florida. All had money and wanted to enjoy spending it.

I was going to see if I could help with that enjoyment over the next few hours.

But suddenly it seemed that wasn't to be.

I was sitting with my back to a wall in the third spot on the table on the right side of the room. From that position I could see most of the room, the main entrance, as well as everyone I was playing against.

A guy, wearing a suit that looked like it was right out of the 1940s stood off to one side of the large archway entrance to the poker room, sort of watching everything. I hadn't seen him come up to the entrance.

He was handsome in a Rock Hudson sort of way, thin and almost dapper, with that classic movie-star chin.

And the more I looked at him the more my warning bells were going off big time. Not danger bells, just warning bells. But he didn't look to be trouble.

I studied him a little closer. He stood maybe five-nine and had a real Fedora on his head that looked to be felt and expensive and he knew how to wear it.

It looked like his natural style, not some costume.

He just flat looked out of place.

Then my little voice changed that to "Out of time."

I knew right then my night of friendly poker was more than likely over.

Chapter Two

I TOSSED AWAY the two cards in my hand and stood, working my way through the crowd of chairs and tables to the front, not really looking directly at the guy, but not letting him out of my sight either.

As I cleared the last table near the wide archway entrance, the sounds of the casino beyond got louder, like I was walking upstream against a torrent of noise.

The guy hadn't moved, but as I stepped closer to walk past him, he glanced at me and nodded.

I nodded back.

"You got time to talk for a second, Poker Boy?" the man asked, his voice level and low.

Now my heart was really racing. The only people who knew who I really was were on my team or other superheroes and gods. And a few of the Ghost of a Chance agents.

"Sure," I said, stopping to face him and he turned to face me. "Don't think we've met?"

"We haven't," the man said. "But we need to talk in private if you don't mind. No one can see me but you. I don't want people thinking you are talking with yourself."

I laughed. "Appreciate that."

I stopped time around the two of us, making everyone freeze suddenly. I actually didn't stop time. From my understanding, no one can do that, not even the most powerful gods. I just took us between moments in time, which had the effect of looking like I had stopped time.

The most striking thing to me every time I used this power was how all sound suddenly stopped. The noisy casino went instantly silent. Everyone frozen.

And trust me, no one looked good in a frozen face.

The guy nodded but didn't seem surprised at stepping between instants of time. "Thanks. I thought you might be able to both see me and help me."

"See you?" I asked.

He reached around and put his hand through the wall and then pulled it back out. "I'm what is called a ghost I suppose."

"You an agent?" I asked.

"Of what?" he asked, looking clearly confused for the first time.

I decided quickly to ignore that and just back up the conversation since it seemed this guy was a real ghost, something I didn't realize could exist outside of the Ghost of a Chance agents.

"Do you have a name and do you know when you died?" I asked, trying my best to keep my heart from pounding right out of my chest. Over the last years I had run into some weird situations, but this was one of the weirdest so far. And that was going some.

Weird and strange tended to go hand-in-hand with the superheroes and gods.

"Lawrence Oakes," he said. "But all my friends used to call me Larry."

He pointed up toward the old hotel tower. "I died upstairs in a room on the sixth floor in 1951. Ticker gave out. Me and my wife Bettie had just celebrated in the old-fashioned way our fifth wedding anniversary, if you get my drift. I had just dressed to go out for dinner."

He shook his head, clearly thinking about the moment. I wasn't real sure I wanted to hear much more but before I could ask another question he went on.

"Bettie was looking really sweet when she came out of the bathroom. She was a stunning woman. My entire life. Then she found me slumped over the bed and started screaming. I just stood off to one side when I realized what had happened and that I couldn't help her or comfort her."

For a moment I thought Larry was going to tear up, then he took a deep breath.

"I just stood and watched the woman I love cry and then they came and took her away and my body away and I stayed. I always wondered how she did after that, what her life was like."

"And what have you been doing ever since?" I asked, almost afraid of the answer.

"Just hanging around and watching the people and the hotel change," he said. "Not sure why I didn't catch a ride out of here on the light. I've watched others die here and they all get a ride. When I saw you and that beautiful girlfriend of yours in the buffet, I knew you two were special and might be able to help me get a ride to the other side if you could see me. I just played a hunch about it when she called you Poker Boy."

So that's how he knew my name. But I was a lowly superhero. No chance I could help him. But I might be able to find some people who could.

"You mind if I call in some help?" I asked.

"Just glad to be able to talk with someone again," he said, shrugging. "More help the better in my book."

"Stan, Ben, could you join me for a moment?"

This was going to be fun getting their take on this very strange situation. Maybe they would have some answers.

At this point, I sure had none.

Chapter Three

STAN, THE GOD of Poker and my immediate boss appeared an instant after I called him. He had on his normal dull clothes. A sweater-vest, tan slacks, and a light shirt under the vest. He looked to be of that indeterminate age even though I knew he had been alive during the time of Atlantis. The guy was so good at looking bland that he could vanish in a crowd and no one would give him a second look.

A moment later Ben, one of the gods of libraries and of knowledge appeared. Ben looked like he belonged in a library. He had the old professor look with the rumpled white hair and the small glasses. He was by far the smartest man I had ever met about everything, including the history of the gods and superheroes.

"Stan, Ben, this is Larry Oakes," I said, introducing my two team members to the ghost. "He died here in 1951 and has just been hanging around ever since."

"Oh, no," Ben said, shaking his head. "Something has gone totally wrong."

Stan just nodded, showing no emotion since as the God of Poker he was the master of no emotion.

Larry shrugged, clearly knowing after over sixty-five years roaming the Golden Nugget Casino that something had gone wrong.

I decided to ask Larry a few more questions to give Stan and Ben time to process what had just been tossed at them.

"Larry, have you ever been out of this building?"

"Didn't know I could," Larry said, shrugging as if that actually didn't matter. "Mostly I only move around at night when there are fewer people because having someone walk through me is very strange. I can read their thoughts and I don't really want to know what most of these people are thinking."

I nodded at that. I didn't blame him in the slightest. The Ghost Agents I had worked with said that being inside people's minds took them a long time to get used to.

"Larry," Ben said, "it sounds like you were intended to be a Ghost of a Chance agent and no one came to train you."

Larry just shook his head. "Second time I have heard that Ghost Agent thing. What are they?"

I quickly explained to Larry that certain people with certain skills who died were picked to be part of a team of Ghost Agents. Their job was to help people.

"So you telling me," Larry said, "that I've been hanging around for sixty-five years doing nothing because someone screwed up?"

Ben nodded. "It appears that way."

Larry just shook his head.

The silence of the frozen casino around us seemed to get very heavy. I was about to break the silence with another stupid question when Larry sighed and said, "Don't suppose we can do anything about what has happened. So how about getting me a ride out of here and to the other side? Wouldn't mind seeing Bettie again."

"Don't think you are going to want to do that?" a voice said from beside me.

I glanced over at Laverne, Lady Luck herself. She was one of the most powerful gods and seemed to run everything. She was the one who had put my team of gods and superheroes with the Ghost Agents at times to save the world.

She was also the one who had given me the power to even see ghosts in the first place.

"Larry," I said, acting calm as if the most powerful god in all the world appeared beside me all the time, "this is Laverne."

Larry nodded. "Nice meeting you. But why would you say I might not want to leave yet?"

"Because," Lady Luck said, smiling, "you haven't been waiting to leave, you have been waiting for your partner to join you."

"I only have one partner," Larry said, shaking his head, almost angry. "And I'm sure Bettie is long dead by now."

"She's not," Lady Luck said. "At least not until one week from tomorrow when she will join you."

At that moment two of the top Ghost Agents appeared beside Lady Luck.

"I'm sure these two will explain everything to you," Laverne said, nodding. "I hope to see you again."

She vanished.

Then Ben and Stan also vanished without a word leaving me standing there between instants of time with three ghosts. Again, weird didn't begin to describe my job at times.

Jewel and Tommy both introduced themselves to Larry.

Both Jewel and Tommy were dressed in their normal evening clothes of jeans, dress shirts, and sneakers. They were a handsome couple, both in their mid-twenties when they died. She had been a doctor, he had been a cop. In the five years since they died they had become the top Ghost Agents.

"I've seen you two in the buffet a lot," Larry said.

Jewel nodded. "We are also ghosts. We knew you were here, but our bosses didn't think we should talk to you just yet."

"Why is that?" Larry asked a half second before I could.

I was starting to get the idea that Larry being on his own here had been part of a plan, not a screw-up.

"Because," Jewel said, "they want to recruit both you and Bettie to our team and Bettie won't pass over for another week."

"Why would Bettie want to spend time with me after all these years?" Larry asked.

"Because she's never gotten over you," Tommy said. "She raised your son and your grandchildren and never met another man. She didn't want another man. She waited for you just as you have been waiting here for her."

Larry looked shocked for the first time since I had seen him. "I had a son?"

Tommy nodded. "Born about nine months after you died."

"And three grandchildren and four great-grandchildren so far," Jewel said, smiling.

I could feel I was smiling as well. Damn hard to keep a poker face in this kind of situation.

I thought for a moment Larry was going to just slump to the floor, but then somehow he pulled himself together. This guy was a lot stronger than I would have been in the same situation.

"Can I see them?" Larry asked.

"After Bettie joins you," Jewel said. "She will look the same as the day you died, just as you still look the same. That is the time she imprinted on just as you did."

"So how come," I said, "someone couldn't tell Larry all this back in 1951?"

Jewel smiled at me. "I asked the same question. It was because they both had to prove they were meant to be a ghost team together forever."

"Unlike how Jewel and I died in the same car wreck," Tommy said, "Many teams die years apart. You met Gail and the Sunset Kid?"

I nodded. Nice couple. Clearly in love and working up in Portland.

"They died almost a hundred years apart," Tommy said. "The Sunset Kid had to basically just work alone for all those years until Gail arrived."

"So if Bettie had met another man and moved on?" Larry asked.

"Then a Ghost Agent would have contacted you and trained you at that point," Jewel said. "But just as you waited, Bettie also waited."

"So guess my job here didn't much matter," I said, laughing.

"Actually," Jewel said, "you just gave us an extra week to get Larry ready is all. The plan was to contact him next week."

"Well," I said, laughing, "glad to be of some help."

I looked directly at Larry. "After you and Bettie are both trained and settled down together, I really want to meet this special woman. And I am sure Patty would as well."

"Oh, trust me, it will be our pleasure," Larry said. "Thank you."

"To the buffet for dinner?" Tommy asked.

Jewel nodded.

At that all three ghosts vanished, leaving me standing there alone with a bunch of frozen people all around me.

Yeah, nothing strange at all about my job.

I tried to remember exactly where I was and in what position I had been when I froze time and then dropped back into the real flow, letting the sounds of the casino smash in around me.

I turned and headed back toward the table where my chips sat. It looked like I might actually get to enjoy the night after all.

As I sat down, one of the guys from Boise asked me why I was smiling so big.

"Sometimes things just go right," I said, laughing.

"Yeah," the guy said, "playing poker in this place is just about as right at is gets."

And to that I could only nod and smile some more.

Can't Get Enough of Poker Boy?
These stories and more are available at your favorite booksellers.

USA *Today* Bestselling Writer

DEAN WESLEY SMITH

HIDDEN CANYON
A Thunder Mountain Story

Professor Margaret Land, Maggie to her friends, loved working with Dawn Edwards, one of the most acclaimed historians of all time.

Maggie, with Dawn's help, tracked the historical facts of a hidden man named Tombstone Dan.

Traveling into the remote Idaho wilderness, Maggie hopes to find more about her elusive research subject.

A Thunder Mountain story with heart and a promise of a future.

Hidden Canyon
A Thunder Mountain Story

One

PROFESSOR MARGARET LAND, Maggie to her friends, sat alone on the balcony of the massive Monumental Summit Lodge and stared out over the valley below and the hundreds of miles of the Idaho mountains and primitive area in front of her.

In all her life she had never imagined a view so spectacular, especially with the setting sun coloring the tops of mountains in shades of pink and orange and red. Many of the mountains were still capped in snow even though it was July.

The air had a slight bite to it, but it felt great after the warm day in Boise and the drive up here. Refreshing, as if she belonged here.

Living in Wisconsin and being born outside of Washington, D.C., she never would have thought she would love the high mountains of Idaho. But she had taken to them like they had always been home.

All her life she had felt a pull to go west, just never had until now.

All fall and winter in Boise, Maggie had been working side-by-side with Dawn Edwards, one of the most famous historical writers of all time, researching a project about the old mining town that had boomed and died in the valley below the lodge.

Maggie had been teaching at the University of Wisconsin, Madison, when Dawn contacted her and offered a position at the Institute for Historical Research in Boise, working on a research project with her. Ten times the money Maggie got paid for teaching and all expenses paid for a year, at least.

The Historical Institute was so prestigious that the university had given Maggie a complete leave of absence with a promise her job would remain any time she wanted to return. That alone had shocked Maggie.

But honestly, for just the chance to go west and work with Dawn Edwards, Maggie would have quit her teaching job and done the work for no money.

Over the winter Maggie and Dawn had gotten along perfectly, once Maggie got over being star-struck working for such a famous historian. Dawn and her wonderful sense of humor made that easy, thankfully.

Both Dawn and Maggie were about the same age at thirty-one, with Dawn having long brown hair and an attitude of calm Maggie had never seen before. Maggie was just an inch taller than Dawn at five-seven and had short black hair.

They both always wore jeans, tennis shoes, and comfortable blouses. And one thing Maggie really liked was that when together they laughed a lot.

Maggie also really liked Dawn's husband, Madison, even though she had only met him once in the last year. Her seemed very kind and smart, as Maggie would have expected for someone married to Dawn.

Maggie had been working on researching the life and people in the bars and brothels of the Old West while teaching. That had been the focus of her doctorial research and her first book, published just a year ago by the university press.

Dawn had wanted Maggie to focus in for the winter on the mining towns in Idaho, including the mining town that Dawn's first book had made famous, Roosevelt, Idaho, an old mining town that had been submerged under water in 1909 after just eight short years of life.

And mostly Dawn seemed to be very, very interested in a man named Tombstone Dan.

It had taken all winter and most of the spring before Maggie finally made a breakthrough with Dan. That guy had been smart and had covered his tracks well. But the Institute had access to resources like no others and Maggie had found him.

It seems his original name had been Dan Gray, a rich cattleman from Kansas City. In 1898, at the age of thirty, he left his business to his partner and disappeared into the west.

In 1900, a year before gold was discovered in the Monumental Creek in the valley below this lodge, Dan had legally changed his name to Tombstone Dan and filed a mining claim and bought all the land in a small side canyon off of the valley below.

Then through a land and investment company set up in Boise, as Roosevelt was formed, he bought parcels on the main street of Roosevelt and showed up at spring melt as the miners were pouring into the valley and built six saloons. There was no record at all of what happened to him when the town went under water in the spring of 1909.

No one was killed since the town had taken days to flood. Much of the furniture in the saloons and all of the pianos were saved and carted out before the town went under.

By that point in time, Tombstone Dan's investment business owned fifty different saloons up and down the west coast.

There was no record of Tombstone Dan surfacing after that.

He simply vanished.

His company continued on and Maggie and Dawn talked with the president of the company who told them the ownership stock in the privately held firm was in trust. He had no idea who controlled the trust and no one from the trust ever had contacted him or the board of directors. The trust just let them run the company and they were all paid well.

So by June, Maggie had hit a dead end on her research on Tombstone Dan, although she had more than enough material about the workings of the saloons and brothels in western mining towns to fill two books, if she ever got the time to write them.

Maggie had no doubt why Dawn had found the man interesting and mysterious. He was to Maggie as well, and the only known picture of him in Kansas City showed he had been handsome as well.

Maggie had a hunch she would have liked the guy if she could have ever met him.

So now, tomorrow morning, Maggie and Dawn were going to go down that harrowing road Maggie could see leading down into the valley below the lodge along a cliff face. They wanted to see if they could find the small side canyon that Tombstone Dan had bought first. Maybe that would give them a clue to what happened to him.

Dawn had been actually shocked when Maggie told her about the small side canyon. Dawn said she thought she knew everything about the Monumental Valley and hadn't known that canyon was even there.

"Here you go," Dawn said at that moment, bringing Maggie a coffee and cream laced with some nice brandy and pulling Maggie's attention away from the wonderful view.

Dawn set the mug in front of Maggie and sighed as she sat down and looked out over the rose-tinted mountains and dark blue sky.

"I never get tired of this view, no matter how many times I see it."

"Neither do I," Madison said, taking a seat beside his wife and sipping on a mug of coffee that looked like it had some brandy in it as well.

Maggie was surprised. Only she and Dawn had driven up here today.

"Great work," Madison said to Maggie, "on finding that canyon and that information on Tombstone Dan. I had no idea there was a canyon down there off Monumental. Looking forward to seeing if we can find it."

Dawn smiled at Maggie. "He's driving that road. Hate that road. Would never drive it."

Maggie laughed. "That bad, huh?"

"It's only terrifying for about ten minutes," Madison said, smiling.

Maggie wasn't sure at all what she had gotten into now. This was a long, long way from the flatlands of Wisconsin. If she didn't feel so naturally at home here, she might actually be worried.

But for some reason, she wasn't.

It felt for the first time like she belonged right where she was.

"Get all the guests tucked in?" Dawn asked Madison.

Madison nodded. "Crews cleaning up the kitchen and everyone is either in their rooms or out here on the deck watching this incredible sunset."

Maggie glanced around and about ten others were scattered along the long, wooden deck of the massive lodge, all facing out at the valley below.

"You own this place?" Maggie asked, clearly shocked.

"We are half-owners," Dawn said, smiling. "We love it up here so much, we try to live here as much as possible."

"I can see why," Maggie said. "It is the most peaceful place I have ever been. So how did you end up owning this?"

Dawn laughed. "Tell you what. We'll give you the entire sordid story tomorrow. But for now we all need rest. We're going to be leaving before the sun hits the tops of the mountains, which is very early in these mountains."

Both Madison and Dawn stood, picking up their mugs. "Enjoy the view and we'll see you in the morning. We'll stay here tomorrow night as well, so no need to pack anything but hiking clothes and sunscreen. We'll take care of the food and water we'll need while down there."

"Thanks for this," Maggie said.

"No, thank you," Dawn said. "I never thought I would get the chance to learn something new about that valley down there. It's exciting."

With that, the two famous historians turned and headed inside.

Maggie turned to stare back out over the mountains, their peaks now growing darker by the moment, the valleys between mountains deep pools of blackness.

What in the world had she gotten herself into? Maybe by tomorrow she would know more.

One thing she did know. After working with Dawn for a winter in Boise and being at the Institute and in these mountains, she didn't want to go back to Wisconsin.

And she had a sense she wasn't going to have to.

Two

MAGGIE WAS STILL trying to catch her breath from the harrowing ride down the side of the cliff when Madison pulled over and stopped.

Madison had driven the white Cadillac SUV like an expert, not too slow, but not too fast either over a road cut out of the rocks of the cliff. The road wasn't much wider than the SUV.

At times Maggie couldn't believe they could even get around corners without scraping rocks along the hillside.

On the other side of the very narrow dirt road, about thirty seconds after they left the lodge parking lot, they had been thousands of feet in the air.

The sun was barely touching the tops of the mountains, so Madison needed full lights going down the cliff and Maggie couldn't see exactly how far down it was to the valley floor. But Dawn had volunteered the fact they were at least two thousand feet in the air and Maggie's ears were going to pop a few times on the way down.

They had.

Maggie was in the back seat, clinging on for dear life. At one point she had asked what happened if they met another car coming up.

"We would have to back up to a wide spot to let them go by," Dawn said, glancing back at Maggie. "Rule of mountain roads, you always back uphill."

"I'll remember that if I am ever stupid enough to drive on a road like this."

Both Dawn and Madison laughed.

So now they were stopped, sitting safely on the valley floor. Maggie worked to pry her fingers from the grip beside the door.

When they had come off the side of the cliff face, the road had crossed over the narrow valley floor, over a small bridge, and then turned down the valley. That was where they had stopped.

"The map shows the small hidden canyon is directly across the valley from us right here," Dawn said.

Madison nodded and pulled the SUV off the road and shut it off.

When the headlights went off, it was very clear just how dark this valley was at this time of the morning.

When Maggie climbed out, the cold air hit her hard. She had already gotten used to the summer in Boise. This was cold and very crisp and the sound of Monumental Creek was soothing.

Not even birds were chirping yet.

It was beautiful. Wonderfully beautiful.

She had on a light jacket, a sweatshirt under the jacket, and a blouse under that. Layers is how Dawn had told her to dress.

Maggie also had gloves and a stocking cap. She sure wasn't going to need the sunscreen for a few hours yet, at least.

"Wow," Maggie said as Dawn and Madison closed the doors. "This is really something."

"This is a very special valley," Dawn said, her voice hushed as if she was in a sacred place.

Maggie could only agree with the feeling. This did feel special for some reason or another.

"Let's head back up the road and over the bridge," Madison said, putting a light pack on his shoulder and turning on his flashlight. "Easier than trying to cross the stream any other way."

He started off and Maggie dropped in behind him with Dawn following her along the narrow dirt road. The only sound in the still morning air was their feet against the gravel.

"Right here," Dawn said as they turned toward the creek, "is where the old pioneer pack trail started up the hillside on this side of the canyon."

Dawn aimed her flashlight at a wide area and Maggie could see the trail heading upward at a fairly steep angle.

Maggie had studied pictures of that trail and of pack trains bringing in supplies to this valley. The trail ended at the top, right at the lodge, which had been there since 1902.

From the records, numbers of people over the years had died on that stretch of trail between here and the lodge.

"No wonder no one ever spotted this canyon," Dawn said, moving on behind Madison toward the road bridge over the creek. "They were either going up or down and would have no reason to look to one side or the other on that trail. And very few people lived up Monumental past this point."

Maggie nodded and just let her nerves calm and enjoy the brisk, cold morning in the high mountains. This was going to be an adventure she would always remember. She wanted to calm down and really enjoy it.

She had always been one to research the past. She had never gotten the chance to actually feel what the past might have really been like until now.

This valley was the past. It was as if she had gone back in time.

They went over the bridge and the road turned up the valley, headed for that terrifying cliff drive.

The three of them stopped and Dawn took out her iPad and pulled up the map. They knew they would get no satellite service in this deep valley, but Dawn had saved the map to her iPad.

She brought up the scale and then overlaid a satellite image she had saved over it.

It was clear where they were standing on the bridge and it was clear the small canyon opening that Tombstone Dan had owned was about four hundred yards down the valley from them along the rock walls.

"Step carefully," Madison said as he shone his light ahead and eased down off the road. "No point in twisting an ankle up here."

With Madison leading, working his way through what openings in the trees and brush he could find, they worked their way down the valley along the rock walls.

Finally, just as Maggie was about to take off her jacket because she was starting to sweat even in the cold air, Madison said, "Would you look at that?"

All three of them stopped and shone their lights ahead. From the direction they were coming, a direction no one would travel along these cliff faces, they could see an opening in the rocks.

It was as if part of the cliff had simply moved about twenty feet away from another part of the cliff, opening a large crack in the wall.

"That would be impossible to see from across the valley where the trail was," Dawn said.

"No wonder we never saw it over all those years of going up and down that trail," Madison said, shaking his head.

Maggie glanced at Madison, then at Dawn, wondering exactly what Madison had meant.

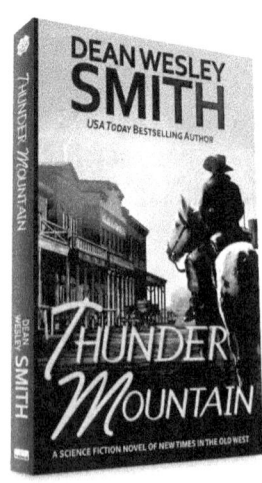

Dawn smiled. "We'll explain later over dinner, I promise."

Madison moved toward the opening in the rock.

"There was a wagon trail here," Dawn said. "Now covered in loose rock, but it was here."

Maggie was feeling more excited by the moment. Around them, the sun was starting to light up more of the tops of the mountains.

And in front of her was the opening to a small canyon that had used to be owned by someone she had worked all winter to find, Tombstone Dan.

She was experiencing real history.

Her heart was beating harder from excitement right at this moment than when they were coming down the cliff road.

She had no idea if they would find anything in this canyon left from Dan's time, but she sure was excited to find out.

And somehow, she believed they would.

Three

MAGGIE FOLLOWED MADISON up the narrow canyon for about a hundred yards, her flashlight making sure the dim morning light didn't hide any wrong steps.

Then the very narrow canyon turned sharply right and after about a hundred more paces opened up into what looked like a round valley in the morning light.

Madison stopped and clicked off his flashlight. Maggie and Dawn joined him and did the same.

"Wow, just wow," Dawn said, looking up at the towering rock cliffs that seemed to go up into the sky around the small valley.

Maggie had seen football stadiums larger than this valley, but not as beautiful. A small stream ran from the far back wall and under some rocks beside them, more than likely joining Monumental Creek on the other side of those rock walls.

Pine trees filled the back half of the valley and a meadow about the size of a football field was directly in front of them.

But what had all of their attention was the log home on a ledge above the meadow on the right side. It had clearly been a wonderful log home in its day.

"Looks like we found were Tombstone Dan lived," Dawn said.

Maggie's heart was racing so hard, she couldn't even speak. Her research had led them here. Her digging through old records and books to find the key to this wonderful place.

She was walking in history. Never in her fondest dreams had she thought that possible. Not like this.

"Let's go take a look," Madison said, starting up what was clearly a wagon trail leading from the opening into the canyon up to the home.

They no longer needed their flashlights and as they climbed the fifty paces up the side of the hill, the day around them had brightened up.

"It's got a metal roof," Madison said as they neared the flat rock ledge the log home was on.

"That had to be put on in the 1930s or so," Dawn said.

"The entire place looks to be in fantastic shape," Madison said.

Maggie had seen lots and lots of pictures of old ruins from the period this valley had boomed. None of them now, in 2017, were anything more than piles of rubble. Yet this cabin stood here like it could be lived in.

"Any signs of anyone living here?" Dawn asked as Madison moved along the front of the porch.

"It has been kept up," Madison said, "So more than likely at some point over the years someone lived here and kept it up since the time Tombstone Dan lived here."

The three of them climbed up on the porch and Maggie turned around and looked at the small valley below them. Also, from the porch she could see the tops of the mountains to the east glowing with the morning light. It was stunningly beautiful.

Madison knocked on the door as if someone might actually be in the cabin, even though they saw no signs of any life being in the small valley lately.

Then he pushed down on the door latch and opened the large wooden front door.

Inside there was furniture in the living room, all covered in white sheets for protection against the dust. A large stone fireplace filled one wall of the massive room across from the main door. Heavy curtains were pulled across the windows blocking all light coming in.

What looked to be a fairly modern kitchen was off to the left, and a hallway led away toward the back of the building.

All three of them clicked on their flashlights.

Maggie felt instantly at home.

Instantly.

"No footprints in the dust," Dawn said, pointing her light at the floor.

Maggie could see the dust was almost a quarter inch thick.

"Looks like about thirty or more years of dust," Madison said, heading down the hallway. It would take that long with this tight a house for this to build up like this.

Maggie just stayed frozen in place just inside the door, not understanding at all what she was feeling and why this place felt like home to her. Nothing had felt like home to her before now.

Nothing.

But suddenly some empty, abandoned cabin in the Idaho mountains did. Strange didn't begin to describe how she was feeling.

Dawn carefully walked over into the kitchen, moving slowly to not stir up too much dust, and looked around.

"This was remodeled around 1970 or so."

"Wasn't this area designated a wilderness area around that point?" Maggie asked.

"Doesn't stop people from living here," Dawn said. "No one to catch them, especially this well hidden."

"Someone spent a lot of money and time getting this place up to date and livable back about that point," Madison said, as he came back from down the hall. "Two beds covered in sheets in two rooms down there and a working toilet and generator just outside the back door. All old equipment from the sixties or early seventies."

Dawn just shook her head.

"So someone found this place before we did," Dawn said.

"A very long time ago," Madison said.

"Before we were all born," Maggie said.

Then finally, she moved carefully toward some framed dust-covered pictures on the mantel over the fireplace.

She carefully wiped off the dust on one and with the light of her flashlight saw the smiling face of Tombstone Dan.

She turned and handed the photo to Dawn. "That's Tombstone Dan when he was about the age he built this place."

Dawn and Madison both stared at the image.

Maggie picked up another photo and carefully dusted it off. It was of two children sitting on the front porch of this cabin. They looked to be around ten or so.

"Looks like there is more to discover about Tombstone Dan," Maggie said. "Maybe they are still alive and were the ones that put this cabin into preservation mode.

Maggie handed the photo to Dawn and Madison.

"A good chance of that," Dawn said, nodding. "Or maybe their children or grandchildren."

Maggie carefully took the last framed photo off the fireplace mantel and dusted it off carefully.

It was a portrait picture done by a Boise photography studio from the label. It had been taken in 1934. It was of Tombstone Dan, the two children, and clearly a woman who was his wife. She was wearing a wide, floppy hat over what looked like short dark hair. She had on what looked to be a frilly blue dress that fit the time. She and Dan and their two kids looked happy.

The woman looked familiar from somewhere. Maggie would have to figure out from where. But the image of the happy family made her smile.

And made her heart race.

For some reason, it seemed to end her search now that she had found that picture. She wanted to know more, sure, about the illusive man who seemed to vanish from history.

But knowing he had been happy just made her happy.

She handed the picture to Dawn and Madison.

"Nice to see he found a wife and was happy, isn't it?" Maggie said.

Dawn looked at the picture, then handed it to Madison who laughed.

"Very nice," Dawn said.

"Now I got to figure out who his wife was," Maggie said, "and who closed up this place to be saved for later."

"We'll have time for those answers later," Madison said and headed for the door.

Maggie took one more look around the cabin and then followed Dawn and Madison back into the morning light on the wonderful front porch.

Maybe later in the month, if Dawn didn't mind, Maggie would come back here with cleaning supplies and get this place back into shape. Maybe spend a month here, actually living in the past she had helped to research.

She had come to love the past over the years. Now she had a chance to come back here and live in the past a little bit.

For some reason, she didn't think Tombstone Dan would mind.

~

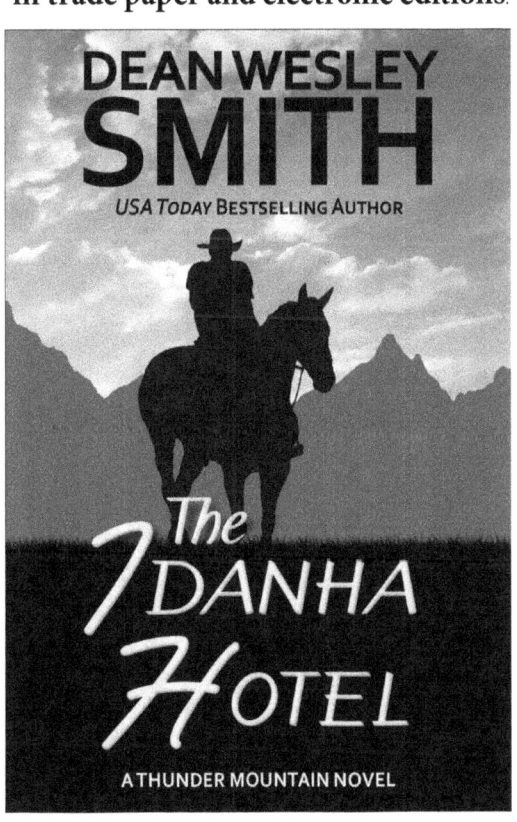

USA TODAY BESTSELLING AUTHOR

DEAN WESLEY SMITH

THE ADVENTURES OF HAWK

USA Today bestselling writer Dean Wesley Smith takes us on a thrill-ride adventure in some of the world's most exotic places.

In search of his missing father, Danny Hawk must survive against all odds and a long way from home.

In 1970, Egypt breeds danger for Hawk and his friends. Hawk's only hope to find his father rests in staying alive and ahead of the dangerous men chasing him.

Sometimes only a half-step ahead.

The Adventures of Hawk

CHAPTER ONE

August 16, 1970
American University, Cairo, Egypt.

NINETEEN-YEAR-OLD Danny Hawk held his breath and tried to listen. He had moved to a position near an open window in the old palace-like building that housed the science department of the American University in Cairo. Outside the window was a concrete ledge six inches wide. He could move along that ledge, three floors above the ground, if he had to.

From what he could hear, two men were threatening Professor Davis in the outer office. The professor was pretending that he had no idea what the men wanted, even though Danny knew that was a lie. The men were after Danny's father's records, just as Danny was.

"He's not going to tell us," one man's voice said. "Kill him and search the place. They have to be here."

There was a sound of scuffling and then a muffled gunshot.

Danny managed not to gasp or make any noise at all, but he wanted to be sick. It wasn't possible that Professor Davis had just been killed.

He couldn't be dead.

Danny's entire body felt like it had turned to Jell-O, but with more noise from the outer office, he made himself move.

And move quickly.

He climbed out the window and stood on the narrow ledge. Holding on to the rough wall as best he could, he pulled the window silently closed behind him. The only other exit out of that back office was through where the professor had just been killed, and Danny certainly wasn't going that way.

The late-evening Cairo air was hot and dry. A slight wind whipped at his loose pants and shirt as he stood with his back against the stone wall. His long black hair blew around his face as he edged inch-by-inch along the stone ledge. He had spent a lot of time climbing rocks back home in Idaho and he had no fear of heights.

But his life also hadn't been threatened in any of those climbing expeditions.

And none of them had been on the side of a building.

He forced himself to concentrate on what he was doing and try to not think about what had just happened inside.

The lights of the massive city of Cairo spread out in front of him. From the ledge, he had a good view over the palm trees and buildings, and in the distance, the Pyramids at Giza were lit up. There was so much light in the downtown area, he felt like there was a spotlight on him. The last thing he needed was to be seen from below and attention drawn to what he was doing.

The door slammed open to the back office and the men's voices got louder.

"Search it and make sure you don't miss anything."

Danny glanced back. Through the edge of the window, he caught a glimpse of a man with a red hood wearing the traditional Arab robe. Except for two eye-holes, his face was completely covered, but Danny caught a glimpse of one of the man's hands. His skin was so pale, he couldn't be Arab. And he had a tattoo on his hand that looked like something with a snake.

Danny glanced away from the window at his path of escape ahead. This wall of the American University Science Building was long, with evenly spaced windows along the ledge. He didn't dare try for the corner. That was too far, and would risk him being seen from either the men in the office or someone on the ground below.

Either would likely get him killed.

The next window to a dark office was locked. Danny glanced back. If one of the men happened to open the window and look outside, he would see Danny.

Danny stepped up onto the windowsill and pressed himself against the glass and the corner of the stone wall. He was a solid five-foot-eight, and people called him husky. But luckily, the windowsill opening was just barely deep enough so that he wouldn't be seen if one of the men looked his direction.

Now Danny just hoped no one below noticed him.

He kept himself perfectly still, using some of the techniques his Native American grandfather had taught him to stay calm.

"Like a stone," his grandfather would say. "Breathe in so slowly, no one can see you, exhale slowly, never stopping.

Keep repeating to yourself: No one can see you."

Over and over, Danny did that, keeping himself pressed against the ledge and the glass, breathing as he had been taught.

Not moving.

I'm invisible. No one can see me.

Danny had never been so afraid in all his life.

His father had gone missing a month earlier, and now Professor Davis was killed because of Danny's father's notebooks.

What had his father found that had caused so much trouble?

Why did these men want that work?

Why was it so valuable?

And what was in the notebooks?

Danny had no answers to any of those questions. The last couple of years, his father had been gone so much, they hadn't talked.

But whatever it was in those notebooks to make them so valuable, if Danny wasn't careful, he would be killed as well for it, before he had any chance to find out what was going on, or what had happened to his father.

His mother insisted that his father was still alive, that she would know in her heart, in her very soul, if he had been killed. And Danny trusted that special connection. His father was being held somewhere. Maybe close by in this very city, as far as Danny knew.

That's why Danny, his best friend, Craig, and his Uncle Steve were in Cairo. The authorities didn't seem to care what had happened to Danny's father, so now he had to go in search.

Danny had expected that his father's notebooks, left with Professor Davis days before his father disappeared, might give him a clue to what had happened.

He never expected the notebooks themselves to get someone killed.

Finally, he heard a clear voice from Professor Davis's office. "There's nothing here."

"Wipe up the blood," another voice said. "Wrap the professor in his rug. We'll haul him with us and make sure his body is very lost in the desert."

The sound of movement echoed out over the night, then one of the men asked the other.

"What do we do now?"

"We trail Hawk's kid," the voice said. "He'll lead us right to the notebooks. His father must have told him where they were. Of that, I'm sure."

Danny was startled at the mention of him. How did these killers know he was in Cairo?

He forced himself to stay perfectly still, to breathe regularly. The last thing he needed at this point, on this ledge, was to panic.

"The kid's here in Cairo?" the other man asked.

"Yeah, he flew in this morning with a friend and Professor Hawk's brother. No reason for them to be here except to find the professor and get his notebooks. Those three will be easy pickings."

Danny was stunned breathless.

Whoever those two men were, they had just confirmed that they were after his father's notebooks. And they knew that Craig and Uncle Steve had come with him to Cairo.

The other man laughed. "Yeah, who knows, we might not have to even kill the three of them."

"Don't count on it," the man in charge said.

CHAPTER TWO

August 16, 1970
American University, Cairo, Egypt.

DANNY HAWK WAITED long enough on the ledge to make sure the men had gone, then when the area below the window was clear of late-night walkers, he eased along the ledge and back inside Professor Davis's darkened back office.

He didn't dare turn on the light. His eyes were accustomed to the dark anyway, so he pulled the window closed and locked it, and then moved quickly over to where Professor Davis had hung his suit coat on the inside door of the closet. Luckily, the coat was still right there.

In the dim light, the room didn't look like it had been searched. Clearly these men were professionals.

Danny wanted, more than anything, to just take his uncle and Craig and head for the airport, go home and forget all of this. Whatever his father had found had gotten him either killed or taken captive. And now it had gotten Professor Davis killed as well. And there was no telling how many other lives had been lost.

Danny knew, without a doubt, that he was in far, far over his head. And there was no one to turn to, no one to trust. The only contact they had had in Cairo had just been killed.

Now it was up to him to get his uncle and Craig to safety and quickly. If there was a safe place anywhere in the world.

The professor's suit coat was the reason that Danny had been in the back office in the first place. The professor's car keys were in his suit coat pocket, and Danny, on Professor Davis's instructions, had gone to get them just as those men had burst into the front office. The professor had told Danny that the notebooks were in the trunk of his car in the faculty parking garage.

Danny searched the pockets of Professor Davis's suit jacket, feeling very odd that he was searching through a dead man's clothing. He pushed that thought back and finally came up with the keys.

He put them in his pocket and moved silently toward the door to the outer office. He opened it carefully, and silently, only a crack. The office was empty, the lights off. It looked cleaned and everything in place.

There was no body.

The rug that had been under Professor Davis's chair was missing. Otherwise, everything looked to be in order. Someone coming in would think the professor hadn't been here. It would be days before anyone reported him missing, since he wasn't married.

Danny moved over to the phone and started to call his uncle at the hotel. Danny couldn't go back there, and he now had to get his uncle and his best friend, Craig James, out of there as well without them being seen.

Then, before he had finished dialing the number, he stopped and put the phone back in the cradle, looking at it as if it were a snake that might bite him at any moment.

"Think," he said softly to himself. "Come on, think."

He forced himself to take two slow, deep breaths, let his mind clear a little.

"Those men are professionals. That phone could be tapped."

He took a few more deep breaths just as his grandfather had trained him to do, and tried to put himself into the mind of a criminal who didn't want to get caught. He'd read enough mystery novels that he should be able to do that.

And right now, he and his uncle and best friend needed to completely vanish from all sight in Africa's largest city.

And quickly.

Danny looked around the dimly lit office. What had he touched?

He took a couple of Kleenex tissues from a box on the professor's desk, then wiped his fingerprints off of the phone. And along the edge of the desk. Then he went back into the inner office and wiped down anything he might have touched in there, including the window. If the professor's body was discovered, there was no point in being connected to this in any way. And since he had an Egyptian visa, he had been fingerprinted when they entered the country.

When he finished, he made himself stand in the center of each room and look around, going over all his movements. He didn't dare miss anything.

"Look carefully," he muttered. "Very carefully."

He then made sure that any surface he might have even accidentally touched was wiped clean. Except for the outer doorknob of the office door, he was finally convinced that he had cleaned off every trace that he had been in the office.

He went out into the hallway and finished the doorknob, then put the tissue in his pocket.

The hallway had very high ceilings and was as wide as some streets. The floor was marble and polished. He walked silently along the empty hall, acting as if he were just a student here who had come later in the evening to see a professor, even though his heart felt like it wanted to explode out of his chest.

So much for the old Indian ways in keeping himself calm. Now he wished he had spent even more time with his grandfather before he died and learned more about self-control. It just never seemed like he would need it. At least, not like this.

He used the wide staircase in the old building and went down to the second floor. An empty receptionist desk filled a large area near the wide marble staircase. A public use phone sat on top of the desk and Danny picked it up and was quickly connected to his hotel.

The hotel was massive and modern. It looked out over the Nile River. Even their room had a river view. They had all been excited getting to it after the long plane flight. Now they were all going to have to run from it, and fast.

His uncle, Steve Hawk, answered the phone. Uncle Steve was the exact opposite of Danny's father. He was friendly, liked to stay at home, and wasn't very smart. Even he admitted that when they had passed out the brains between him and Danny's father, he had got a half serving.

Craig and Danny had the room next door to Uncle Steve's room. Craig was much taller than Danny, standing just over six feet. He had blonde hair and a smile that never seemed to quit. He lived in the same small ski town in central Idaho and his father tried to run a restaurant for tourists, but he drank more than he worked. During the summer for the past few years, Craig had helped Danny and his uncle on their tourist boat on the big mountain lake just to get away from his father.

To Danny, Uncle Steve had been there for him far more than his world-traveling archeologist father had ever been. And even when his father was at home, he was always up north at the University of Idaho, doing research and getting ready for his next trip.

"Uncle Steve," Danny said quickly when he answered the phone. "Don't say anything, just listen to me. I need you and Craig to meet me at the south entrance of the U.S. Embassy. Go down a back staircase and out a hotel back door. Make sure you are not followed. Bring your luggage and what you can of my stuff as well. You're never going back to those rooms. If I'm not there beside the embassy, wait for me without being seen. Move fast. Your lives are in danger."

Then Danny hung up without giving his uncle a chance to argue. More than likely, the call had just scared the poor man half to death. And that was good. After what Danny had just been through, they all needed to be scared if they were going to have any chance of surviving.

Danny forced himself to take another deep breath and think about staying calm.

The seemingly empty old building loomed around him. He had read that a long time ago this building had housed the University of Cairo, before that school moved across the river to larger grounds. It had been some sort of ancient palace before that.

He stood silently, working to calm his racing heart. No one seemed to be listening, to even know he was there. But after what happened to Professor Davis, he could never completely trust that feeling again. He was going to have to be careful every moment and try not to do anything too stupid.

What he really wanted to do was call the police and then just curl up behind the desk until they arrived. But he couldn't do that either. He was in Egypt. A country that was going through a change of government and unrest. Nassar, the leader since 1952, had just died and a man by the name of Sadat looked like he was going to take control. The last thing

Danny needed was to get involved with the Egyptian police at this point. Instead of trying to find his father, he might spend the next year in a jail cell even though he hadn't done anything.

Danny had no doubt at all that the three of them were very much on their own. And next what he had to do was take a huge risk and get his father's notebooks out of the trunk of Professor Davis's car. Those notebooks were the only chance he had of finding out exactly what was happening.

And why his father had disappeared and Professor Davis had been killed.

CHAPTER THREE

August 16, 1970
American University parking garage, Cairo, Egypt.

DANNY MOVED SILENTLY into the two-story parking garage and up to the second floor where Professor Davis had said his small red sedan was parked. The car was tiny compared to American cars, but after spending only a half-day so far in Cairo, Danny understood why all the cars here were small. The streets were jam-packed and, except for the main boulevards, as narrow as an alley. You had to have a small car to even get around.

He stood to one side of the garage in a deep shadow and just watched and waited.

Nothing was moving at all.

But he didn't trust that.

He stayed there, silently in the dark, watching, listening, breathing slowly and deeply as his grandfather had taught him.

No movement.

Nothing.

Finally, he stepped forward as if he belonged there, walking with the gait of someone who was heading to his car to go home.

The key fit perfectly in the trunk of the car, even though Danny's hands were shaking.

The trunk looked empty.

Danny's stomach twisted. Oh, no! Had he heard the professor wrong?

Or had someone else gotten to the notebooks first?

He dug in the trunk, moving first an old blanket and then the spare tire. In the well under the tire, was a dark blue backpack, blending into the bottom of the trunk.

Danny recognized his father's brown notebooks inside. Six of them.

He replaced the tire and blanket, made sure the backpack was securely closed, then put it over his shoulder.

He finished his search of the trunk, finding nothing more that belonged to his father.

Using the tissue still in his pocket, he wiped off his fingerprints from everything he had touched, including the trunk lid, then unlocked the front door, wiped off the keys as well, and tossed them in the tray between the seats.

He quickly locked the door again, closed it as silently as he could, and then turned and walked away toward a side entrance.

He was sweating, his hands were shaking, and his breath was coming fast and hard. What he had taken from the car belonged to him, his father's notebooks, and Danny had had permission to get into the car. Yet, it still felt as if he had just robbed something.

And with Professor Davis dead, Danny would have a very hard time proving that he hadn't robbed the car.

Or, for that matter, killed the professor. Who would believe his story of a red-hooded man?

This garage in Cairo, Egypt, was a long way from the tree-covered mountains of central Idaho where he had grown up, and the tourist boat his mother and Uncle Steve ran.

In two weeks, he was supposed to start back at Boise State University in his second year, and even though he got good grades, he didn't work hard at it. He was much more worried about what was going to happen in two years when he graduated with a degree in English. He didn't really believe in all the fighting and killing going on in Vietnam, so for the moment staying in college was the best thing he could do.

All of it seemed so overwhelming to face.

At least, until his father had disappeared and the next thing Danny knew, he was trying to stay alive in a parking garage in Cairo, Egypt. Worrying about being drafted into the Vietnam War suddenly seemed very tame.

At the edge of the garage, Danny opened the door to the staircase, then let it close without going through. He stayed in the shadows, listening, watching for any movement at all in the garage. He needed to know if he had been followed out of the main building.

He stood perfectly still, his jeans and dark shirt blending into the shadows.

Nothing was moving.

The warm wind blew strange city smells through the garage, and in the distance, sirens cut through the night sounds.

Finally convinced that he hadn't been followed to the car, he walked down the curling ramp to the ground level and out the main entrance, turning toward the U.S. Embassy.

He kept one hand on the backpack strap as he turned south on a wide boulevard, trying to keep his pace the same as the few other walkers out this late at night. He knew he looked like a tourist of some sort or another. His long black hair and dark complexion from his Native American heritage helped him blend in a little, but not much.

He forced himself to keep an eye on everything as he walked.

No one seemed to be paying him any attention, but he had to be sure. Even though the American University was in the same general area of Cairo as the U.S. Embassy, he still had almost a mile to walk. Cairo was a huge city, the biggest in Africa. And Craig and his Uncle had a good mile to travel from the hotel to the embassy as well, coming from the north along the river.

He stopped two blocks from the embassy, ducked into an open restaurant and then stood out of sight near the front door, making sure no one was following him.

No one was, at least that he could see. But he was convinced that someone with real skill could be following him easily, and he would never know it.

If that were the case, he was as good as dead.

Finally, after waiting long enough to give himself a little confidence that he was alone, he went the last few blocks to the south side of the U.S. Embassy.

Craig and his uncle were standing hidden from the street between a fruit stand and a dark alley.

Danny walked up in front of them, then pointed at the street as a black and white taxi approached. He had been told that was what he needed to do to catch a cab in the city, but he hadn't tried it yet. The taxi slowed, its window down.

"Airport!" Danny shouted at the driver, and the driver pulled over to the curb quickly.

Danny kept the backpack on his shoulder while, without a word, his Uncle and Craig loaded the bags they had brought into the trunk and back seat of the small Fiat taxi.

Danny slid in beside the driver, indicating that no one should say a word. In broken English, and what little Arabic Danny knew, he and the driver worked out a fare by the time they were halfway to their destination. Six Egyptian pounds. That was just under two dollars U.S. Danny knew that was high, but at the moment, he didn't care.

He had the cab driver leave them at the international terminal, then Danny led the way inside and to a hidden restaurant off to one side of a large concourse.

After they were settled at the table, Uncle Steve turned to Danny. "All right, you want to tell us why you scared us to death and brought us here?"

Now Available
from all your favorite booksellers.

Danny took a deep breath and let himself relax a little for the first time in the last two hours. He figured he might as well tell them the important detail first, then fill in the rest later.

"Professor Davis was killed tonight by two professional killers looking for my father's notebooks."

Both Uncle Steve and Craig stared at him with their mouths open. If it hadn't been so serious, it might have been funny.

"They're going to come after us next to find them," Danny said. "And they will kill us to get the notebooks. Actually, more than likely, they will kill us anyhow."

"Oh," Uncle Steve said, his face suddenly drained of any sign of color.

"And we have them?" Craig asked.

Danny patted the backpack he had on the floor beside his chair. "We have them."

"Oh, great, now what are we going to do?" Uncle Steve asked, his face white.

"Get on an airplane and get out of here," Craig said. "I'll even buy the tickets."

Craig stood up and reached for his wallet. "I think I have enough money."

Danny shook his head. "Nope."

Craig dropped back into his chair. "How did I know you were going to say that?"

"We're not leaving?" Uncle Steve asked, his voice cracking.

"Nope," Danny said. "We're going to find a safe hotel and hole up while we read my father's notebooks. Then we're going to do what we came here to do."

"Find out what happened to your father," Craig said.

"Exactly," Danny said. "And besides, we can't go home. They would just go there and kill us, and maybe my mother, and there is no way I'm putting her in danger."

He looked around at the three of them. "I heard the men talking about when we arrived in town and how easy we would be to deal with. These people are very real and connected and they seem to have eyes everywhere. We have to find out what they want and why. We're the only hope my father has at this moment."

"So we're committed to this search," Craig said.

"Very," Danny said.

Uncle Steve didn't say anything. He just looked like he might be sick at any moment.

CHAPTER FOUR

August 17, 1970
Gizera Hotel, Cairo, Egypt.

MAKING SURE THAT they weren't followed, Danny Hawk, his best friend, Craig, and his Uncle Steve left the airport restaurant and hailed a cab to a hotel that Danny had found a small ad for in the airport. It was on the west side of the river on Gizera Avenue. The hotel was spread out around a number of court-yards, each filled with decorative rock and a few palm trees and nothing more. It wasn't an upscale tourist hotel, but it wasn't bad. It looked like it catered more to businessmen from the area.

The area smelled lightly of dirty water and animals. Not at all a smell Danny would have expected in the center of a big city.

Again, they got a room for Uncle Steve while Danny and Craig shared a room with two beds. They registered under false names, booking the room for three days. The night clerk had been so tired, he hadn't even asked to see their identification or passports like the bigger hotel had done.

Craig just passed out, snoring lightly, his six-foot-plus frame dangling over the edge of the bed, but Danny didn't sleep much during what was left of the night. But he managed to rest and think. So by breakfast in the small hotel restaurant, he was feeling more in control.

Scared and completely over his head, but in control.

The men who were looking for them would have no way of tracing them through the thousands of hotels in Cairo. More than likely, they were still watching the Continental where they had been staying. And would for a few days at least, since Uncle Steve had paid for three nights and they hadn't checked out when they left.

"What's the plan this morning?" Craig asked Danny.

"We should contact the authorities," Uncle Steve said, using his confident voice. The voice Danny knew he always used when trying to get something from someone.

"And say what?" Danny asked, staring at his uncle. Sitting in the airport restaurant last night, he had told them the entire story of how he managed to escape and get the notebooks.

Uncle Steve looked flustered, his face growing slightly red which was accented by his gray hair. "I don't know, but we should."

"For all we know," Danny said, "the police were who killed Professor Davis."

Uncle Steve started to say something, but Danny held up his hand. "We don't know, do we?"

Uncle Steve just shrugged.

"We're not in the United States, remember." Danny patted the backpack he had carried with him from the room. "And we have no idea just what's in these notebooks or how valuable they are."

"Valuable enough to kill for," Craig said, shaking his head and looking worried. "That's for sure. We need to read them, find out why."

"Agreed," Danny said. "And that's the plan for the day."

After breakfast, they went back to Uncle Steve's room.

When Danny opened the first book bound in leather and full of his father's writings, he was almost instantly disappointed. This was going to be a lot more difficult than he had thought.

The notebooks were in a combination of English, Italian, Latin, and Egyptian hieroglyphs. Danny knew his father was fluent in all four languages, plus a few others, including some Arabic, since he had worked so often in Egypt. Clearly, he had no trouble writing in all the languages as well and had done so from one paragraph to another, changing without any seeming reason.

Danny knew some Latin and some French, but that was all. Not much help.

"Who can read what language?" Danny asked, handing the notebook to Craig and picking up another to see if it was the same. It was.

"A little Spanish," Craig said, shrugging.

"Nothing," Uncle Steve said, looking apologetic. "It would figure my brother would protect his notes with something like this. He always did like to show off how smart he was."

Danny ignored the old family chant he had heard his uncle say hundreds of times. "Well, let's read what we can and figure out how to get help with what we can't read later."

Danny took back the first notebook and started into the record of the last ten years of his father's research. It felt like reading his father's private thoughts was snooping on something his father had never wanted him to see.

Three hours later, Danny put down the last notebook and sat back, trying to make sense of what he had been able to read.

It seemed that his father had been focused on finding archeological records of what he had started to call "The Fountain." That was short for the Fountain of Youth.

Danny had been around his father and his work enough to know that with any myth coming up through history, there was usually some sort of factual basis somewhere in the past. His father clearly didn't believe in any water that could keep a person youthful, so he was searching for the start of the myth.

And why the myth existed the way it did.

Somewhere, in the second year, the word Taccola had come into the notebooks. Danny knew a little about Taccola because his father had been so interested in him when Danny was ten. Taccola was an engineer in the late fourteen century in Siena, and his inventions were amazingly ahead of their time. Many of the inventions concerned moving water to the city of Siena, which was a landlocked city without a good water supply.

But later in Taccola's life, he had been interested in finding older inventions and had led expeditions into parts of Egypt, where he vanished without a trace somewhere around 1458.

His father had underlined a phrase that bothered Danny a great deal. "Could Taccola still be alive?"

That was the last mention of Taccola in the notebooks, at least in the parts that Danny could read.

The next book dealt with Napoleon's interest in ancient culture and the archeological searches he funded and went on in Egypt and other areas around the Mediterranean. It seemed that, as with Taccola, Napoleon was focused on water in his searches, possibly even something that was rumored to give his men an invincibility.

At one point, his father had written "He was searching for the Fountain."

It was in the fourth journal that the words *Hydra Journals* were written, then underlined.

Danny couldn't tell from what he could read in English what the Hydra Journals were about, but from that point onward, they seemed to be a focus for his father. Five years of intense focus, as a matter of fact, from what Danny could tell from the dates in the notebooks.

The very last entry in the last notebook had been in English. It had basically said that Danny's father had made a breakthrough, but somehow he was going to have to keep his find from the *Hydra League*.

Then he wrote a few notes in Egyptian hieroglyph and the journal ended.

From the last date in the notebook, Danny's father had taken them to Professor Davis for safekeeping the next day and then vanished two days later.

Danny stared at the words *Hydra League*.

Was the red-hooded man who killed Professor Davis part of that league?

Was it the league that had taken his father?

Hydra, an old Greek legend was about a snake with many women's heads.

Hydra Journals. Water. Fountain of Youth. Taccola. Napoleon. Hydra League.

Danny sighed, sat back, and closed his eyes while Craig and Uncle Steve kept reading.

At least he knew a little more of where his father's research had taken him. But now Danny was more confused and scared than he had been last night.

And he had no idea what to do next.

CHAPTER FIVE

August 18, 1970
Gizera Hotel, Cairo, Egypt.

THEY HAD SPENT the entire previous day reading what they could of the notebooks a second time and talking about them and what they contained. They hadn't left the hotel and had turned in early to get rested, with the understanding that at breakfast they would decide what to do next.

Danny barely slept, even though he was exhausted. Every time he closed his eyes, a red-hooded snake with many heads would come up out of a black pool of water and chase him.

He wasn't sure he was having a vision dream, as his grandfather would sometimes call vivid images like that, or just a nightmare. Danny had a hunch it was a little bit of both.

But he did know that he was his father's only chance of survival if he was still alive.

And Danny had to believe his mother that his father was alive. Somewhere, being held by someone.

And now, just like his father, Danny was in too deep. There was no turning back, no going home, back to the easy life of going to school.

Across the restaurant table the next morning, Danny looked at his best friend and his uncle, then laid out simply what he thought they should do next.

"Uncle Steve, Craig, I want you two to take a flight from here to London, then on home."

"What?" Craig asked.

Danny held up his hand. "Let me finish. Uncle Steve, I need you to get my mother out on your boat into the upper areas of the lake. The old cabin up on the point should be safe for a time. Lock up the house and just go, get on that boat and stay away from contact as much as possible.

Uncle Steve shook his head and Craig looked disgusted.

"We're not leaving you," Craig said. "And who do I have to go home to? My drunken father?"

Danny knew Craig was right. There was no one at home for Craig. His mother was dead and his father spent more time in bars than at home. Craig pretended to live with his father, but in reality, he spent most of his time at Danny's house. Not only were they best friends, but Craig was like the brother Danny never had. And Danny's mother considered him her second son.

"Your mother would kill me if I left her son over here alone," Uncle Steve said. "And she'd have a right to."

"Uncle Steve," Danny said, "the men who took my father, and who killed Professor Davis, are not going to stop at the border of Egypt. They know we're here, they know we left my mother alone. Once they can't find us, where do you think they're going to go next?"

Uncle Steve's skin turned a sickly white and he instantly started sweating. He clearly hadn't thought of that.

Danny stared into the fear-filled eyes of his uncle. "Someone needs to protect my mother, and you're the best man for that. Get out on the boat on that lake and up to the cabin on the point."

"But you can't stay here alone," Uncle Steve said.

"He's not going to be alone," Craig said, his voice full of anger. "I'm staying with him and there's no argument on that point."

Danny looked at his best friend, then smiled. He had been hoping that Craig would say that. Together, they had more of a chance than Danny did alone, that was for sure.

Craig then turned to Uncle Steve. "But Danny's right, you have to go back and get his mother safe."

Uncle Steve sighed and slumped in the booth.

Danny knew that he had put his uncle in an impossible situation. He either had to leave two boys he still considered his "babies" in danger in a foreign country, or he had to live with the fact that if he didn't go back, Danny's mother more than likely would be killed.

"Remember," Danny said, "we may be young, but we are considered adults. We'll be fine."

Uncle Steve didn't even nod at that, just stared down at his hands.

"One other thing," Danny said. "We're going to need money at times if we're going to try to find out what happened to my father and stay hidden from the men after the notebooks. Craig and I can live pretty cheap here, and stay out of sight easier if it's just the two of us than if you are with us. But even still, we're going to need someone we can contact for money."

Uncle Steve again just sighed, but this time he nodded as well.

Danny knew that his uncle had a pretty good sum of money stashed from the settlement from his wife's death.

"You're going to be our anchor," Danny said. "You and my mother have to stay safe, and yet be in contact with us. And from the looks of these notebooks, there's no telling where this is going to take us, or how long it's going to take."

Craig laughed. "I suddenly feel like I've been tossed into a quest fantasy."

"I just wish this was a fantasy," Danny said, smiling at his friend. "It's just a little too real and deadly for my tastes."

"No argument there," Craig said.

CHAPTER SIX

August 19, 1970
International Airport, Cairo, Egypt.

LATE THAT NIGHT, just after midnight, the three of them went back to the international airport. Uncle Steve booked them all tickets to London, then on to Seattle. From there Uncle Steve would drive back to central Idaho. The idea was that if the men who were after the notebooks thought all three of them had left, they would follow Uncle Steve to Seattle.

"Are you sure you want them after you?" Danny had asked his uncle when he suggested the idea.

Uncle Steve nodded. "Don't worry, they'll never find your mother and me after we get on that lake. The old cabin has no entrance road and no one really remembers it's out there. Besides, looking for you in Seattle will keep them off your trail here for a while at least."

Danny didn't like it, but he had agreed to the plan.

The plane didn't leave until six in the morning, so for the rest of the night, the three of them sat in a secluded place where they could see people in the international airport coming and going. They planned as much as they could during those hours, including how and when Danny and Craig would check in with Uncle Steve and his mother.

The first thing Danny and Craig had to do was try to get new identification. Uncle Steve left them with enough money to last them for a few months in Cairo, and they set up how more money could be wired to them.

As Uncle Steve got ready to go through customs, he turned to Danny. "You're mother's going to kill me, you know."

Danny laughed. "Just make her close up the house and get away from there."

"Oh, I will," Uncle Steve said, the worry in his lined face clear. "Twelve hours after I reach home, we'll be gone."

"Good," Danny said. He gave his uncle a hug, then Craig did the same.

"Be careful," Uncle Steve said. "And find my brother, would you?"

"We will," Craig said for both of them.

Uncle Steve nodded, then with a worried smile turned and headed into the customs area.

Danny and Craig stood off to one side, watching all the people coming and going through that area of the airport. No one seemed to be paying them any attention, so after a good half hour, they went out the door and took a cab into the old heart of Cairo, right to the Khan Al-Khalili bazaar.

Neither of them spoke on their ride into the center of the city. Danny felt completely overwhelmed by what they faced, and very much afraid. Chances were he and Craig would be killed far before they found Danny's father. But they had to try.

They had no other choice.

CHAPTER SEVEN

August 19, 1970
Khan Al-Khalili bazaar, Cairo, Egypt.

STEPPING OUT OF the modern city of Cairo and into the bazaar was like stepping through time back centuries, much like turning off a modern boulevard in New Orleans and going into the French Quarter. The narrow streets were jammed with everything imaginable being sold on both sides, and the noise level was intense, with people bargaining for everything, often at the top of their lungs.

Ancient two-story buildings and many cloth overhangs and tents kept out the early morning sunlight, making the long, crowded market seem like a carnival without any lights turned on. From what Danny understood, it was this crowded all morning and into the early afternoon every day. At least for now, the shade kept the temperature down. Later this afternoon, with the sun directly overhead, this street would be almost too hot to walk on.

"Oh, wow, does that smell good," Craig said, walking past a booth where a woman was cooking something in a large pot.

It did smell wonderful, like a combination of beef stew and baking bread, but Danny wasn't sure if he was up to eating from a street vender just yet, even though he was starting to get a little hungry.

They passed one booth after another, all cooking something different. And the cooking smells mixed with the smells of incense and new rugs hanging from almost everything.

The booth and the crowds stretched as far as Danny could see, and the moment they got into the crowds, he became separated from Craig for a moment. After they got back together, they agreed that if they did get separated, they would meet back on the corner where the cab had just let them off.

"So, where do we start?" Craig asked.

Danny looked at the crowds and booths selling food, incense, rugs, lamps, and just about everything else. "I don't have a clue. Let's just walk and see what we see."

They were looking for help with languages reading the journals, and Uncle Steve had suggested that the best place to find help, and maybe a guide to the city, was at the famous bazaar. So it was the first thing Danny and Craig were going to try.

They had walked the crowded street for most of an hour, not even beginning to see all of the bazaar yet, when a short, young Arab man approached them and motioned that they should move to the edge of the street, near a building, so they could talk.

The guy was short, no more than five-three, and both Danny and Craig towered over him. He looked to be about their age, maybe younger, and had a robe on that clearly had seen better days. He wore the traditional sandals of the city, and nothing on his thick, unruly black hair.

As they got to a place near a building wall where the crowd wouldn't bang at them like a river trying to go around a rock, the guy said, "American tourists?" He spoke in clear English with a slight British accent that seemed really odd coming from a short Arab boy in ragged robes.

Danny nodded.

The guy introduced himself, rattling off a name that was long, complex, and that Danny had no chance of following. Then he smiled and said, "But my American friends all call me 'Bud'."

"Nice meeting you, Bud," Danny said without giving him their names.

Bud looked at each of them, then shrugged. "You looked like you were looking for something since you entered the bazaar. I just thought I'd offer my services in finding what you are searching after."

Danny felt a shock of fear hit him, and clearly Craig wasn't happy with the sound of that either. This guy named Bud had been following them since they entered the bazaar and they *hadn't* noticed. And Danny had been watching for anyone following them.

"You were following us?" Craig asked, sounding as worried as Danny felt.

Bud shrugged, his tattered robe moving like waves on a calm sea. "Sure. You looked like you needed help. That's what I do, I offer my help."

"For a fee," Craig said.

Bud smiled. "Of course. But it is a very *small* fee."

"I'll bet," Craig said.

"Was anyone else following us?" Danny asked.

"No," Bud said. "I would have seen them. Were you expecting someone to be?"

"We're hoping not," Danny said. "But for all we know, you were paid by the people looking for us to follow us."

Bud laughed. "Oh, trust me, anyone could have followed you. They would not have needed to hire me."

Danny had to agree the short guy was right. He was starting to think that this guy might be able to help them, or at least, for a small fee, point them in the right direction.

"Do you know the city well?" Danny asked.

Bud laughed. "I have survived on these streets since I was ten. Of course I do. The streets are my home."

"Can you read other languages besides Arabic and English?" Craig asked.

"Some Italian, some French," Bud said, now looking puzzled. It was clearly not a question that he had been expecting.

Danny glanced at Craig, who nodded.

"Can you find us someone who also can read Latin and knows some hieroglyphs?"

Bud again shrugged. "Of course."

"Can you wait here for a moment," Danny asked Bud. "I need to talk to my friend."

Danny and Craig stepped a half dozen steps away. "He might be exactly what we're looking for to start with," Danny said.

"As long as you keep an eye on your wallet at all times," Craig said, "I agree."

Then he smiled the devious smile that Danny had come to know over the years. It was a smile that tended to get them into trouble more than anything else.

"How about we make up some sort of treasure?" Craig said. "Tell him that we're searching for it, and offer to let him join us. That way he's got a stake in it as well and won't charge us when he helps us."

"You mean like the Hydra Journals and the Fountain of Youth?" Danny asked, smiling.

"Yeah, that treasure," Craig said, laughing. "I guess we really are after a treasure, aren't we?"

Danny nodded. "I have a hunch we find those Hydra Journals, we find my father."

"I bet you're right," Craig said. "And let's just hope the Fountain of Youth is real as well."

"So," Danny said, "let's hire this Bud to help us find someone else to do languages, tell him we're in danger and ask him what he suggests for places to live and hide, and then if we like him, we'll tell him everything."

"A good plan," Craig said.

Together, they returned to Bud, who had been leaning against a building, waiting and watching things around them. He seemed almost invisible, he blended in so well. And his eyes didn't seem to miss anything. Danny didn't know why, exactly, but he trusted this guy. He just hoped he and Craig wouldn't pay later for that trust.

"We'll talk money in a few minutes," Danny said to Bud, "but we first need to know if you can get us to someone who can read Latin and hieroglyphs."

"Sure," Bud said. "The twins. They're staying in a small apartment near here."

"Twins?" Danny asked.

"Ernie and Ed," Bud said, shrugging. "That's more than likely not their real names, but that's what they go by here. They're from South Africa and have skin as black as the night. They say they're traveling the world searching for treasures, but I think they're trying to escape something."

"How old are they?" Craig asked.

"You two look about twenty," Bud said. "The twins are about your ages I'd say, but they've never told me."

Danny was shocked at how smart this short guy was.

"How old are you?" Craig asked.

The guy shrugged. "I am close to your age, but I have lived a long time in those short years."

Danny didn't doubt that at all. "How do you know these twins can read Latin?"

"Because I watched them one day in an old palace underground near here. They're the smartest two people I've ever met."

Danny looked at Craig, who nodded.

Danny turned back to Bud. "Can you help us find a place to live that will be hidden from those chasing us?"

"Sure," Bud said. "Where are you living now?"

"A hotel," Danny said, not wanting to give him the actual name just yet.

"Real tourists," Bud said. He looked at Danny, then at Craig. "But you're here alone?"

Danny nodded.

"And someone might be following you and you need a place to live and hide while you translate some sort of language problem. Right?"

"Right," Danny said, knowing exactly what Bud was doing. He was starting to bargain for a rate to help them. "Twenty pounds for the day for you to help us."

"Fifty," Bud said. "And if you don't like the twins, I'll find you someone else."

"Thirty," Danny said, "and not a penny more."

"Thirty-five or you find yourself another guide. And you have to show me you have that much on you."

"Deal," Danny said, flashing a fifty-pound note. "And if you do us a good job today, we may have another offer for you after we're finished."

Bud smiled. "I like the sound of that. What first? A safe place to live or meet the twins?"

"The twins," Danny said and Craig nodded.

"Follow me," Bud said and turned, almost vanishing into the crowds of shoppers at once.

Danny quickly checked his wallet. It was still there. He had a hunch that with Bud, he would be checking for his wallet all the time.

CHAPTER EIGHT

August 19, 1970
Khan Al-Khalili bazaar, Cairo, Egypt.

BUD HAD TO wait for them a number of times in the short two blocks through the bazaar to an ancient stone building on the right of the street. The heat of the day was increasing by the minute and Danny not only found himself even more hungry than he had been earlier, but also sweating.

Craig was sweating as well. They needed to get out of the heat pretty soon and get something to drink. The Pacific Northwest just didn't have this kind of dry heat.

When Bud finally stopped and waited for them one last time, he said as Danny stopped in front of him, "We're going to have to get you both some better clothes for this heat and not being followed. You stand out like a fire on a dark night."

Danny nodded. He had thought of that, but hadn't expected Bud to.

"Wait here," Bud said, indicating a place still in the shade against a building. "I'll see if they are home and if they are interested in seeing you."

With that, Bud turned and disappeared through an archway that led somewhere into the shadows of the buildings.

"We're going to need food and water pretty soon," Craig said.

Danny nodded. "Bud can tell us which booth is safe to eat at."

"If you buy him lunch," Craig said, laughing.

Danny had no doubt he was going to have to do that. Luckily for them, the exchange rate made staying here very cheap. The thirty-five pounds he had offered Bud for his services was less than five U.S. dollars.

Less than a minute later, Bud appeared near Danny silently, startling both Danny and Craig.

"You two seem very jumpy, even for Americans," Bud said.

"It's been a long few days," Danny said.

"How bad are these people you are hiding from?" Bud asked.

"Bad," Craig said and Danny nodded.

Bud frowned, then said, "The twins will talk with you if you bring us all some lunch." He pointed to a cart making some sort of wrap of meat and bread. "Five of those, five bottles of Coca-Cola."

"Heaven," Craig said, as all three headed toward the booth where a woman worked and two children sat in the shade on the ground behind her. The entire lunch cost Danny two pounds, including five warm small bottles of Coke, and the woman seemed very happy with that much.

As they walked away, Bud said in a disgusted voice, "You should have only given her one. You two Americans really do need my help."

Danny was starting to believe him.

The twins' apartment, as Bud had called it, was no more than a room not much larger than an average bedroom. It had two sleeping pads against the back walls, one window that was open, and one table with two chairs. If there was a bathroom, it was down the hall or outside.

The place actually felt slightly cooler than out on the street, but Danny wasn't sure if that was because they were out of the sun or if it actually was cooler.

Bud had been right about the twins being Danny's age. They actually looked a little younger, with startling dark black skin, short-cropped hair, and smiles that seemed to light up the room.

They were clearly identical twins and Danny could see no difference at all, not even a mannerism that separated Ernie from Ed. Thankfully, Ernie had a small silver stud earring in his right ear, while Ed had the same earring in his left. Otherwise they were completely identical twins, so much so that they even finished each other's sentences and wore the same color brown robe.

Bud handed them the food and drink, and Ernie thanked Danny in a polite British accent.

No one sat at the table, since it was covered in papers and books, so all five of them ended up sitting on the floor with their backs against the bare, paint-peeling walls, eating.

Danny was stunned at how good the bread and meat tasted. Almost like a Sloppy Joe back home, only with a much sweeter spice and a very thin, dry bread. And he was so thirsty that even the warm Coke tasted great.

Danny thought he ate the food fast, but when he finished and looked up, Ernie, Ed, and Bud were sitting watching him, clearly waiting. Craig was still eating.

Ed looked at Danny, then at Craig. "We thought all young Americans your age were killing women and children in Vietnam."

Danny was stunned at the directness. He had spent the last few years worrying about being drafted and going to Vietnam. He hadn't realized that the rest of the world paid attention as well.

"College deferments," Craig said, staring back at Ed.

"I must apologize for my brother," Ernie said. "We just do not believe in what your country is doing."

"Half of our country doesn't either," Danny said. "It's why our cities and college campuses are being destroyed by bombs and people are marching in the streets."

Ed nodded. "I am sorry."

"Not a problem," Danny said, waving it off.

"So, what can we do to help you?" Ernie asked.

Danny didn't know where to start, so he figured a little background might ease him into what they needed. He introduced himself and Craig, using first names only, and told them where they were from in general.

"My father is an archeologist. He went missing a few weeks back and we're here looking for him."

"Professor Kenneth Hawk?" Ernie asked, suddenly sitting forward, clearly excited and very interested.

"You're his son?" Ed asked, also excited.

"You have his notebooks, don't you?" Ernie asked.

"And you need help reading them," Ed said. "Oh, this is so amazing."

Bud stared at the twins, then at Danny.

Danny didn't know what to say. Or do for that matter. He just sat there stunned.

Beside him, Craig's mouth was open.

"We would be honored to help you find your father," Ernie said.

Ed nodded. "Very honored. I hope my rude comment about your country's stupid war did not upset you too much. We have already been doing what we can to find your father."

"Without success," Ernie said.

"Sadly," Ed said.

"Yes, your father was a brilliant scientist and archeologist," Ernie said.

"He was onto something very large when he was taken," Ed said.

"Very large. Very important," Ernie said.

Danny held up his hand and stopped the constant talk of the twins. He was suddenly very worried that they had come to the wrong place. "How did you know my father?"

"We met him many times, and worked with him some on his latest dig," Ernie said.

"Only as brushers," Ed said.

"And dirt haulers," Ernie said.

"But we were still honored," Ed said.

Ernie only nodded in agreement.

"Oh, I knew these two could help you," Bud said, smiling. "I'm so good."

Danny glanced at Craig, then back at the twins, trying to clear his head. Finally he managed in the silence of the room to get back to what they had come here for. "Can you read Latin, Italian, or hieroglyphs?"

"Yes," both twins said at once.

Danny glanced at Craig, who was nodding. "Might as well tell them everything."

Danny shrugged. He had no choice. He was going to have to trust some people. Not everyone could be on the other side. His uncle wasn't even a few hours away from Egypt and they were making better progress in getting help than Danny could have hoped for in weeks. Assuming these two were not members of the Hydra League.

"My uncle Steve, Craig, and I arrived in Cairo two days ago," Danny said, "to start a search for my father, since the authorities and U.S. Embassy seem to have had no luck."

"They wouldn't either," Bud said. "Not with everything that's going on with the new government."

"And your father was taken by forces far more powerful and older than any government," Ernie said.

Ed nodded.

Danny didn't like the sound of that at all, but he went on. "Professor Davis at the American University had been given my father's notebooks to keep, since clearly my father was worried something would happen to him."

Ernie and Ed both nodded. "Yes, Professor Davis, a good man."

Danny took a deep breath. "I was in his back office when two men burst in and threatened him to get the notebooks. I ended up hiding on the ledge outside his back office window and they didn't see me."

"Oh, no," Ernie said.

"Professor Davis refused to tell them that he even knew what they were talking about," Danny said, going on. "So they killed him and searched his office. Then they cleaned up his office and took his body away, saying they would dump it in the desert."

Now it was Ernie and Ed's turn to look shocked. And Bud didn't look very happy now about even being with them.

"I also overheard them say that they would come looking for my uncle, Craig, and me, since we had just arrived and must have the notebooks."

"That's who you were afraid of following you in the bazaar?" Bud asked.

Danny nodded. "We managed to escape without them seeing us and found another hotel where we registered under false names. Then we bought three tickets back home to lead them in the wrong direction, but only my uncle used his ticket to go home and get my mother to safety. We stayed to continue the search."

"Very smart thinking," Ernie said.

"Yes, very," Ed said.

"So these killers may not know you are even still in Cairo," Bud said.

"That's what we're hoping," Craig said.

"So, you don't have your father's notebooks?" Ernie asked.

"No, I have them," Danny said. "They are very safely hidden. But we could only read a part of them, since my father alternated between English, Latin, Italian, and hieroglyphs."

"Do you have training in archaeology?" Ernie asked.

"Some," Danny said, "but not officially. Just from being around my father growing up, and listening to his stories when he came home."

"So," said Ed, "even if you could read it all, you might not understand it."

Danny nodded. He had considered that as well.

"So what was your father looking for that got him kidnapped and this Professor Davis killed?" Bud asked.

"The Fountain of Youth," Danny said.

Bud laughed, but Ernie and Ed both nodded.

"It is very real, and has been known about for centuries," Ernie said. "Your father had become the leading expert on it."

"But it is not a fountain," Ed said, just as seriously as Ernie. "Your father, of course, knew that."

"Actually, no one knows exactly what it is," Ernie said.

"But it is the world's most protected secret coming down through the centuries," Ed said.

"It is believed that many people have lived thousands of years because of what is called the Fountain," Ernie said.

"Who protects it?" Danny asked, worried that he already knew the answer. "Men in red hoods?"

Ernie and Ed looked stunned, but slowly both nodded.

"The Hydra League," they said together.

Craig shook his head and stared at the floor. "We are so screwed."

CHAPTER NINE

August 19, 1970
An apartment near the Khan Al-Khalili bazaar, Cairo, Egypt.

THEY TALKED FOR another hour or so, and the more they talked, the more Danny came to trust all three of their new friends. He learned that the Hydra Journals his father was searching for weren't really journals in a traditional sense, but a series of clues that when put together would lead to the secret of the Fountain.

The Hydra League had supposedly been formed six centuries ago to protect the secret, and the journals' clues had been placed in various places around the globe. Taccola searched for one of them, as did Napoleon and his people.

"Both are said to have found one part of the Hydra Journals," Ed said.

"Do you think my father was close to finding another piece?" Danny asked.

The twins shrugged. "There was a reason he was taken. It was rumored he found the key to finding them all."

"So he's been killed," Danny said, very much afraid of the answer the twins might give him.

"I don't think so," Ed said.

"I think he was taken to the Fountain," Ernie said, and Ed nodded.

"What?" Danny said, surprised. "Why would a group that killed Professor Davis spare my father?"

"Even the Hydra League is rumored to have rules," Ed said. "Very old rules."

"You father cracked their secret code, we're sure," Ernie said. "And thus he would have earned the right to go to the Fountain, the world's greatest archeological treasure."

"But he's being held?"

"Of course," Ed said. "How else would the Hydra League protect its secret?"

"Sure," Ernie said. "They would only have to hold him for a hundred years or so. All of his family and friends would be dead, and who would he tell? And if he tried, who would believe him then?"

Danny felt all the energy drain out of his body. If these two were right, the chances of seeing his father again didn't exist.

"So, we crack the Hydra Journals and go rescue him," Craig said.

"Oh, sure, nothing to it," Bud said. Then he seemed to realize something and brightened. "If we did find this Fountain, it would be worth a great deal of money, wouldn't it? Count me in."

Ernie and Ed both shook their heads with looks of identical disgust.

Danny closed his eyes and leaned back, banging his head slightly on the wall. His father's only hope was him and these guys with him in this tiny Cairo apartment. But at least, as long as they were still alive and looking, trying to find him, there was still hope. No one else was going to go looking for his father, that was for sure.

The image of his father, tall, lean, hungry eyes, boarding the plane for Egypt the last time came to Danny's mind. His work had always consumed him, often more than his family. And Danny had always thought it somewhat stupid, digging in the ground for old things to put in museums.

But it seemed that the past held secrets that were deadly even to the present, and those secrets could change the world if they were exposed. Maybe it was time to tell the world that the Fountain of Youth was real.

The only chance of ever seeing his father again was to find the Fountain. They all needed to pick up the quest where his father had left off. And somehow not get taken by the Hydra League.

He had to actually follow the Hydra Journals, find all of its clues, and go to the Fountain and rescue his father. More than likely the quest would kill him, but he had no choice.

He had to try to save his father.

Danny sat forward and opened his eyes. "Ed, Ernie, would you help Craig and me search for my father?"

"Of course," both said at the same time.

"I will pay all expenses," Danny said, "including food and travel if we have to change cities."

Both nodded in agreement to the terms.

"And if we do find treasure, we divide the value evenly."

"I agree," Ed said, "but I would argue for the archeological treasure we might find be sold to museums."

"Of course," Danny said.

"Then I agree as well," Ernie said.

"How about a five-way split?" Bud asked. "You're going to need someone like me along on this adventure. I know how to find things. I got you four together, didn't I?"

Danny smiled at the short guy. "I was hoping you would want to join us. You're right, we are going to need you."

"You know," Craig said, "we all may get killed going after this."

"It's highly likely," Ernie said.

"But it is a great treasure," Ed said. "And great treasures are worth great risk. Danny, your father believed as much."

"I like that part," Bud said. "Great treasure."

Danny looked at them. "I have no choice. My father needs me. I'm his only hope."

Then he smiled. "But finding the Fountain of Youth wouldn't be all that bad either."

CHAPTER TEN

August 19, 1970
Gizera Hotel, Cairo, Egypt.

THE SUN WAS dropping over the desert to the west when they finally left the twins' apartment. The bazaar had wound down in the heat of the day, and now the street looked almost deserted.

Waves of shimmering heat came off the pavement and Danny, this time with Bud's help, bought them all bottles of Coke again. Bud paid less than a quarter of a pound for the five bottles, and seemed upset that he hadn't gotten a better deal.

The five took two cabs to the hotel where Danny and Craig were staying. The twins and Bud took a cab to the hotel first, to scout out the area to make sure no one was waiting for Craig and Danny, who followed in a second cab a few minutes later.

There was no one, Bud swore to that, but Danny was convinced that their luck wouldn't last. He and Craig had to move to a safer place near the bazaar that couldn't be traced. Bud said he knew the best place, but he wouldn't be able to get it for them until tomorrow morning. So they decided to risk one more night in the hotel and all read Danny's father's journals while there.

Danny brought them all food after getting the notebooks from the hiding place in the ceiling tile. The twins were well into the notebooks, writing like crazy. They had brought second spiral notebooks, and were going to copy by hand every word Danny's father had said.

And put it all in English.

"Your father is an amazing man," Ernie said as he ate and read at the same time. "He put together clues from diverse sources that no other archeologist would have thought of doing."

"Yeah," Danny said, "but he wasn't much of a father."

"Never home?" Ed asked.

Danny nodded.

Bud shrugged. "Never knew my father. Or my mother for that matter."

Danny glanced at Bud. He had said it so matter-of-factly, it seemed like he actually didn't care. But Danny had a hunch that under that tough shell, Bud actually did care.

"Our father was killed in prison for speaking out against the South African white government," Ed said.

"Our mother never recovered," Ernie said. "She was also killed for the same cause."

Bud glanced up at them, surprised. Clearly they were not runaways as he had suspected, except maybe running away from their country.

"My father drinks, can't hold a job, and gets mean," Craig said. "I try not to be around him much, but I still like the old guy."

Danny looked at his new friends, suddenly understanding just how lucky he had been to have the father he had.

His mother had never complained, and neither had Uncle Steve. They had just accepted Professor Kenneth Hawk for what he was, a driven scientist in search of something mythical.

Danny had been the only one angry at him for not being home more. And now it was up to Danny to save his father.

After they finished eating, all five boys went back to reading, with Bud going out to check the surrounding area around the hotel every fifteen minutes.

Craig dozed off around one, and Danny finally fell asleep at two.

When he woke to the sun streaming in through the window, the two twins were still writing as fast as they could, and Bud was napping in a chair near the door.

"We almost have it finished," Ernie said without slowing down.

"Another fifteen minutes at most," Ed said.

"But I can tell you this much," Ernie said. "We're going to have to go to your father's apartment here in Cairo."

"Why?" Danny asked.

"We're not sure, but we need to go there."

Danny shrugged. More than likely it had been cleaned out, but if the twins thought it was a good idea to go there, they would do it.

"And we need to go to the Giza Pyramids," Ernie said.

"So you can see something your father found and understood," Ed said.

"Was my father's last work site there?"

"No," Ed said. "His dig was farther to the south."

Now Danny was really puzzled. "Why go to Giza then?"

"A clue to the Hydra Journals is there," Ed said. "We think you should see it."

"Wouldn't my father have taken it with him, or the Hydra League hidden it after they took him?"

"No," Ernie said, pointing to a place in the notebook that was written in hieroglyphs. "Because it's been in plain sight for years. Every tourist looks at it without understanding what it is. Your father finally put meaning behind what everyone sees."

"Oh," was all Danny could say.

The twins both went back to writing at full speed, so Danny decided he would get them all some breakfast.

"We're not going to either of those places without me checking out the area first," Bud said before Danny could stand. "And right now, I need to scout this hotel again. No one leave until I get back."

Bud moved quickly and went out the door, closing it carefully behind him.

Danny stayed in the chair he had been sleeping in and watched the twins work. He was very glad they had suggested making a copy of the notebooks and hiding both. That way, if the League did catch up to Danny, he could surrender the originals and still have what they needed to start their journey toward the Fountain and his father.

"Done," Ernie said.

"As am I," Ed said a moment later.

They quickly wrapped the original notebooks and put them back in their pack. Then they quickly took the four notebooks they had written in and hid them under their robes, in pockets that didn't seem to show the books at all.

"We have company," Bud said, coming back in quickly and closing the door.

"These guys are good," Craig said, sitting up and rubbing sleep out of his eyes. "Only two days to find us here."

The sound of the shot killing Professor Davis came back clearly in Danny's mind, but he pushed it away. "How many and where?"

"Only two, and they are at the front desk," Bud said. "But they have a picture of you, Danny, and the front desk clerk is chattering like a bird at sunrise."

"You three go out the window," Danny said, handing Bud a fifty-pound note. "Circle around to the front and take a cab back to the bazaar and wait for us. They don't know you, so you'll be safe."

Danny grabbed his bag and then put his father's backpack over his shoulder.

Craig grabbed his suitcase.

"How are you two getting out of here?" Bud asked, a worried look on his face.

"Right through the front lobby," Danny said. "We're even going to check out and everything, then head for the airport."

Bud smiled. "I'm starting to like you two more and more. You have some courage."

"That is taking a great risk," Ernie said.

"They know what we look like already," Danny said as he opened the window to hold it for the three new friends. "They won't dare confront us in a public place. We'll try to lose them at the airport, but if we don't we're going to need cover when we reach the bazaar."

"You'll have it," Bud said, going out the window right behind Edward.

"Good luck," Ernie said and ducked out as well.

"We're going to need it," Craig said as Danny closed and locked the window, then turned and headed for the door, glancing around the room as he went to make sure that they hadn't missed anything.

Danny was happy that at least now copies of his father's notebooks were in the hands of two twins who would never be suspected of having them.

Danny knew his plan of escape rested on the two men staying in the lobby or outside waiting and not trying anything until they had privacy and red hoods, as they had done with Professor Davis. It was a gamble, he knew that.

And he was betting his and Craig's life that he was right.

CHAPTER ELEVEN

THE HALLWAY WAS thankfully empty, so Danny led the way down the hall toward the front desk. The restaurant was on the right of the big lobby. There were plants, small palm trees, and a dozen places to sit.

The two men that Bud had described were still standing at the front desk. Both were white. One looked British and very properly dressed in an expensive black suit. The other was of what looked like Italian descent, with big arms and a black suit that was two sizes too small. He looked mean, and his face had a nasty scar on the right cheek.

Clearly, the British-looking man was in charge. As Danny got closer to them, he could see that their skin had a weathered look to it all over. Not scarred, just weathered.

Danny had no idea if that was the same two who had killed Professor Davis, but if they were asking about him, he had no doubt they were with the same group.

"Remember," Danny whispered to Craig, "don't look at them. We don't know them. We're just checking out and heading home."

"You're nuts, you know that?" Craig whispered back as they crossed the open tile of the lobby and walked up behind the two men.

"Ah, Mr. Hawk," the desk clerk said loudly, looking over one man's shoulder.

Both men seemed to jump just slightly. Then one of them said to the clerk, "Thank you for the information. Please keep this to yourself."

"I understand," the clerk said, giving the man a sickly smile in return.

Danny wanted to just cut and run. He knew that voice. It was the man who had been in charge in Professor Davis's office, the man who had ordered the other to shoot the professor.

As the two men stepped off to one side, stopping close enough so that they could hear, Danny nodded to the clerk and gave him their room key.

"Checking out, going home," Danny said, pretending to be in a good mood.

"So soon?" the clerk asked, his voice trembling slightly. Clearly the two men had threatened him in some fashion or another.

"We've got to get ready for school," Danny said, trying his best to sound calm and relaxed, even though his heart was about to pound a new path right out of his chest. "It starts for us at the end of the month."

Craig stood beside him, pretending to read some sort of flyer that was on the counter. He had his back to the two men which, considering Craig's lack of a poker face, was a good thing.

"Where's your uncle?" the clerk asked as he wrote up Danny's receipt for the room.

"He left early yesterday," Danny said. "My mom needed his help. We wanted to stay and see the pyramids and everything yesterday, so he let us. Plus, we got my father's notebooks, which is what we came here to get."

He made sure his voice was loud enough that the men could hear him, and then to make it really clear, he patted the backpack he had on his shoulder.

Craig coughed and pretended to keep reading.

"Your father?" the clerk asked.

"Yes, he was an archeologist. These are his notes that I hope will help lead to where he is, but I can't read them. They're all Italian, Latin, and hieroglyphs. I figured someone back home can help me figure out what they say."

Craig coughed again and kept reading. Clearly Danny's little play was giving him a near heart attack.

"Well," the clerk said, glancing at the men, "have a good flight home."

Danny pocketed the receipt the clerk had given him and picked up his suitcase. "We will. Great food on the planes these days."

With that, he and Craig walked right past the two men who had killed Professor Davis.

Right past two members of the Hydra League.

Outside, in front of the door, was a cab that wasn't at the taxi stand twenty paces away. It had pulled up near the front door and had its back door open.

Bud must have set that up for them.

"Airport," Danny said as he started to climb in. A cab a few feet behind them honked long and loud, like a warning.

Danny suddenly realized that maybe Bud *hadn't* set up the taxi. Maybe it was the men inside, and the cab driver worked for them.

Danny quickly backed out, bumping into Craig and pushing him away. "Never mind," he said to the driver as he slammed the door.

The cab driver glanced back at Danny with an almost angry look on his face. Danny had a hunch they might have just escaped once again.

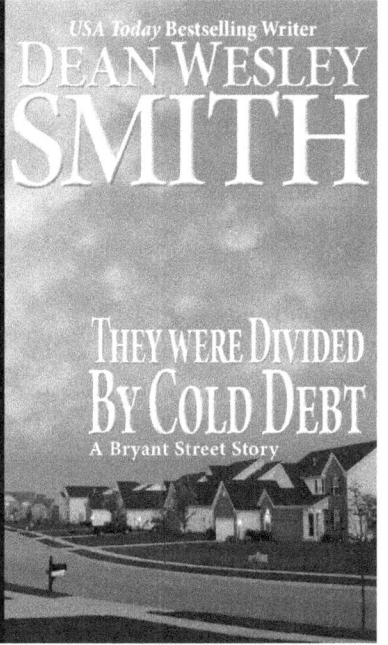

Some Classic Dean Wesley Smith Stories
Available at your favorite booksellers.

The two men came out the front door and watched as Danny and Craig moved toward the three cabs at the taxi stand.

Sitting behind the wheel of the second cab was Bud, smiling, a taxi driver's cap pulled down low over his head.

"Second cab," Danny whispered to Craig in case he hadn't seen Bud.

They quickly piled in the back seat, luggage and all, and before the door was even closed, Bud had the cab headed out of the cab line and toward the highway.

Danny glanced back as the two men got into the cab in front of the door and started to follow.

"Okay," Craig said to Bud, laughing, "how did you get this cab?"

"Driver had to use the bathroom and he got a little *tied* up," Bud said, shrugging as he focused on driving. "So I just thought we'd borrow it. We'll leave it at the airport, blocking traffic, of course. The twins took another cab and they will be waiting for us at the bazaar."

"The two men are in the cab behind us," Danny said, glancing back as if he were looking at the sights, not at the cab following them. His heart was still racing, and even though it was cool in the early morning hours, he was sweating.

"I know," Bud said. "Don't worry, we'll lose them in traffic or at the airport."

"You had me scared to death with that act at the front desk," Craig said, sitting back and shaking his head at Danny. "I thought they would just step up and grab the journals right there."

"I knew they wouldn't, once I had them convinced we didn't know they were following us. They'll wait for the right time."

"Was it the men in Professor Davis's office?" Bud asked.

"It was," Danny said, trying not to shudder. "I recognized one of their voices."

"They are mean-looking, that's for sure," Craig said. "Cold eyes."

"Very cold," Danny said, forcing himself to breathe evenly. It was one thing to talk about going after his father and risking his life, but it was clearly another matter to actually be in danger.

"And nice job telling them we hadn't read the journals yet," Craig said.

"You did?" Bud asked, glancing back with a smile. "Nifty trick."

"You think that might save our lives when they do catch up with us?" Craig asked.

"Probably not," Danny said, sinking into the seat. "But it was worth the try just in case."

CHAPTER TWELVE

August 20, 1970
Cairo, Egypt.

BUD, EVEN THOUGH he was barely tall enough to see over the dashboard, wound the cab through the thick Cairo traffic like a racecar driver trying to gain the lead.

As Danny watched, the cab with the two Hydra League killers behind them was cut off time after time, falling farther and farther behind in the thick traffic as they got closer to the airport.

Finally, they were so far back, Danny wasn't even sure which cab they were in in the sea of black and white cabs heading for the International Airport.

"When I pull up at the terminal," Bud said, "open both doors, then close them and duck down so you can't be seen. And stay down until I say otherwise, even if we're moving."

"Got it," Danny said. He was trusting Bud completely with his life at this point.

Danny tossed his suitcase over the seat and onto the front seat floor as Craig crammed his suitcase down onto the floor.

"Okay, get ready," Bud said.

He swung across two lanes and into a spot against the curb just in front of a small van. The sidewalk was crowded with passengers and their luggage going into the international terminal.

Craig opened the side door and Danny opened the door on the road side.

Then they both slammed them closed and ducked down onto the floor, trying to get as low as they could. The backseat of the taxi was cramped, but unless someone looked in, Danny was sure no one passing by in another cab would be able to see them.

"They're going past us," Bud whispered, sitting up on his legs so that he looked taller than he really was.

The seconds seemed to tick past as Danny held himself in the cramped position tucked down low.

"I'm going to ache in the morning from this," Craig whispered.

"Better than being dead in the morning," Bud whispered back.

"They have seen me," Bud whispered, pretending to count cash. "The cab is pulling in three cars ahead of us and the two men are getting out. Stay down."

Bud suddenly pulled the cab back out into traffic and moved over two lanes.

"The two men are going into the terminal," Bud whispered. "And the other cab is waiting for them. Stay down a little longer, until we get out of sight completely."

The cab bumped and jerked, and in the position Danny was, crammed on the floor of the back seat, his head down against his knees, he had no doubt that

Craig was right, they were going to be very sore from this in the morning. And bruised from every bump that Bud hit.

The cab jerked right, then picked up speed.

"Clear," Bud said.

Danny tried to stretch his cramped muscles as he climbed back onto the seat.

"Great work," Danny said to Bud, reaching forward and patting him on the shoulder. "I'm really glad you're with us."

"Yeah, me too," Craig said.

Bud laughed. "Makes the days interesting."

"What, trying to stay alive?" Craig asked, laughing.

"I've been doing that for five years," Bud said. "But I will admit, this is new."

"Next stop, while we have them busy searching the airport, is my father's apartment," Danny said. "We need to know if the twins are right in there being something in the apartment that we need to see."

"Address?" Bud asked, like a regular driver would do.

Danny gave it to him, then sat back and tried to once again get his heart to calm down and stop racing. He really wished he had spent more time in training with his grandfather. Staying calm would come in really handy right about now.

CHAPTER THIRTEEN

August 20, 1970
Cairo, Egypt.

BUD DROVE PAST the small apartment building twice before finally backing the cab into a hidden driveway and stopping in the shade.

The neighborhood around the two-story apartment building looked to be an older residential one, with small buildings packed in tight together. No lawns or shrubs like in the States, just rocks and peeling paint. Some of the houses had laundry hanging in the front or side yards. It was far too hot for anyone to be outside in the sun, so everything felt abandoned.

"I'll keep the car running and if you hear a honk, come running. It will be hard to escape this neighborhood."

"Got it," Danny said. "We won't be long."

"So, what's the plan?" Craig asked as they climbed up the exposed outside stairs to the second floor and faced the wooden door.

Danny dug for the key in his pocket that his mother had given him. His father had sent it to her as a backup, in case something happened to him and she needed to come here. He always kept the rent paid up for months in advance so nothing would be disturbed by the landlord at least.

"We gather up what we think might be important, then get out of here," Danny said. "We'll let the twins figure out if what we got is important or not."

"As good a plan as any," Craig said.

"No talking inside," Danny said. "It might be bugged."

Craig nodded. "Good thinking. I've just got to get more paranoid."

Danny unlocked the door and slowly pushed it open.

There were no lights, so he stepped inside and let Craig follow before shutting the door and flipping on a light switch.

The place smelled musty and unused. At least it was much cooler than outside.

The living and dining areas were almost empty. A wooden table with two metal folding chairs were in the dining room, and a couch that had clearly seen far too much use was the only thing in the living room.

Danny glanced at Craig who was shaking his head at what greeted them.

The tiny kitchen had a few glasses and chipped bowls in one cupboard and that was it. Not even a dirty dish in the sink.

Everything had been cleaned off and wiped down. Danny knew his father was known for being a slob. His mother complained about it all the time, sometimes even going so far as wishing he would leave on another dig so that the house would be clean again.

Danny knew that his father put all his attention into his work. Keeping a clean apartment was just an annoyance left up to others.

If Danny's father had lived here, someone had gone to a lot of trouble to make sure nothing was left of how he lived.

Or any of his personal things.

The one bedroom had a made bed against one wall and a small wooden desk against a second wall. The desk was empty. As was the closet and bathroom. The bed was made like a maid had done it.

Danny wasn't really that surprised. At least not as surprised as he would have been if he had come here first from the airport three days ago. Someone clearly had come in and taken all of his father's things and cleaned the place. The only thing left was a large world map that somehow his father had glued like wallpaper to the wall.

Craig pointed to it after Danny finished checking every corner of the closet.

Danny stepped over to the map. Small "x-marks" had been made in blue ink, at least a dozen of them all over the world.

South America's western coast area had two. One over New York City, three over London and the surrounding area. Another in the Soviet Union behind the Iron Curtain. Even more in Egypt, China, Mongolia, and India.

Danny studied the marks, not having a clue what they had meant to his father. But his father had put those marks on that map for a reason, Danny was sure of that.

Danny tried to pry the map off, but it was glued completely. It would completely destroy the map and the wall to take it off.

The only reason he and Craig were seeing the map with the marks was because the map had been impossible to peel off and the people who had cleaned out the apartment had just left it.

Danny leaned over to Craig and whispered in his ear. "Memorize the exact locations of all the marks."

Craig nodded and both he and Danny stood in the nearly empty apartment for the next few minutes doing just that, like they were both studying for a geography test in school.

After Danny felt like he had the dozen or so marks clear in his mind, he motioned for Craig that they should get out of there.

He locked the door behind them and quickly went through the heat down the stairs to where Bud waited in the running cab.

Bud was clearly happy to see them. "Starting to worry me. Find anything."

"Place had been cleaned out," Craig said as Bud pulled out of the driveway and headed back into town.

"Except for a map glued to the wall with a bunch of marks on it," Danny said. "I just hope we can remember where all the marks were. We need to write them down later, while it is still fresh."

"Yeah," Craig said. "And better yet, at some point figure out what they mean."

Danny couldn't agree more.

"One more stop," Danny said. "But we have to pick up the twins before we go there."

"The Pyramids of Giza?" Craig asked. Danny nodded.

"Well," Craig said, "at least I get to be a tourist before some goon kills me."

CHAPTER FOURTEEN

August 20, 1970
Giza Plateau, Egypt.

ONE BLOCK AWAY from the bazaar, Bud parked the cab in a shaded alley so narrow that Danny was amazed that Bud could get the cab backed in and still get the door open. Bud was small enough to squeeze out the door somehow and vanished around the corner, leaving Danny and Craig sitting in the cab, clearly trapped. They were both too big to even climb out the open windows between the car and the walls.

And on top of that, the alley smelled of urine and some sort of fried meat. The two odors did not combine well.

"You ever wonder what has just happened to our nice, normal lives?" Craig asked.

"Most of the last three days," Danny said. "So much for football practice starting next week."

"And the homecoming dance I suppose is now out of the question as well," Craig said, shaking his head. "I was really looking forward to maybe asking Karen. I would have loved dancing with her."

"Slow-dancing," Danny said, smiling at his best friend. "You fast-dance like a monkey."

"It's all the rage," Craig laughed. "Or haven't you heard?"

At that moment, Bud slid back into the car and pulled the car to the front of the alley where Ernie and Ed had room to climb in, Ernie in the front seat, Ed in the back beside Craig.

"Field trip," Craig said as Bud pulled out into the busy traffic, narrowly missing another cab and causing at least three cars to swerve to miss him.

"You have your translations in a safe place?" Danny asked, feeling the backpack on the floor beside his leg with his father's original notebooks.

"Hidden safe and sound," Ed said.

"Don't tell us where," Craig said, holding up his hand. "I think it's better that we just don't know."

Danny nodded.

Bud turned west and headed out a wide highway, picking up speed and making it impossible to talk with all four of the windows rolled down. He was going faster than Danny thought any street kid

should be allowed to drive. And just like he had done on the main streets, Bud was swerving in and out of traffic.

Danny just held onto the door handle and let the wind blow in his face from the four open windows.

Ahead of them, the three larger pyramids of Giza seemed to grow like mountains as the road climbed out of the city and up to the sands of the desert. Actually, the pyramids were very close to the edge of the city. Danny had no doubt that in forty years, the city would surround the entire Giza Necropolis. From what he had heard, the smog was already starting to eat at them, and just recently, people had been barred from climbing on the pyramids anymore.

There was no way to describe the awe that Danny felt seeing those huge stone pyramids grow bigger and bigger in front of him. How could anyone have built them? Now he understood that age-old question. Pictures just didn't do them justice and there was nothing in the United States that even compared.

For a few miles, all of them just stared. Craig his mouth slightly open, just kept shaking his head, as if he wasn't believing what he was seeing. Danny understood that feeling.

The most famous of the pyramids was the Great Pyramid of Khufu, the second was the Pyramid of Khafre, and the smaller one, still a giant structure but dwarfed by the other two, was the Pyramid of Menkaure. There were a lot of other smaller pyramid-like structures scattered around the base of the big three. They were called The Queen's Pyramids by many.

Three smaller Queen's Pyramids were between Khufu and the Eastern Cemetery. The Western Cemetery was on the other side of Khufu, and three smaller still pyramids were lined up beside Menkaure.

The entire area was huge. But it was the three monster pyramids that dwarfed everything.

"So, where are we headed?" Bud shouted to Ed.

"The Great Sphinx," Ed shouted back over the winds.

Bud nodded and headed to the east to a parking lot there.

Danny wanted to ask him why the Sphinx, what his father had said in the notebooks that was taking them here, but decided to wait until they stopped so they could talk normally. The idea of rolling up the windows in this hot air was just an insane thought.

Finally, Bud pulled the cab into a place facing the Great Sphinx and shut off the engine. There were only two other cars in the parking area, and Danny could see no other people around at all. The stones and shallow valleys were such that hundreds of people could be in the area and not be seen from the parking lot.

The silence was like a thunderclap to Danny. He was startled by it, after being in the cab and in the city and the bazaar. Out here there was only the wind blowing over the sand and that seemed to suck away noise like a soundproof room.

They all piled out of the cab and headed up the tourist sidewalk.

The Great Pyramid towered over everything, a good fifty stories tall. Danny couldn't believe how large it was. He just kept staring up at it.

Finally, after a dozen steps in silence, Danny got his head together and asked the twins, "Where was my father's dig from here?"

"Abusir," Ed said.

"To the south and east of here about twelve kilometers," Ernie said, pointing up the Nile.

Ed nodded. "Your father believed that under the Fifth Dynasty cemeteries of Abusir were remains of a much older civilization, dating back to far before King Scorpion in what is called the Archaic Period."

"Far older than four thousand years B.C." Ernie said.

"That's old," Craig said, shaking his head.

"Isn't the Great Sphinx believed to be much older than the Fourth Dynasty pyramids built here?" Danny asked.

Both Ed and Ernie shook their heads no.

"It was built in the stone quarry for the Great Pyramid, by Khufu's men," Ed said.

"But," Ernie said, "the famous Hall of Records from the legendary civilization of Atlantis is supposed to be buried somewhere near the Great Sphinx."

"Edgar Cayce predicted that would be where it was found," Ed said.

"Your father believes it is here as well," Ernie said.

"Atlantis?" Craig asked.

Ed nodded. "It is believed to have existed before the great dynasties of Egypt, and the survivors from the great disaster flocked to the Nile valley and other places around the world to live and rebuild."

"The Hydra League was formed in the time of Atlantis," Ernie said.

Danny just shook his head and stared up at the ancient pyramids, amazed at what it must have taken four thousand years ago to build them. If he had been sitting at home, on his couch, he would have never believed any of what Ed and Ernie were telling him. But Danny had men from this Hydra League after him now, and he was facing giant pyramids that he doubted that 1970's technology could build. So he was willing to believe just about anything at the moment.

They moved past the Valley Temple and up a dirt walkway until suddenly the giant cat-like stone figure sort of appeared in front of them, towering over them with the Great Pyramid behind it.

"Oh, wow," Craig said, stopping and staring up at the towering carving. It was a man's head on a lion's body, with huge paws extending away from the body. Clearly the air and time had done a lot of damage to the Sphinx, since its nose and part of its face were missing. But it was still very, very impressive.

"Nose fell off about a thousand years ago," Ed said.

"Napoleon's artillerymen were rumored to have used the Sphinx for target practice as well," Ernie said. "When only its head was sticking out of the sand."

"But for most of its life, it was buried," Ed said. "The sand around its base, in fact, was just cleared away twenty years ago."

Danny's mind just didn't want to accept that the huge stone creature in front of him was even real. But yet it was.

For the first time, Danny was starting to understand his father's passion toward archeology. So many questions, so few answers.

CHAPTER FIFTEEN

August 20, 1970
Giza Plateau, Egypt.

I'M GOING TO keep an eye out for our friends," Bud said. "You enjoy the tour."

The short kid turned and just silently vanished behind a huge stone before Danny could even agree that it was a good idea. He couldn't imagine how the men could follow them from the airport to here, but anything was possible. Better to have Bud watching their backs.

The twins led the way into what they called the Valley Temple, a series of tall blocks to the left and in front of the Sphinx.

Over what looked like a main entrance to the temple was a stone placed between two other stones. Carved into the stone were a series of hieroglyphs.

Ed pointed to them.

"What does it say?" Craig asked, staring up at the very old writings.

Danny had a hunch what it said because he could see a number of snakes seemingly flowing together.

"What many think it says is simply a blessing for those entering this temple built in the Fourth Dynasty," Ed said.

"But Danny," Ernie said, "your father believed it meant something else, and that the stone was put there to mark the entrance or the general location to the Hall of Records."

Ed nodded. "It says, basically, that knowledge is protected by many snakes and the ten great puzzles of life."

"Hydra League," Danny said softly.

"The term Hydra is commonly thought to have an ancient Greek origin," Ernie said. "But the idea of snakes was common along the Nile, and they were often worshipped or feared as evil spirits or powerful gods, depending on the time. So this is not out of place."

"Ten puzzles?" Craig asked.

"This saying," Ed said to Danny, "got your father started putting together what he believed were ten clues called the Hydra Journals."

"Clues," Ernie said, "actually riddles that would lead to the location of the Fountain of Youth. And from there, maybe even the exact location of the Hall of Records."

"The Hydra Journals are a series of riddles?" Craig asked. "Great. I hate riddles."

"These riddles are as old as time, and your father had found three of them," Ed said.

"We have company!" Bud said as he came running around a large stone and skidded to a halt in the sand. "The three guys in the cab from the hotel just pulled up out front and parked next to a tour bus and a few other cars that just arrived. I don't think they saw our car."

"How did they follow us to here?" Craig asked, looking stunned.

Danny felt just as stunned as Craig felt.

"They know the details of your father's work," Ed said.

"This would be a logical place to check out," Ernie said.

"That's right, they may not know we are here," Bud said. "They weren't acting like they did."

Ernie pointed up at the second pyramid, talking quickly to Bud. "The main road comes in on the north side of the Pyramid of Khafre. There is a side road that runs up near the Western Cemetery. Think you can get the cab without being seen and meet us there?"

"I can," Bud said, nodding and again vanishing between the large stones.

"We need to head to the north and into the cover of the Eastern Cemetery," Ernie said.

"Isn't there a causeway the Pharaohs built between here and the Pyramid of Khafre?" Danny asked, remembering some of his reading about these pyramids.

"There is," Ed said. "But it is too exposed and we would be seen easily."

Danny nodded. "Lead the way."

At full run, the boys headed out through the stones, staying as low as they could as they moved behind the Sphinx.

There was on open stretch of sand between the back of the Great Sphinx and the first blocks and mounds and small pyramids of the Eastern Cemetery.

Just the run along the length of the Sphinx had Danny sweating and breathing hard. The heat was intense, and he had no doubt that he and Craig couldn't stay out in this very long.

Ernie motioned for them to stay in the slight shade of the back of the Sphinx and quickly climbed up its side, moving like he had done it a hundred times in his sandaled feet. Danny was impressed. Clearly the twins were a lot stronger and in much better shape than they looked.

And they were used to working in the intense heat of the desert.

Ernie found a spot where he must have been able to see back toward the temple and the parking lot. With one quick look, he came scrambling back down.

"The three men are going into the temple," Ernie said. "We have to run now!"

He led the way out into the sun and across the hot sand, with Craig right behind him and Danny following his best friend very closely. Ed seemed to almost be pushing Danny from behind, and clearly wasn't working as hard as Danny was.

Running in the sand was like a football coach's dream for how to torture his high school team. As sophomores, their football coach had had them run sand dunes for exercise one day. Danny had hated that, and he hated running in the sand now.

It seemed to take an eternity for them to reach the tall stone blocks of the cemetery. And when they finally did, Ernie didn't even slow down. He turned to the west, staying between the smaller pyramids and stone funeral structures of the cemetery. He led them toward the southern edge of the Great Pyramid.

Up close, Danny couldn't believe the size of the blocks that the pyramid was constructed out of. They were taller in places than he was. He couldn't believe people used to climb them for sport.

The four of them ran along the hardened tourist path that framed the south wall of the Great Pyramid, then on around to the west side. They ducked into the cover of the Western Cemetery, finally stopping in the shade near the north side of the Pyramid of Khafre.

Danny worked to catch his breath, and he could feel the heat making him light-headed.

"We're going to need water," Craig managed to choke out between sobbing breaths.

"Only if we live," Danny said, his throat feeling like sandpaper had been scraped along the inside of it.

Suddenly, in a cloud of dust and sand, a cab appeared, bouncing off the main road and fishtailing over the dirt toward where they were hidden. Behind the wheel, Bud grinned like a kid enjoying a new Christmas present.

They all piled in almost before Bud had slid the cab to a stop. A moment later, he was accelerating out of the western parking area, headed toward the main road.

Danny had climbed into the front seat this time, and he turned to Bud. "Did they see you leave?"

"Nope," he said. "They were up in the temple area and I doubt they even heard me start the cab."

Danny leaned his head out the window and let the hot wind cool him some. Was this going to be the rest of his life? Staying just a few steps ahead of sure death at the hands of the Hydra League?

He hoped not, but if that was what it was going to take to save his father, then so be it.

"Now," Bud said, shouting over the wind so everyone could hear, "anyone got a problem getting back to the bazaar? I have to get out of this cab before the police spot it. I have no desire to spend the next twenty years in jail while you four go on and find the treasure without me."

"We'd visit you," Craig said.

"Yeah," Danny said, taking a deep breath and trying to get himself to relax a little. "As long as we're alive."

CHAPTER SIXTEEN

August 20, 1970
Khan Al-Khalili bazaar, Cairo, Egypt.

DANNY HAWK FELT like he might end up with a sore neck at any moment because he was twisting around so much, looking at the crowds around him, like every man or woman could be after him.

And they just might be.

He kept waiting for a knife to be thrust into his stomach from a man walking past, or a gunshot to rock him backwards into a booth. His imagination was making everyone look like a Hydra League member out to kill him.

He stared at everyone's hands, looking for the tattoo of the snake's head rising out of a pool of water that indicated Hydra League membership. Or at least Danny thought it did. The two men who had killed the professor both had the tattoo.

And in the crowds of this bazaar, there were thousands and thousands of people crammed into the streets.

Thousands of possible enemies.

There was an old man sitting on an ancient WWII motorcycle. Could he be the enemy?

Or what about the sinister-looking jewelry vendor with the thick brows and a gold tooth?

Anyone could be the one who kills him and takes his father's notebooks.

Anyone.

That had Danny scared to death, gripping his backpack with a death grip that made his hand ache.

The narrow streets of the bazaar felt like it must have felt a few thousand years ago. The smells of rich food, new carpets, and incense filled the air like a thick shield. Everyone was dressed in the traditional loose Arab robes, and all the women had their heads covered. The street was so jammed with booths, small tents, and people that it was almost impossible to move anywhere.

Since Danny and his best friend, Craig, were Americans, still dressed in their jeans and light shirts, everyone in the bazaar looked at them with suspicion, while at the same time seeming to want to sell them something.

Danny kept a firm hand on his backpack, which held his clothes and his father's original journals, and checked it every time it got bumped.

After twenty halting paces into the crowd, Danny felt the tug of Bud's hand on his shirt. He was yanked hard down and to the right, close to a stone wall.

"Get down!" Bud shouted to the other three.

A moment later, a shot rang out over the bazaar and a bullet smashed into the wall near Ed Black, one of the twins, not more than ten feet from Danny.

The echo of the first shot sent the thousands of people in the bazaar into a panic. Everyone tried to get out of the way at the same time, all moving in different directions.

The sounds of the screams and shouting was deafening.

Chaos.

A second shot rang out. It hit the wall close to Danny, between him and the twins, and just above their heads.

"Too close!" Craig shouted from behind Danny.

People screaming and running smashed into Danny as he tried to stay down and against the wall. He got kicked hard twice, and had yet another man trip over him a moment later.

From what Danny could see, his four friends were taking the same punishment. He had no idea where the shots had come from, but they were clearly aimed at the five of them. And where they were crouched, they had no real cover.

"The shooter's on the far roof!" Bud shouted, pointing up through the swirling crowds at the other side of the bazaar. At that moment, another shot cut through the screams and shouting and a man fell just a few feet from Danny.

"Follow me!" Bud shouted and headed along the right side of the bazaar, staying low.

Bud was short, and he looked more like a bum because of the tattered clothes. But Danny already knew the clothes were just a disguise to make Bud not be noticed in his many scams and tricks on tourists. Bud had lived on these streets for years. He could move through the bazaar crowds like a ghost, and Danny was noticing that Bud never seemed to miss a detail. It was a special talent he had, and Danny was happy to have him helping them stay alive right now.

Staying low, below the level of the frightened crowds, Danny ran along the wall, following Bud.

Craig was right behind him, and the twins brought up the rear.

Another two shots sent stone chips flying from the wall near Danny.

Another man fell face first onto the street.

Danny had to get out of these crowds. Too many innocent people were getting hurt.

All this was because of the notebooks Danny carried on his back.

His father's notebooks.

They ran past booth after booth, staying low and against the stone walls of the buildings. There were no more shots. They must have outdistanced the shooter for the moment, but Danny had no doubt the man, or men, would be right behind them.

Two-story buildings blocked some of the mid-morning sunlight from reaching the street, and Bud stayed in the shadows, leading them at full run through the vendors.

Suddenly Bud turned into an alcove and went down a dark side alley. The intense sounds of panic in the bazaar were cut off by the narrow alley like someone had thrown a switch. It became only a background rumble, like waves on a distant beach.

At a fast run, they all went up a long, narrow staircase without handrails and turned left at the top toward the twins' apartment.

"Everyone all right?" Bud asked, stopping for a moment in the narrow hallway as Ernie Black pushed past and fumbled to open a door across from their apartment.

Danny nodded, trying to catch his breath as he glanced around at his friends. All of them looked like they had escaped the shooter, at least this time.

Next time, they might not all be so lucky.

"We also rent this apartment under another name," Ernie said, indicating a door he was fighting to open.

"I really don't think it's a good idea to stop here," Craig said, glancing back down at the staircase behind them.

"We're not," Bud said.

"I need to hide these," Danny said, patting his backpack and his father's original journals. The twins still carried the copies that they had translated last night in the hotel room. But the men chasing them were after the originals.

Ernie shoved the door open finally. Everyone crowded inside except Bud, who said, "I'm going to see how far behind that shooter is." He turned and headed back down the stairs toward the alley.

The room was tiny, the size of a small bedroom, and completely empty except for two chairs and a small wooden table with a scarred top. A window led out to a rooftop.

The twins' other apartment was across the hall.

"Why two apartments?" Danny asked, turning from the window. "One for each of you?"

Ernie shook his head. "Safety." He pointed to the window. "Another way of escape from this top floor. We're going out that way."

"Why?" Danny asked. "Something to do with what my father found?"

Ernie shook his head. "Our father."

"The South African government?" Craig asked before Danny could.

Ernie nodded. "They killed our mother trying to get to us. We were very vocal after they killed our father, and led demonstrations against them. We are criminals in our own country."

Danny was shocked. That was the exact reason he had sent his uncle home to protect his mother, in case the Hydra League would go after her to get to Danny and the notebooks.

"I'm afraid," Ed said, "that if we help you, we will all also be running from not only the ancient and powerful Hydra League, but the South African government."

Ernie nodded. "In fact, it may be some of their operatives shooting at us, not the Hydra League."

Danny didn't much like the sound of that, but at this point, he had no choice. He needed their help if he was to ever find his father. He smiled. "Well, at least that will make it interesting."

Danny just wished he felt as confident as he had tried to sound.

At that moment, Bud slammed into the apartment and quickly closed and locked the door.

"Three men in brown suits," he said breathlessly. "Headed up the stairs."

"Hydra?" Danny asked.

Bud shook his head. "I don't know. Couldn't see their hands. But I've never seen them before and they're all carrying big guns."

"Great," Craig said. "Now we have even more people out to kill us."

CHAPTER SEVENTEEN

August 20, 1970
Near the Khan Al-Khalili bazaar, Cairo, Egypt.

BUD RAN TO the window and pushed it up and open. "Let's go."

"We'll be right behind you," Ed said as he moved to one corner of the room and quickly pried up a loose floorboard. It didn't come easily, but it was clear Ed knew it would come.

"Put your father's journals in here," Ed said as Bud climbed out of the window and onto the roof. "We have paid for this apartment for a year. They will be safe."

Danny quickly took the notebooks out of the pack, knelt down, and shoved them between the floor joists, off to the right under a board still in place. If anyone did pry the board off, they would never see the notebooks.

Outside the door, the sounds of heavy footprints filled the hallway. It sounded like a herd of elephants had filled the building. Danny wasn't sure if the sound of his pounding heart was louder, though.

Ed quickly and silently replaced the board. It looked like it had never been removed. Danny knew that if something happened to the five of them, no one would ever find his father's work. It didn't seem like the right thing to do, but at this point, anyone who Danny might send those journals to would more than likely be killed. And Danny just couldn't put someone else at risk, no matter how much work his father had put into the research.

Ernie was half out the window, and Bud and Craig were already running across the rooftop.

"Hurry," Ed whispered to Danny.

With one last look at where he had hidden his father's life work, he ducked out the window and onto the hard, white sand of the flat rooftop. From here, he could see mostly roofs and walls of buildings. Laundry was hung in different places, blowing in the hot wind, and on another roof, a couple of children played a game in the shade.

Ed came out behind him and carefully closed the window. Then the two of them ran to follow the others. From inside the building, the sounds of someone banging on an apartment door could be heard even outside. Those men weren't going to be far behind, that was for sure.

"Run fast," Ed said breathlessly from behind Danny. "You have to jump."

Danny didn't have time to ask how far or when. He could see when.

Right in front of him Ernie, at full run, leaped into the air and disappeared downward over the edge of the building.

Danny wanted to ease up to the edge and look at what faced him, but instead he just kept running. If a fall killed him, so be it. More than likely it would be a quicker death than having the men behind him catch him.

He hit the edge of the roof in mid-stride and full running speed and jumped.

"Oh, nooooooo!" he shouted as he flew over the hard stone of a dark alley two stories below.

The distance across the alley to the next building, which was lower than the one they were on, was a good eight or nine feet.

He focused on it, willing himself to make it.

Everything seemed to move in slow motion as he sailed through the air, finally landing solidly on the other roof, stumbling, but still running.

Ed cleared the alley right behind him.

Ahead of them, Ernie turned and quickly started down a metal ladder attached to the side of the building. It led into yet another alley.

Danny got to the ladder as below Ernie reached the ground and then ducked inside a building. There was no sign of Bud or Craig.

Danny half climbed, half slid down the ladder, hitting the ground hard enough to jar his knees, but not hard enough to hurt himself.

The door led into a long, dark hallway that went through the middle of the entire building. On the other end, through a door, Bud was waiting like a doorman, holding open a cab door.

They had come out onto a main street of Cairo a few blocks to one side of the bazaar.

Danny piled into the back of the cab with Craig and Ernie.

A moment later, Ed jammed into the crowded back seat with them, then Bud slammed the door of the building closed and climbed into the front seat beside the driver.

Bud said something to the driver in Arabic that was clearly instructions. A moment later, the cab sped off, moving at full speed down the narrow side street and finally onto a wide boulevard.

All of them fought to catch their breath as the cab swerved through traffic, putting distance between them and the men with the guns.

Danny was sweating like he had never sweated before, and the hot wind coming through the open window didn't seem to help much.

They had escaped again.

For the moment.

Finally, Danny breathlessly asked Ernie, "Where are we going?"

"Your father's last dig," Ernie said. "You said you wanted to see it, remember?"

"Yeah," Danny said, sitting back in the seat and wishing his heart would stop racing. "But that was before people started shooting at us."

CHAPTER EIGHTEEN

August 20, 1970
Cairo, Egypt.

"STOP HERE," BUD shouted, pointing to a place beside a food cart on the sidewalk near the four-lane highway. The cab crossed two lanes and almost slid to a stop, half up on the sidewalk.

"What's wrong?" Craig asked, looking around, his blue eyes wide with worry. Before this trip to Egypt, Craig and Danny's biggest fear was making it to work and their college classes on time.

They were both in far, far over their heads.

Bud didn't say anything and motioned for them to stay in the cab.

Danny had no idea what the short Egyptian kid was up to.

Bud jumped out, talking quickly to the man in the food cart. A moment later, Bud started handing into the back seat what looked like wrapped meat sandwiches and warm bottles of Coca-Cola.

Food. Bud was getting them food.

It looked and smelled like heaven to Danny. He had forgotten they had skipped breakfast that morning and had had no time to eat in the bazaar. They needed food and drink, and Bud had been the only one to think of it.

It was like a fast pit-stop in a sports car race. Less than thirty seconds later, Bud was back in the cab and the cab was again speeding toward the western edge of town.

Bud said something to the cab driver in Arabic, then handed him a bottle of Coca-Cola.

The man seemed very happy to have it.

The wrapped meat tasted like a mild Sloppy Joe. And Danny had never thought a warm Coke could taste so good.

Danny ate, watched the neighborhoods of Cairo flash past, and thought about what he had read in his father's notebooks last night. Those notebooks were the key to all of them staying alive.

While reading them, it had become clear that over a decade ago, his father had decided to try to track down the historical background for the myth of the Fountain of Youth. From the dates in his journals, it had taken a few years for his father to get any traction at all on the goal.

Then the famous engineer Taccola came into the research about the time Danny would have been in his early teens. Taccola lived in Fifteenth Century Siena and was known for being ahead of his time in inventions concerning the movement of water. During the last of his life, Taccola had become focused on Egypt and had actually disappeared there in 1458.

In hieroglyphs, Danny's father had written a simple phrase that Taccola had found.

"Belief. The Water flows uphill."

His father had then later labeled that phrase "Hydra Journals Entry One."

Danny had no idea what that meant, and it seemed from what he read, neither did his father.

Napoleon was next in his father's research. It seemed that the French leader had been focused on discovering in Egypt a way to give his troops fantastic strength and long life. It seemed Napoleon didn't find what Taccola had found, but something different, which Danny's father had labeled "Hydra Journals Entry Two: The birth of a snake, the path of elephants."

His father had found reference to the Hydra League in some ancient texts and on stone hieroglyphs. As Danny read, it became clear that his father became more and more worried that the ancient organization still existed. And that he believed that some of the members might have been alive for far longer than humans normally lived.

By the end of his notes, it had become clear Danny's father believed the Hydra League did still exist, and its purpose was to only allow those worthy to find the Fountain of Youth.

He knew there were ten parts to the Hydra Journals, that must be followed to find eternal youth, and he again underlined the word "Map."

His father had then underlined another key phrase. "Fountain of Youth. Not Water. Something else."

His final entry in his notebooks was "Hydra Journals #3: Under the teeming masses, the river becomes clear, the path muddy."

Danny looked out at the buildings of Cairo flashing past. He had no idea what to do next. And he didn't even want to admit to himself how scared he was. He just kept those thoughts pushed back, out of the way, covered with the idea that he had no choice.

To find his father, he had to find the Fountain of Youth, and he had to find that Fountain by following a trail of ancient riddles.

He had never been much good at solving riddles. They just made him angry, and now his father was somewhere at the end of an ancient riddle, protected by men who thought nothing of killing innocent people to protect their secret.

Impossible.

Finally, with one last drink from his bottle of pop, Danny looked around at his friends crowded into the cab. "Do any of you have any idea what to do next, when we get to the dig?"

"We follow the clues," Ed said.

"That's our only logical path to the next clue," Ernie said, "and then the next."

Craig laughed. "Yeah, that's going to work."

"Belief: The water flows uphill," Bud said from the front seat, shaking his head. "What in the world does that mean?"

"You must put yourself in the shoes of ancients who lived six thousand years ago," Ernie said.

"The water flows uphill was a belief about the Nile in ancient times," Ed said. "And on a map with North up, the water of the Nile flows uphill as well."

"Wish I'd paid more attention in history class now," Craig said, shaking his head.

"But the Nile is a very long river," Danny said, at least glad that he now understood the first Hydra Journals Entry. The easy one. "How does that help us?"

"It doesn't," Ed said.

"Unless you have the second clue," Ernie said.

Bud shook his head. "The birth of a snake?"

"The headwaters of the Nile," Danny said, suddenly realizing what that phrase meant. "The Nile is a long snake on a map."

"Exactly," Ed said.

"And the path of elephants?" Craig asked.

Both twins just shrugged.

"So, we go to the headwaters of the Nile, find an elephant, and follow it," Bud said, shaking his head. "Where will that get us? And that third journal entry seems really crazy."

"That it does," Ernie said. "But if we go to the head of the snake, we may find something that will help us understand it."

"And maybe find the next riddle?" Bud asked.

Danny turned to the twins. "What are we going to see at my father's last dig?"

"Not much, to be honest," Ernie said. "More than likely, by this time, since it hasn't been protected, blowing sand has filled back in much of it."

Danny nodded. He had thought as much. "Then I don't need to see it. It might put us at risk again. They might be watching the site, assuming I would go there. We need to get out of this city. Let's find a way to get started up the Nile."

"Anything is better than hanging around here waiting to get shot," Craig said.

The twins nodded, so Bud turned to the driver and gave him new instructions in Arabic. A moment later, the cab was headed south, toward the edge of Cairo.

They rode in silence for a few minutes, then Craig laughed. "This has got to be the biggest wild-goose chase ever imagined. Actually, an ancient, deadly wild-riddle chase."

"True," Bud said, "but with a fantastic treasure at the end."

For Danny, the treasure at the end would be finding his father alive.

CHAPTER NINETEEN

September 1, 1970
Upper Lake Nasser, Sudan.

THE FIRST PART of the trip up the Nile had been fantastic, at least from a tourist perspective.

They had somehow managed to get out of Cairo without being seen and book a boat going south up the river. They had slept the first night on the wood plank floor of one small cabin, taking turns because there was only room for three to sleep. For Danny, that felt better anyway, since the two who weren't sleeping stood guard.

At every major port, they got off the ship and hid, then changed ships and kept going, sometimes booking a nice tourist ship, other times catching rides on fishing boats.

With every face that looked their way, Danny imagined it might be one of the Hydra League.

Or one of the brown-shirted men who had chased them out of Ed and Ernie's apartment.

From Cairo, for the first 400 miles, between Abu Roash and El Kula, there seemed to be a mountain range of pyramids along the west bank. Many times, Danny wished he and the others were there to sightsee, but they weren't. Even the slightest halt at this point might be enough to get them killed.

When they had crossed out of Egypt and into Sudan on a ferry on the great Lake Nasser behind the Aswan Dam, they had been asked for their passports, but were paid no attention to after that.

Danny had been surprised that Bud even had a passport. Later, Bud told him he had found it in the street a few years back and just kept it. The kid's name on the passport was Anthony Penn, and it was British, which fit Bud's accent.

Both of the twins also had British passports, but Danny didn't want to ask them how they got those. He was just relieved to have no further trouble. It looked like they had made a clean escape.

But that night, as the ferry pulled into Wadi Halfa, Sudan, two men climbed on board. It was just after midnight, but the air was still hot. The night sky was full of stars, brighter than any night sky Danny could remember seeing.

Danny, who was standing guard at the time, knew at once that they had been found. It was the same two men who had killed Professor Davis back in Cairo. He would recognize those two men

anywhere, especially with the distinctive snake-rising-out-of-water tattoo on their right hands.

Hydra League.

Danny wanted to be sick. They were six hundred miles up the Nile River, yet these two men had found them.

How was that possible?

"They found us," Danny whispered to the others, waking them. They were on the top deck of the three-level ferry, near the rear. "Hydra League men."

"How?" Craig asked, shocked. "Are they human?"

"I would not bet on it," Bud said.

Below, the two men split up, one going toward the bow, the other toward the stern.

Danny looked at the lit dock and the large Sudan village beyond. It seemed impossible to reach without being seen. The ferry was about to pull out, and clearly the two men planned on riding along. Once the ferry was into the middle of the huge Aswan Lake, the boys would have no chance of escape.

"We need to get down to the next level," Danny whispered.

"Then what?" Ernie asked, looking panicked in the faint light.

"We're trapped," Ed said.

"When the two come up the stairs to the second level," Danny said, "we go over the side to the first level. We'll have to be quick. We'll only have a few seconds."

"We'll need to wait there until just as the ferry is pulling out," Bud said, nodding. "Then make a jump for it."

"Exactly," Danny said, trying to breathe evenly to slow his heart from pounding right out of his chest.

They made a dash for the second deck, moving as silently as they all could on the wooden stairs. On the second level, Bud went on down the stairs to the first level to see where the men were while Danny, Craig, and the twins moved quickly to a place in the middle of the ship away from both staircases.

A moment later Bud came running back. "Get over the side," he said as he went past Danny and flipped himself over the railing, sliding down a support pole to the first deck.

All four of them followed Bud, with Danny going last. As he slid down, he caught a glimpse of one of the Hydra League killers coming up the stairs near the front of the ferry.

At that moment, a signal sounded, echoing through the night air. The ferry was going to pull out. The engines got louder and the ferry lurched into motion.

"We jump at the last minute," Danny said, running along the edge of the ferry's lowest deck. He got to a point near the stern, swung himself over the railing, his backpack on his shoulder, then waited for the dock to come sliding past.

The other four were in the same position beside him on the outside of the rail. He would be the first to jump, and the dock looked like it was getting farther and farther away from the ferry.

He had to wait.

Time it right.

Too soon and he would hit the water, too late and he would do the same on the other side of the dock.

The ferry had really gained speed as he finally said, "Now!"

He jumped with all his strength.

The blackness of the water between the ferry and the dock seemed to be a vast expanse, but somehow, he cleared it, hitting the dock with a few running steps before stopping.

The others did the same. Craig, the last one off, actually hit and rolled, but came up all right.

On the boat, one of the men standing on the second deck yelled something in Arabic at them that Danny didn't completely understand, since most of it was swearing.

Danny waved at the man like he was a relative going on a cruise.

"Now, that's not nice," Craig said, laughing. "You really shouldn't tease the big man with a gun."

"True," Danny said, turning and heading for the city of Wadi Halfa as the ferry vanished into the darkness of the big lake. "But what's he going to do? Kill me twice?"

CHAPTER TWENTY

September 11, 1970
Upper Lake Nasser, Sudan.

DANNY FIGURED THE two men would circle back by land to the city to look for them, so they took another ferry an hour behind the last one and for the rest of the trip up the river didn't see anyone following them. It took another full week, making good speed, before they had reached Lake Albert. It wasn't the headwaters of the Nile exactly, but it was close. The river that led to Lake Victoria fcd off of Lake Albert.

They stopped on the Republic of Congo side of the lake because of a conversation Ernie had had with a boat pilot a few hundred miles back. It seemed what was called "the path of elephants" by the natives was from the bank of Lake Albert, over a range of mountains and into the deep jungle of the Congo.

The elephants had been using the same path for thousands of years.

Danny had been stunned. There really was a "path of elephants."

"The area is haunted," Ernie had told them. "It's never really been explored. The pilot said it goes through what is called the Land of the Dead. None of the native tribes go near the area."

Bud had laughed. "Well, at least we won't have that problem. But we're going to need someone to guide us."

Ernie had nodded. "The captain gave me a name of a guide who would take us along the elephant path to the Land of the Dead."

In the small village of Bumia, ten miles inland along a mud road from the lake, they had found their guide, a skinny, older man with long grey hair and rotted teeth named Hassett.

At first, Danny wasn't sure the old man could help them, but then after watching him move around his hut-like home, it was clear the man was still in great physical shape.

Danny had told him what they wanted and his answer had been to laugh. When none of them laughed with him, he had asked simply. "Why would I take you five into the jungle?"

"I'm in search of my father," Danny said. "And our only clue is to walk the path of the elephants."

"Path of the elephants?" Hasset asked. "What do you know about that?"

"Nothing," Danny said. "That's why we want to hire you to walk it." Danny had made no mention of the Hydra League or anything else. Hassett had finally agreed and Bud had helped him with the negotiations for Hassett's fee and buying the supplies they would need.

Twenty-two days and nights of travel after leaving Cairo, they started off into the jungle.

In all his life, Danny had never been so scared. He was leading an expedition into an area of the world that had never been explored.

And he had no idea what he was looking for.

CHAPTER TWENTY-ONE

September 15, 1970
Deep in the jungle, Republic of Congo.

WALKING THE PATH of the elephants had actually turned out to be fairly easy, considering the thick underbrush of the jungle that bordered the half-mile-wide band of brush and trees trampled down by the passage of thousands of elephants twice a year. Danny couldn't imagine even trying to walk through that jungle. It looked like a two-story green wall on both sides.

Except for watching for the mounds of what Craig called elephant chips, they made good time. And the dried elephant chips made great fuel for fires at night.

They never saw an elephant, either, but did see a few scattered remains of ones, rotting and smelling in the hot, humid air.

Hassett had warned them that if they felt the ground shaking, get off into the jungle fast. Elephants mostly moved along this path slowly, but at times they moved a lot faster, and then they were real dangerous.

At first, the bugs that seemed to be everywhere had driven them all crazy, but as Hassett had said would happen, they all got used to them, and from what Danny could tell, as soon as they did, the bugs seemed to almost stop bothering them.

After five days of hiking, mostly uphill toward what Hassett called Elephant Pass, Danny was getting frustrated. He and the others had no idea what they were looking for. The only clue was the words "teeming masses" in the Hydra Journals entry #3. And in this jungle, it sure didn't look like they would find any teeming masses of anything except insects.

"When do we enter the Land of the Dead?" Danny asked Hassett just after they started out on the fifth morning.

Hassett laughed, a sort of choking sound that Danny still wasn't used to. "Son, we've been in it for a day now."

"Can we stop and talk for a minute?" Danny asked.

Hassett shrugged and pointed to some shade to one side.

With the pack off his back, Danny told the twins that they were all in the Land of the Dead, and what Hassett had said.

"Are there any ruins in this area?" Ed asked Hassett.

"I wouldn't know," Hassett said. "Never been off this trail. Never had any reason to go bushwhacking out in that stuff." He pointed to the high wall of what looked to be solid green that bordered the path of elephants.

"Any high place we could look over the Land of the Dead area?" Ernie asked.

"Sure," Hassett said. "Later today we'll reach Elephant Pass. To the right there's Ishango Peak."

"Ishango?" both Ernie and Ed said at the same time.

Hassett nodded, surprised.

"Ishango is the name of an ancient people," Ernie said.

"Rumored to exist before the first Pharaohs," Ed said.

"Can you get us to that peak where we can look out over the Land of the Dead?" Danny asked Hassett.

"Sure," he said. "But before I do that, you are going to have to tell me the truth."

He looked around slowly at each of them, but no one said a word, so he kept going. "Two men have been following us for days, staying behind us, pacing us. What kind of trouble are you boys in?"

Danny thought his heart was going to stop. Craig dropped to the ground and just sat there shaking his head. Clearly, they had been found yet again.

Danny looked at Hassett, then at the twins, who both nodded that they should tell Hassett everything.

"How familiar are you with archeology?" Ed asked.

Hassett did his laugh, then said, "I have a degree in it from Oxford, back before any of you were born."

Now Danny was even more shocked.

Ed smiled. "You're Dr. Steven Hassett. Expert in pre-Egyptian empires. Discredited for your beliefs that at one time an advanced civilization had spread around the world on the equator."

Hassett bowed in acknowledgement.

Ed pointed at Danny. "We are looking for his father, Professor Kenneth Hawk. He was taken by the Hydra League."

Now it was Hassett's turn to be shocked. His face went white and he had to swallow before he spoke. "Ken was taken? Then he must have found the third Hydra Journals entry?"

"He did," Danny said, surprised that Hassett had known his father. "And I have his notebooks well hidden. We are after the fourth entry in the assumption that the only way to find my father is to follow the Hydra Journals."

"And that means those two men who have been following us are Hydra League," Hassett said, clearly suddenly very afraid. Now he too sat down, so Danny and the rest did as well.

"Have I said before how screwed we are?" Craig asked, shaking his head.

"I know these Hydra League men on sight," Danny said. "If you can take me back close enough so that I can see them, I will tell you for sure."

Hassett shook his head. "They have been pacing us very carefully. They are not hunters, and are clearly out of their element here in the jungle. They are after you, and clearly hope you will lead them somewhere, and I will not take you to the old city if they are following."

"Old city?" both Ed and Ernie asked at the same time.

Hassett nodded. "Why do you think I've been living here, pretending to be a guide? This is called the Land of the Dead because of a city buried by the jungle centuries ago." He pointed to the right off the trail. "I have worked it, explored it, for twenty years now."

"We will give you the first three Hydra Journals entries if you take us to the city," Danny said.

Hassett stared at Danny for a moment, then nodded and stood. "I have the first two, but I need the third. You have a deal. But first we got to make sure we're not followed."

He turned and started up the path, moving at a good pace.

"Where are we going?" Danny asked, scrambling to get his pack on his back and follow.

"We're going to hide your friends," Hassett said. "then you and I are going to get rid of the men behind us."

CHAPTER TWENTY-TWO

September 15, 1970
Deep in the jungle, Republic of Congo.

HASSETT HAD CRAIG, the twins, and Bud hide in the jungle to the right of the path of elephants and warned them to not move for any reason, no matter what they heard or what happened. Then he used a branch to brush away their footprints where they had all entered the deep underbrush. Danny and Hassett also both left their packs, but Hassett kept a rifle he had been carrying over his shoulder.

"This way," Hassett said, turning and moving uphill through the jungle. Danny stayed with him for ten minutes, breathing hard and sweating even harder. Finally, Hassett held up his hand for Danny to be quiet, then moved to the edge of the jungle.

"Make no sudden movements," he whispered.

He then led Danny over a shallow rise along the edge of the jungle. It took a moment for Danny to realize what he was seeing. The half-mile-wide path had turned almost gray under the high trees ahead. Thousands and thousands of elephants were grazing and moving slowly down the hill.

"How did you know they were here?" Danny whispered.

Hassett pointed at the circling flocks of small birds. "They go where the elephants go."

The elephants' smell was thick in the air, like baskets of apples that had been left in the sun for days.

Danny had never seen an African elephant, and was stunned at their size, and of the size of the tusks the bulls had. He had heard that ivory poaching had been bad in some areas, but it didn't look like this massive herd had been found yet.

Danny stayed close to Hassett, moving as silently as he could as they worked their way past the elephants, past the lead bull who stood guard.

Hassett moved the two of them slightly out into the path above the elephants, then handed Danny some dry brush. "Get ready to wave this and run at them," Hassett said.

Danny finally understood what Hassett was planning.

Hassett grabbed another handful of long, dry grass, then took his rifle off his shoulder.

He lit Danny's brush with a pocket lighter, then his own, and said, "Now!"

Waving the burning grass in his hand, Danny ran at the herd of huge beasts, shouting as loud as he could.

Hassett did the same, firing his rifle into the air at the same time.

The noise and the sight of the flames spooked the herd almost instantly.

The bull trumpeted a warning, as did others, and almost as one, the entire herd turned and started down the path at a full run.

For a moment, all Danny could see was a massive wall of elephant butts disappearing into a cloud of dust.

Thousands of huge animals, all weighing thousands of pounds, all running at the same time. It was a sight that Danny had never imagined, or thought of ever seeing.

Danny dropped his torch and stamped it out.

Hassett did the same.

A couple of bull elephants trumpeted so loudly that Danny bet it could be heard miles below on Lake Albert.

The elephant stampede shook the ground like a strong earthquake, and the rumbling echoed over the jungle. The huge dust cloud drifted out over the jungle.

"How far will they run?" Danny shouted to Hassett over the intense noise.

"Far enough to take care of our friends and cover our tracks!" Hassett shouted back.

They stood and watched the amazing sight for a few moments, then Hassett led Danny back to the edge of the jungle. They plowed into the underbrush, staying in the deep jungle as they moved back down the hill toward Craig and the others.

He and Hassett joined up with Craig and the others, and with Hassett indicating they should be very quiet, he turned and led them deeper into the jungle, away from the path of elephants.

A very long, hot hour later of fighting their way down what seemed to be a narrow animal path, Danny finally asked Hassett, "When are we going to get to the lost city?"

Hassett laughed and kept going. "You've been in it for fifteen minutes."

That got all of them looking around, and now that Hassett had said that, Danny could see odd shapes buried by the dense growth of the jungle.

"How big was this place?" Craig asked, shouting his question over Danny's shoulder to Hassett.

Hassett entered a small meadow and stopped, dropping his pack in the shade under some large trees. "I figure that over a half million people lived here six or seven thousand years ago."

"Half million?" Danny said softly. He couldn't even imagine that, standing here in the jungle now. It would be like standing in downtown Los Angeles, after it was overgrown and all the tall buildings knocked down, and trying to imagine the size of the city.

"Welcome to the city of Ishango," Hassett said, waving his arm around in a wide circle.

He moved about twenty steps to one side of the meadow, beside what looked like a wall of vegetation and yanked on some growth, pulling aside the green to show stone blocks underneath.

Danny followed the angle of the green wall up through the trees, stunned as his mind tried to grasp what he was seeing.

"It's a temple," Ed said, his voice hushed.

"It seems we found our teeming masses," Craig said, shaking his head and looking around.

"Teeming masses?" Dr. Hassett asked.

Danny nodded. "Under the teeming masses, the river becomes clear, the path muddy."

"The third Hydra Journals entry?" Dr. Hassett asked.

Danny nodded. "It would seem that the teeming masses were the half million people who lived here."

"Well, I'll be," Hassett said, shaking his head and laughing. "I was so busy looking up, I never thought in twenty years to look down. I have no idea what's under this ancient city."

Danny had no doubt that to continue the search for his father, they needed to find out.

CHAPTER TWENTY-THREE

September 17, 1970
Lost City of Ishango, Deep in the jungle of the Republic of Congo.

TWO LONG DAYS of searching later, Danny finally had some luck, but not the kind he had hoped for. The ground dropped away under him like an elevator suddenly falling.

Danny had been using a burning torch for light to explore a dark room in the back of the old temple while Craig went on down a narrow hallway. The thousands of years of jungle and hot weather had left nothing of the old city except the stones with which the Ishango people had built the city. If there had ever been wooden doors, they were long gone. And every stone structure was completely covered by jungle and shaded by tall trees. In the dark rooms inside the stone buildings, nothing lived except small animals and insects.

In two days, Danny had seen more large spiders than in a bad horror movie. So far, all of them had avoided the huge creatures hovering in webs in the dark rooms. The last thing any of them needed thousands of miles from any civilization and good doctors was to be bitten by a poisonous spider.

Or any other jungle creature for that matter.

As the floor dropped out from under him with a loud crack and Danny fell, he did two things, almost instinctively, and at the same time.

First, he shouted. "Craig!"

Second, as what he thought was a solid rock floor dropped away into blackness, he twisted around like a drill the coach had made them do in football practice last year. That way he was facing what he thought was the outside wall of the building.

He found himself falling through an open space filled with twisted roots.

He frantically grabbed for anything to slow his fall. Everything went into slow motion as he grabbed and ripped out handfuls of thin roots.

Finally, one of the roots held, but his grip didn't, and his momentum yanked his hand off the root as it swung him around.

But it slowed him enough to grab more roots, and they held, and after a moment, he found himself swinging in midair, close to what looked like a tall stone wall, holding on with all his might to handfuls of tree and plant roots.

His hands and shoulders hurt, but he was still alive.

Around him was complete darkness.

He couldn't even see his arms going past his face.

The air was cool and smelled of damp earth and mold. And there was a faint, distant sound of water running.

He forced himself to remain as still as he could and take deep breaths to let his pounding heart slow and his eyes adjust. It became clear that he wasn't in complete darkness, but close.

Carefully, he then looked down.

His torch had fallen all the way through the roots and somehow remained lit, showing faint outlines of the huge cavern-like room. He could see that he still had a good fifty feet to drop from where he was hanging.

His breath caught. Oh, wow, luckily, the roots had been here, like a false ceiling on the huge underground area, otherwise he would have been very dead on those rocks below.

Above him, the hole into the room he had been in was an impossible twenty feet over his head. And there was nothing to climb on. The layer of roots didn't extend all the way to the hole.

And besides that, he didn't trust himself to let go of the roots he was holding.

He forced himself to take yet another deep breath. His hands and shoulders were aching. He couldn't hold himself here for very long.

He twisted carefully around and searched for any kind of ledge on the rock wall near where he hung.

At first, he couldn't see anything, but then he spotted a crack between two stones where more roots were growing out into the open area just below him. The crack didn't look to be more than a few inches wide, but it was more than he had now, if he could get to it.

He got swinging gently, almost holding his breath for fear he would break or pull out the roots holding him.

Finally, he managed to get one foot on the ledge. It was more than a crack. It was actually a thin ledge about an inch wide.

He eased around and pressed his back against the cold wall, using the heels of his shoes to take the pressure off his arms.

The ledge felt solid under his feet, but after falling through the floor of that room, he wasn't trusting anything at this point. He still kept his tight grip on the roots that had saved him. But at least they weren't holding his entire weight anymore.

"Danny!"

Craig's voice echoed down to him from what seemed like an impossible distance away.

"Down here!" Danny shouted back. "But be careful. It's a long fall!"

The dark around him seemed to swallow Danny's voice. And it felt like something scampered across his feet on the ledge, but he ignored that. He didn't dare try to bend over. If he did, he would swing back out into space holding on to only the roots.

And he wasn't sure if he wanted to know what it was that lived in this dark cavern.

Above him, the light from Craig's torch outlined the hole where the rock floor Danny had been standing on had slipped away. Then Craig poked his head over the edge.

"Danny!" Craig shouted. Danny had no doubt that all Craig could see was his torch seventy feet below him on the rocks.

"About twenty feet below you," Danny said. "Stuck like Spider-Man on the wall."

"Oh, man, are you all right?" Craig asked, finally seeing Danny. "And how did you get there?"

"Just luck," Danny said. "But I think I found how to get under the old city."

"Yeah, I'd say," Craig said. "Can you hang on there? I'll go get the others and some rope. Actually, a lot of rope."

"I'm not going anywhere," Danny said. "But hurry, would you?"

"Right back," Craig said.

His face and light disappeared from the hole over Danny's head.

He kept staring upward at the blackness, trying to let the training he had from his Native American grandfather take over and control his breathing.

Right now, more than anything, he needed to just remain still and calm.

Standing on the narrow ledge fifty feet over rocks, holding on to roots for dear life, there was just nothing else he could do.

Then, he felt something again move across his foot in the pitch darkness of the jungle cavern.

It felt very real and had weight.

Then the horrible thing started up his leg.

CHAPTER TWENTY-FOUR

September 17, 1970
Under the Lost City of Ishango, deep in the jungle of the Republic of Congo.

DANNY PRESSED HIS back against the stone wall. He took a slow, shallow breath to try to stop himself from screaming and panicking. On a thin ledge, with only a bunch of roots holding him in place, he didn't dare panic. That would be the quickest way to get himself killed, no matter what was crawling up his leg.

Slowly, using his left hand to hold onto all the roots that had saved his life, he pressed his back against the rock wall then took a swipe at the creature as it came above his knee in the dark.

The back of his hand hit something fairly solid and covered in some sort of fur. It felt huge, but Danny figured it was about the size of his fist. More than likely one of the big spiders.

Whatever it was went flying off into the darkness. He just hoped it went far enough that it wasn't coming back.

He sure didn't need to be fighting a mad spider in the dark while clinging to the face of a cliff.

He took a deep breath and forced himself to try to calm his racing heart and try to listen.

Nothing seemed to be moving around him.

Only the distant sound of running water broke the intense silence.

Under the teeming masses, the river becomes clear, the path muddy.

That was the third Hydra Journals entry Danny's father had found in Cairo.

It was the riddle that had led them here, to this ancient lost city. The half million people who lived here when the Hydra Journals were written were the teeming masses. And now Danny could hear the river, or at least it sounded like a river.

He had no idea what "the path muddy" meant, but he had a hunch, as with anything in this adventure so far, it wasn't going to be easy to figure out.

And even here in the dark, pressed against a cliff face, he half expected the men from the Hydra League to show up. The League had seemed to be able to track them just about anywhere they went. Their only hope, Danny figured, was that the elephants had taken care of them. Otherwise, they would show up here soon, if they weren't already here somewhere, just watching them.

The Hydra League had been formed when this city was still alive and had a half million people in it. They clearly knew these ruins were here. They were the ones protecting the secret of the Fountain of Youth.

And they were the ones who had kidnapped Danny's father.

Danny figured the only way of ever seeing his father again was to stay alive long enough to find and solve all ten of the Hydra Journals' clues. A tall order for a guy stuck in the dark on a cliff ledge.

"Danny!" Craig shouted from above. "Hang on, we're coming!"

Danny glanced up as a number of torches lit up the hole above him.

"Careful on that floor," Danny shouted up to his friends. "More sections of it might give way."

"You found the way under the city I see," Hassett said as he poked his head over the edge and looked down.

"I think it found me," Danny said. "And I hear running water."

Hassett laughed. "Perfect. Hang on, we're hooking up enough rope to get you all the way to the ground."

"Not going anywhere," Danny said, trying to adjust his grip on the roots that he had been holding onto with a death grip for what seemed like an eternity now.

A moment later a rope started down toward Danny. Craig stuck his head over the edge and watched it.

"That's enough," Craig said as the rope with a few knots in it got to Danny's level. It looked to be a thick rope, clearly something Hassett had in his camp hidden in the center of the old city.

"How far down do you think it is from there?" Hassett called out.

"Fifty feet, maybe sixty!" Danny shouted back up, glancing down at his flickering torch on the rocks below.

"Hang on," Craig said.

Danny watched as he looked around, then leaned back over the edge. "Okay, we're ready. You want a ride down?"

"I would love one," Danny said.

Craig took the rope and got it swinging slightly until finally the end got close enough for Danny to reach with one hand.

"Are you ready?" Danny shouted back up. "It's going to have to hold all my weight."

Craig glanced back over his shoulder, then shouted down, "Ready."

"Here goes," Danny said.

Letting go of the roots, he grabbed the rope right above one of the knots tied in it and swung out into space, twisting in the hundreds of roots that filled the space. He wrapped his legs around the rope, like he had done in gym class in junior high.

He was living a childhood dream. He was in a jungle playing Tarzan, only he was underground, fifty feet above rocks, in the dark, with huge spiders, and scared to death.

Tarzan had it good.

The rope held and Danny swung through the maze of roots, breaking many of them, and wrapping others around his body. He used his arms to keep the roots away from his neck. The last thing he needed was to slip and have a root hang him.

He used his legs to support most of his weight on the rope, then with one hand he pulled off many of the roots before shouting, "Lower away!"

Less than five minutes later, he was on the rough rock surface of the cavern's floor.

He hadn't felt anything so good as solid ground under his feet. He hadn't realized until he was down just how frightened he had been. Now his hands started to shake.

"I'm down!" he shouted up to a tiny hole of light at least seven stories over his head.

All the way up, the rope had knots tied every five feet to make it easier to hold and climb. That was going to be a nasty climb to get back out of here.

"Tie the rope around a rock or anchor it in some way," Hassett shouted down, his voice echoing in the large, dark cavern.

Danny did as Hassett said, then shouted that it was secure.

"Coming down," Hassett shouted.

The old archeologist had a large pack on his back and he came down the rope like a monkey, faster than Danny could have done it. For a man in his sixties, Hassett was in great shape, that was for sure.

He got to the bottom and then worked on starting another few torches.

The twins followed next, dropping quickly hand-over-hand, clearly also used to climbing ropes. They both had packs of equipment as well. Bud came down next, with a bag of something in his mouth. He was slower, clearly more afraid of the height than of climbing down the rope. Craig was last and the slowest, not taking any chances.

Craig patted Danny on the shoulder after they were all standing on the rough floor of the cavern. "Glad you're all right."

"Thank all the roots," Danny said.

Now Available
from all your favorite booksellers.

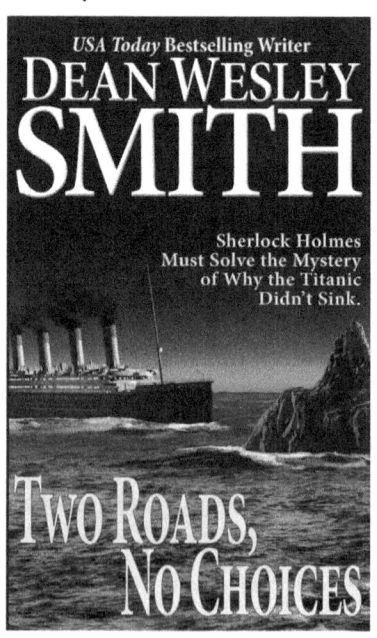

"Well, at least we found this," Hassett said, holding his torch up and studying the huge cavern around them. "The original residents clearly used these caverns."

He pointed to some old stone stairs leading down toward a lower cavern in the direction of the water, now clear in the light of six burning torches. The smoke from the torches twisted upward into the dark of the maze of roots.

Danny finally took time to really look around at the cavern he'd found.

Some of the walls were stone blocks as well. And part of the ceiling was the stone floor of the temple above them. A lot of rock had fallen in places, and the hole over their head seemed to be the only way out. The temple had been built over this cavern for a reason, of that there was no doubt. Now they just had to find the reason.

"Well," Craig said, shaking his head. "At least those Hydra League thugs won't find us down here."

"I wouldn't count on it," a distant voice said from over their heads.

All of their heads snapped to look up as if tied to the same string. There was a faint light in the hole above, and a few shadows moving around.

Danny knew that voice. It was the same man who had killed the professor back in Cairo.

How could they have found them?

Clearly they had escaped the elephants and had just been watching them the last few days.

As all six of them stared upward, the rope fell toward them, forming a huge pile with a thump at their feet.

The end had clearly been cut.

Now they had no way out.

"Enjoy your stay," the voice above them said.

Then he laughed, the sound echoing in the huge chamber like a bad villain in a bad movie.

Only this was real.

Very real.

CHAPTER TWENTY-FIVE

September 17, 1970
Under the Lost City of Ishango, deep in the jungle of the Republic of Congo.

"HAVE I SAID lately how screwed we are?" Craig said, staring at the pile of rope.

Above them the hole in the floor of the temple seemed like an impossible distance away to Danny. Totally impossible.

And the men that had been chasing them were up there, more than likely standing guard.

Before anyone else could say anything, Hassett held up his hand for all of them to remain silent. "We need to get away from this area quickly," he whispered. "Just in case they decide they need a little target practice."

Danny glanced back up. Hassett was right. Shooting them now would be like shooting fish in a bowl.

Hassett pointed to the rope on the ground. "Bring that." Then he motioned that they should follow him.

Danny picked up the huge pile of rope and his torch, and then he followed Hassett and the others down through the cavern, heading for old stone stairs that led deeper underground. At some point, the stairs must have led to something in the big cavern, but rocks now covered whatever it was.

Danny was glad that at least they were still alive. But they wouldn't be for long if they didn't find another way out of this cavern. Clearly, the two Hydra League men above didn't think there was another way out.

And Danny bet they knew the ruins.

The six of them quickly wound their way down through a series of linked smaller caverns, following the ancient stone path and stairs carved six thousand years before. Danny, on one trip to the Southwest, had gone into Carlsbad Caverns. These caverns seemed very much like those. The deeper they got underground, the more stalactites and stalagmites they wound their way through.

The colors of the stones shimmering in their torchlights were fantastic. Bright reds and blues and greens.

The deeper they got, the louder the sound of the river became, filling everything. If Danny hadn't been so worried about finding a way out, he would have enjoyed the cave exploring a lot more than he was.

Finally, the series of small caverns opened up into a huge cavern with a river running through one corner of it, crashing down over rocks and then disappearing into a wall, clearly going deeper in to the ground than it already was.

The stalactite-covered ceiling of the cavern was a good hundred feet over their heads. And from what Danny could see, there were a dozen smaller caverns leading off in different directions from this one. There was a maze of caverns under the ancient city. A maze that could easily get them lost forever.

Hassett, who had been leading them down the stone path of the ancient people, stopped in an open area and dropped the pack he had been carrying. "I don't think they can hear us down here."

"You think they're going to follow us?" Bud said.

Hassett shrugged. "Not for a week or so. Then they'll come looking for our bodies."

"Great," Craig said.

Danny glanced down at the river. "We have water, that's for sure. Anyone bring any food?"

"A day's worth for everyone," Hassett said.

Everyone else shook their heads no.

"We can stretch that to last a lot longer," Hassett said. "As long as we can drink that water."

"True," Bud said. "Many times I've gone without food for a week, but I had water."

Danny glanced at his short friend. He didn't want to know what the Cairo street kid had been through while trying to survive alone on the streets, but with comments like that, he was getting a good idea.

"So," Craig said, glancing at Danny, "what's the plan?"

Danny shrugged. "We find the next Hydra Journals entry. Then find a way out of here."

"How about we do both those things at the same time?" Bud asked.

"Seems like a good idea to me," Hassett said, smiling.

Danny agreed. They needed to find a new way out, since their way in was blocked to them, and more than likely guarded. Clearly, the ancient people used these caverns under their city, so it would be logical there would be more than one way in and out. If those ways were still open after six thousand years.

Ed glanced around, then quoted the third Hydra Journals entry. "Under the teeming masses, the river becomes clear, the path muddy."

"Shall we try to find the muddy path?" Ernie asked.

"As good a plan as any," Danny said. "And the farther we get from those men back there, the happier I will be."

"I'll second that," Craig said.

All six of them glanced back into the dark where they had come, then as one, they turned and headed down the stone pathway toward the loud river crashing over the rocks below them.

CHAPTER TWENTY-SIX

September 17, 1970
Under the Lost City of Ishango, deep in the jungle of the Republic of Congo.

"A PATH," ED said an hour later.

Danny was up on some rocks above the river, climbing to see if he could see anything from a higher position that they had missed. The stone path they had followed down through the caverns had just ended at the edge of the river like a docking port.

But the river was tumbling over the rocks so hard just below the path that Danny couldn't imagine even taking a raft down that river and into the dark tunnel.

Hassett had suggested that back when the path was built, the river had been calmer, and the tunnel led to other caverns. Maybe, but Danny doubted it. Six thousand years just wasn't that long in the life of a river cutting through solid rock.

"It's a debarkation platform," Ernie had finally said after they had explored the edges of the tunnel below the platform. "The ancient people were coming from up the river to here."

There must be something back in the cavern they had started in that the ancient people would raft to here, then walk the rest of the way. Whatever it was had clearly been covered in cave-ins and rockslides. Danny hoped the next entry in the Hydra Journals wasn't back up there.

That was when they had focused their attention upstream and Ed had found the path.

Unlike the stone path they had come down into the cavern, this path was more natural and wound its way around and past rocks. The spray from the river caused it to be wet and slick and slightly muddy.

"Well," Craig said, "we found all the parts of the third Hydra Journals entry. Now what?"

"We follow the path," both Ernie and Ed said at the same time.

"Might as well," Danny said, glancing back up the cavern to where Bud had stationed himself as a lookout for the Hydra League goons. He waved for Bud to join them, then turned to everyone. "I want us all roped together in case we slip and fall in that river."

All of them agreed, and they waited until Bud joined them to put him in the middle.

"I'll lead," Danny said. "I'm a good swimmer. Dr. Hassett right behind me. Then Bud and the twins. Craig, you bring up the rear."

They all tied themselves into the heavy rope that they had lowered themselves into the cave with, spacing themselves four paces apart.

"Everyone be careful," Danny said. "Watch your step, but keep your eyes open for any ancient writing."

Danny took a couple of deep breaths, then, holding his torch high over his head to keep it as far from the river spray as he could, he started forward.

The path wound its way along the rocks just above the water. In the tunnel, the river seemed almost calm and very black. Danny had no desire to go in that cold water and find out what lived in there.

He wasn't thirty paces into the darkness of the river cave when he noticed two things. The first was a giant spider web across the path, its web glimmering in the faint light and dampness.

He eased forward and lit the bottom of the web on fire, using the flaring torch to break the web apart. Out of the corner of his eye he saw something move in the rocks, but he forced himself to not turn to look. It was just better to not know what lived down here in normally total blackness.

Then, as he held the torch out directly in front of him, he noticed it was blowing back slightly toward him, the smoke catching him in the eyes.

A breeze.

He stopped and glanced back along the trail where everyone else had stopped waiting for him to move forward. "Notice the breeze?"

"An opening somewhere ahead," Hassett said, smiling.

"Now if it is only big enough for us to get through," Ed said.

"We'll make it big enough," Ernie said.

Danny nodded, hoping Ernie was right.

Danny led the way along the slick, muddy path beside the river's edge. The path seemed to wind on forever. Clearly, this tunnel was not normally walked. There weren't any rapids in the river, so whoever used this usually floated down from some place up ahead.

"Any idea which direction we're heading?" Craig asked from behind Danny.

"I think we're going west," Dr. Hassett said. "Toward the mountains beside the city."

Danny didn't know if that was good or bad. He just kept going, moving slowly and carefully through the rocks.

Finally, just about at the point he was going to have them stop and rest, the tunnel opened up into a giant cavern.

Some Classic Dean Wesley Smith Stories
Available at your favorite booksellers.

Danny stepped a dozen steps out into the huge space, held up his torch, and stopped cold.

From what he could see, the cavern was huge, bigger than even a massive football stadium back home. On one edge, the river had turned into a decent-sized lake, with a high platform right in the center of the room beside the lake.

The platform faced a thousand stone seats that formed an amphitheatre around the platform.

"The Great Council Chamber," Dr. Hassett said beside Danny, his voice hushed. "We found the ancients' Great Council Chamber."

"There's got to be treasure here," Bud said.

"Amazing," Ernie said.

"A stunning find," Ed said.

"Wow! Big place," Craig said.

All Danny could do was stare.

And wish his father were here to see this.

CHAPTER TWENTY-SEVEN

September 17, 1970
Under the Lost City of Ishango, deep in the jungle of the Republic of Congo.

"WHAT IS THE Great Council Chamber?" Danny asked Dr. Hassett after another minute of all of them staring at the huge cavern in front of them.

"From everything I can gather," Dr. Hassett said, "the ancient people who lived here and in other great cities around the globe were governed by a group of ten elders. These elders were elected and served like a city government, representing the adults, both men and women, of the city. This is where everyone met to listen to the council debate, act and vote."

Dr. Hassett pointed to the main platform beside the lake. "The Great Council would meet there and anyone who wanted could watch and listen. The important issues and elections would fill this place I'm sure. I had always hoped to find the remains of a Great Council Chamber, but never in this good a condition."

Dr. Hassett started off toward the huge platform beside the lake. The floor of the cavern was paved in stone blocks and perfectly smooth. This entire room was an amazing piece of construction.

Danny and the rest followed, moving slowly, staring at everything around them.

Danny almost wanted to hold his breath as he climbed up the stone steps to the giant stage.

A stone table with a polished top filled the center of the stage, but nothing else was left but dust. After six thousand years of being in the open, even in a dark cave, that made sense. No wood or cloth would survive the moisture down here.

Behind the table on the stage was a stone wall. And across the top of the stone were carved hieroglyphs, large enough for everyone in the room to read, even from the top seats. It was the first writing of any type that Danny had seen in the ancient city.

Dr. Hassett, Ernie, and Ed stared at the hieroglyphs.

"What does it say?" Danny asked.

"Hopefully it's an exit sign with an arrow," Craig said.

"From the greatest city," Dr. Hassett said.

"No, highest city," Ed said, stopping him.

"I agree," Ernie said. "Not greatest, highest."

Dr. Hassett studied the carvings for a moment, then nodded. "From the highest city, power flows to the many."

"The fourth Hydra Journals entry?" Danny asked, sick to his stomach that it looked like the trail to rescue his father would end right here, in a cave deep under a jungle.

"More than likely, yes," Dr. Hassett said. "The ancient people wrote very little in stone. This is written in an early form of Egyptian hieroglyph, as the others were."

"Well, that's that," Craig said, sitting on the edge of the Great Council table. "That's not going to lead us anywhere."

Dr. Hassett looked at Craig, then at Danny and laughed. "Of course it is."

"From the highest city, power flows to the many," Danny said, repeating the phrase. "Assuming we can get out of this cave, how is that going to help us?"

Again Dr. Hassett laughed and even Ernie and Ed looked puzzled. "Danny, your father and I both believed that this ancient civilization existed, and we both believed that it spanned the globe and was of a high degree of engineering and civilization before it died off for some reason. Many different races are descendants of this first civilization, and many races built in their ruins."

Danny nodded, as did Ernie and Ed.

"That was in my father's notebooks," Danny said.

Dr. Hassett pointed back at the images carved in the stone over the great stage. "The highest city?"

Suddenly Danny realized what Dr. Hassett was talking about. "Machu Picchu?"

"Exactly," Dr. Hassett said.

"But wasn't that an Inca city?" Craig asked.

"Later," Dr. Hassett said. "The Incas took it over, built new parts, and made it their own. But there is much evidence that the city was older than the early Incas."

"Power flows to the many?" Danny asked.

Dr. Hassett shrugged. "That's something you'll have to figure out there."

"So the next clue is in the Andes?" Bud asked.

Danny nodded. "Looks that way."

"Great," Bud said. "Glad we found it and figured it out. But right now we're trapped a long way underground in the center of Africa with bad men stalking us. First things first, I always say."

None of them had an argument for that.

CHAPTER TWENTY-EIGHT

September 17, 1970
Under the Lost City of Ishango, deep in the jungle of the Republic of Congo.

AS DR. HASSETT, Ernie, and Ed studied the rest of the main platform of the ancient council chamber for any other clues to anything, Danny decided that he and Bud and Craig would look for the way out.

Danny watched as Craig held his torch up. The faint smoke from it drifted to his right and toward the tunnel they had come through.

The three of them climbed down off the large stone platform. "Craig," Danny said, "go toward the left wall. Bud, you go up the right staircase, I'll go up the left. Using the smoke from our torches, we should be able to get some sort of reading on where the draft is coming from."

Danny quickly climbed the stone staircase that went upward between the stone benches. Even fifty rows up in the stands, he could clearly hear everything Dr. Hassett and the twins were saying. Amazing acoustics in this cave, that was for sure.

He stood about halfway up the staircase and let the air around him calm, watching the smoke. It drifted still toward the tunnel, so the entrance was above him.

"Nothing down here," Craig said from down by the left wall. "Smoke just sort of swirls."

"Mine shows the entrance is up top," Bud said.

"Go slow," Danny said, turning and starting up. "We may have someone waiting for us up there."

Bud nodded and moved at the same pace as Danny up the staircase.

At the top, there was a wide area inside yet another cavern. The entire floor of this cavern had also been paved with stones. The breeze felt clearly more noticeable, and the air was warmer as well.

Craig joined Bud and Danny in the center of the room. They let the air settle, then headed to where the wind was coming from.

At the back of the room were over a dozen tunnels, some made of stone blocks, others cut out of the natural stone. All of them led off the back of the room like spokes on a wheel. Clearly, at one point there had been a lot of entrances to this great chamber, so that a lot of people could come in at once. But now the breeze was only coming from one.

Bud led the way, moving so silently that after a moment, he motioned for Danny and Craig to just stop and he would scout it out. Danny watched Bud's torch disappear around a corner in the stone tunnel.

The waiting seemed to stretch as Danny worked to not hold his breath as he tried to listen for any problems Bud might have.

Then, after what must have been the longest two or three minutes on record, Bud came back, smiling.

"The tunnel was blocked at the entrance a long time ago," Bud said. "Clearly on purpose, so no one would find this place."

"That doesn't sound good," Craig said.

"There was a cave-in just short of the blocked entrance," Bud said, smiling. "We can climb up the rocks and get out just fine."

"Okay, so we can get out," Craig said, clearly feeling as relieved as Danny felt. "Now what do we do next?"

"We look for treasure," Bud said, smiling.

"Besides that," Craig said, laughing.

"I think that's a discussion for everyone," Danny said. "But I'm voting for South America."

"Yeah," Craig said. "Why did I know that?"

Two hours later, sitting on the benches of an ancient civilization's Great Council Chamber, they worked out their plan.

CHAPTER TWENTY-NINE

September 22, 1970
Bunia, Republic of the Congo, on the shores of Lake Albert.

FOUR DAYS AFTER leaving the Great Council Chamber, they made it back down the Trail of Elephants to the shores of Lake Albert.

Dr. Hassett left them almost at once, headed back down the Nile. He didn't dare stay since he was easily recognized in the area. He planned on holing up in an apartment in London and writing up his notes and publishing a few papers on the great lost city. He had enough pictures, enough evidence, that he hoped to get some decent publications, even though his name had been discredited.

Danny wasn't happy with him leaving them, but they really didn't have any choice if they didn't want to draw attention to themselves. With luck, they would meet him in London after they had found the next Hydra Journals' entry in Machu Picchu.

The problem they faced was how to get out of Africa.

At first it had been suggested by Bud that they try to make it across the Congo and to the west coast, but that was ruled out by everyone. Even Danny knew enough about that jungle and the tribes and governments of the Congo to not go that way.

And none of the boys wanted to try going back down the Nile to Cairo, following Dr. Hassett. Going that way felt to Danny like walking into a huge trap.

Right now, he was convinced that if they stayed hidden, they would have a head start on the Hydra League men still guarding their old camp up in the ruins. It would still be days, maybe weeks yet, before those men discovered that they hadn't died in the cave, but had escaped.

After leaving the cave, Bud had worked his way back down into their old camp in the ruins. The two Hydra League men had been sleeping close by, so Bud had managed to get all their money and a few personal things in packs that the two men wouldn't know were missing. So at least they had money for whatever they needed to do.

"We go east," Ed said after they had all stared at the maps for a time.

"Aren't we trying to go west?" Craig asked. "Seems that South America is west of here, if I remember my world map correctly."

Danny agreed. "Going east across the Indian Ocean and then the Pacific is a long way out of the way."

Ed nodded. "But we need to go east to get out of Africa. Then we go south and west."

"I agree," Ernie said. He pointed at the huge body of water on the map. "We need to cross Lake Victoria and get into Kenya."

Ed traced the path they were proposing with his finger on the map. "We land in Kisumu in Kenya, take overland transportation of some sort to Nairobi, then a train down to Mombasa on the coast. From there we can get a ship to take us down the coast to South Africa. In Cape Town, we know people who will help us get to Brazil."

Danny looked at the two twins shocked that they would even think of the idea. "You can't go back to South Africa."

"Yeah," Bud said. "They were shooting at you in Cairo, remember?"

Both Ed and Ernie nodded. "We don't have a choice. It is our best chance from here."

Danny didn't like it, but after a few hours of studying the maps, he knew they were right. The twins had to go right back into what might be a death trap if they were all to get out of Central Africa and get on with the search for the Hydra Journals.

CHAPTER THIRTY

October 2, 1970
Cape Town, South Africa.

THE FREIGHTER DOCKED at just after twelve noon in what was clearly a huge, industrial port to one side of Cape Town. From the deck of the freighter as they moved into the harbor, Danny could see at least a hundred ships of all sizes, if not more. It was a very busy international port.

The city itself looked beautiful, tucked in under a long mountain with a flat top the twins said was aptly named Table Mountain. Ernie pointed out Devil's Peak and Signal Hill to the right of Table Mountain. The place would have been interesting to explore if it wasn't so deadly to the twins. They had to get in and out of this port fast.

The sun was high overhead and the air was hot and thick with the smell of oil and sewage. Hundreds of workers swarmed over the docks, loading and unloading the ships.

Danny and Craig were standing on the deck as the crew finished the tying up of the ship. Ed and Ernie had insisted that as a group, they couldn't be seen together. Only Danny and Craig dared do anything, so the twins, with Bud, had stayed hidden below decks, with Bud standing guard for them.

With the apartheid form of government, and the high levels of segregation, two white boys and two black boys were not allowed together. Just doing that would be enough to get Ed and Ernie tossed in jail, and then once the police discovered who they were, they would be killed without trial.

So it was up to Danny and Craig to find a British ship of some kind and book them all passage to Brazil. Danny had no doubt, looking at the busy docks, that wasn't going to be an easy task.

An hour later, they finally found the headquarters of a British ship company, tucked just off the docks on a side street.

The man inside, behind the desk, was dressed in a blue uniform of some sort, with a tie and hat. A fan was working hard in the window to keep the air in the room moving, but it still felt like a sauna bath in the small office.

Danny introduced himself and Craig and told the man that they and three other friends were looking for a way to get to Brazil.

"Americans?" the man said in a fairly proper British accent.

Danny nodded. "Washington State."

The man nodded and chuckled to himself. "We get a lot of American boys these days, traveling the world, trying to stay out of your infernal war in Southeast Asia. Do you have money or do you need to work your way there?"

"We have some money," Danny said. "But we don't need anything fancy. In fact, we would rather not be on a fancy ship."

"Hiding are we?" the man asked, looking at them.

"In a manner of speaking," Danny said, letting the man go ahead and think they were running away from the draft. It was easier than telling him the truth.

The man nodded. "I have a freighter leaving in two days for Brazil. It will be running mostly empty to pick up coffee. I have two spare crew cabins you could have."

"That would be perfect," Danny said.

"All five of you need to be on dock 86-B before seven in the morning, October 4th, with your passports."

"Not a problem," Danny said.

"See to it that it isn't," the man said.

The five tickets cost Danny almost half of the money he had left, but it was worth it. And once in Brazil or Peru, he could wire Uncle Steve and get more.

"That went surprisingly easy," Craig said as he and Danny headed back toward the freighter.

"Yeah, now we just have to hide for the next two days. And try to keep the twins from being spotted."

Now Available
from all your favorite booksellers.

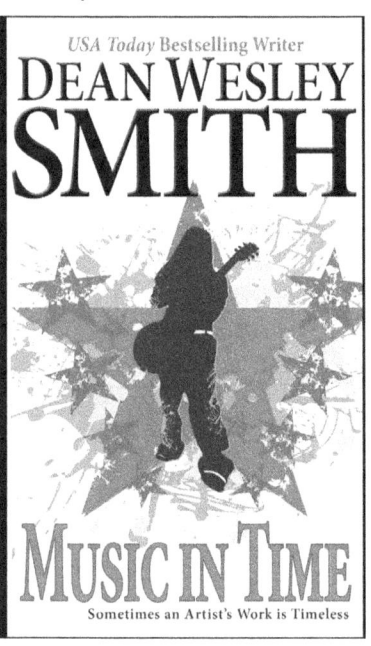

"From the sounds of it," Craig said, shaking his head, "just being seen with us could be just as bad."

"Yeah," Danny said.

In America, he had watched night after night of civil rights demonstrations on television. He had watched the replay of the assassination of Martin Luther King. Being part Indian, he understood some of what the blacks were going through, but not much. He had been lucky to be raised where he had been raised.

And until Ed and Ernie had mentioned that they couldn't be seen together, Danny hadn't even thought of them as anything but two others his age. Sometimes the world was just a stupid place.

As Danny and Craig moved between two large crates and were just about to step into the open in front of the freighter, Bud appeared beside them.

"Stop! Hide!"

He motioned for them to duck back in behind the crates.

Just as they did, two white men in brown dock police uniforms escorted Ed and Ernie past the crates.

Both men were carrying guns, and had them pointed at the twins.

Danny could feel his stomach twist. They couldn't lose the twins now. They had to do something.

"What happened?" Danny whispered.

"Captain turned them in as being suspicious," Bud whispered back, spitting on the ground in disgust. "I barely got away."

"As soon as they find out who they really are, they're dead," Craig said.

"I know," Danny said, doing his best to keep his heart from beating right out of his chest. He was sweating harder than he should be in the heat. "We follow them."

Bud nodded and led out, motioning to them when it was clear or not.

They didn't have far to follow the two policemen. The twins were taken into a large warehouse two ships down from where their freighter had docked. On the small side door of the warehouse, a sign said simply, "Port Police."

Danny had no doubt that the twins were as good as dead unless he and Craig and Bud could do something, and do it fast.

But what? Danny had no idea.

CHAPTER THIRTY-ONE

October 2, 1970
Cape Town, South Africa.

THE POLICEMAN RAISED his gun at Danny Hawk and shouted, "Halt!"

Danny stopped, then carefully turned and raised his hands above his head.

Never, in all his life, had he been so scared. He had been in a lot of rough situations over the years, and even more since his father had gone missing. But having some large man in a brown uniform point a gun at him was the most frightening.

Around him, the huge three-story tall warehouses of the Cape Town shipping docks felt like huge child's blocks. They blocked the sun from getting down into the narrow alleys between the buildings, but didn't block the heat. And right now, Danny had sweat running down the side of his face. He wasn't sure if it was from the heat, or from the fear.

Probably both.

If this plan didn't work, he just might spend a lot of years in a South African prison. And right now, standing here with his hands in the air and a gun pointed at him, he wasn't sure about anything

working, let alone getting his friends, Ed and Ernie Black out of jail.

For all Danny knew, he might be shot where he stood.

"What are you doing down here?" the man asked, not lowering his gun. The guy was huge, carried the gun like it was a toy, and looked mean, with a pockmarked face and balding head.

"Looking for my dad, sir," Danny said, in his best British accent, following the cover story he and Craig and Bud had decided on earlier. "He was supposed to be down here. His name is Carl Conley. My name's Carl Conley Junior."

Carl Conley was a name Bud had seen on an office sign near the dock headquarters. The guy either ran this entire docking facility, or was near the top. Danny had no idea if he had a son or not, but he had to take a chance that the guard wouldn't know if the big boss did or not. After all, this was a huge docking facility.

The guard lowered his gun instantly and smiled a sickly smile. "Oh, sorry. I was just doing my job, you understand."

Danny took a deep breath and lowered his hands, going on with the plan he, Bud, and Craig had come up with. "No harm done."

Bud had said that the best plan was the boldest plan. Right now, Danny didn't feel so bold. He just hoped the guard didn't notice that his hands were shaking.

The guard put his gun away and then smiled again, stepping closer to Danny. "Any idea where your father was supposed to be?"

"His secretary said he was going to be at a jail," Danny said, continuing his bold lie. "I think she called it a holding area. She said it was in one of the warehouse buildings. He was coming down to see two prisoners. She gave me directions to the building, but I got lost."

Danny knew he was only one building over from the jail holding the twins.

"You didn't miss it by much, young man," the guard said, laughing. "And don't worry on getting lost. I still get turned around in this maze of buildings and I've worked here for years. Follow me."

He led the way between the two buildings and then to a door in the side of one warehouse that Danny had seen the twins taken through.

Danny walked in ahead of the guard, trying to act like he belonged where he was.

The small jail was just like an office, with two desks, a few extra guns on the wall, and a refrigerator tucked down a small hall behind one desk. The small window was barred and dirty.

The place was stuffy, hot, and smelled stale and sickly, like some drunk had thrown up the night before.

Another large guard sat behind the desk to the right, and through a barred window in a door behind him, Danny could see one of the twins in a window-less cell.

"Conley is on his way down here," the guard who had escorted Danny into the room said to his friend. "This is his kid."

The guard behind the desk stared at Danny, clearly not believing his story.

Danny knew he looked rough and his clothes were slightly dirty from being in the jungle, even though they had managed to wash most of their things while on the ship from Kenya. Danny knew he didn't look like an executive's son.

"Thought Conley's kid was younger," the guard behind the desk said, frowning and looking at Danny carefully.

This was going badly. This guy knew Conley.

"I grew up," Danny said, shrugging.

Suddenly, a loud crash filled the room. Something large had slammed against the building near the jail door.

Danny ducked for cover behind the desk, still playing his part, acting like he was suddenly afraid. Both guards headed for the door, guns drawn. Danny just hoped Craig and Bud stayed out of sight.

As the two guards reached the door, another crash echoed from the next building.

"Stay here, kid," one guard said to Danny over his shoulder as they went outside on the run.

The moment they went through the door, leaving it wide open, Danny headed for the twins. The keys to the jail cell were hanging on a peg beside the door and Danny grabbed them.

Outside, one of the guards swore in pain.

Clearly, Craig and Bud were distracting them. Danny wasn't sure he wanted

to know how. Bud had said to trust him, the guards would be distracted.

Danny sprinted into the darker cell area.

Ed was in the cell to the right, Ernie to the left. The place smelled of urine and vomit.

"Danny!" Ed said, moving to the bars.

"What are you doing here?" Ernie said.

Both looked shocked and very happy.

"Jailbreak," Danny said. "But if we don't move fast, I'm going to join you."

And Danny didn't like the sound of that at all.

CHAPTER THIRTY-TWO

October 2, 1970
Cape Town, South Africa.

THERE WAS ANOTHER crash outside as Danny fumbled with the keys. He finally found the right one after what seemed like an eternity and opened Ed's cell door.

From outside, one of the guards again swore in pain. Then there was a gunshot.

The sound froze all three of them.

Danny's stomach twisted even tighter at the thought of Bud or Craig getting shot.

"Hurry," Ernie said as Danny again fumbled with the keys.

"I'll get our passports and papers," Ed said, sprinting for the front office. "I saw where the guard put them."

More swearing and shouting from outside, this time a little more distant.

Danny finally got Ernie's door open and the two of them ran for the outer office.

Ed slammed a drawer and held up his and Ernie's papers with a smile. "Got them, and the money those two took from us as well."

At the outer door, Danny had the twins stop and he went out first, looking around. No sign of either of the guards. Just sounds of swearing from the other side of the warehouse across the paved alleyway.

There was no one else in sight.

The plan had been for Craig and Bud to lead the two men to the west, while Danny and the twins went in the opposite direction. They were to meet up somewhere near dock 86-B.

Danny indicated that the twins should follow him, then at a run, they turned left and went down the side of the warehouse, then a quick left again around a corner of the building. They ran for the length of two large warehouses, turned right, ran the length of yet another, and then turned left again.

Danny was really starting to get winded in the heat when Ed said, "In here."

They ducked into an area between two buildings that was stacked with dozens of piles of wooden pallets.

"You are amazing!" Ed said breathlessly to Danny, patting him on the back.

"We thought we were dead for sure," Ernie said.

"We all might be if we don't find a good hiding place," Danny said, looking both ways down the narrow alley between the warehouses. He was sweating so hard, it was stinging his eyes. They all were going to need something to drink pretty soon as well in this heat.

"We can't keep going together," Ed said.

Ernie nodded. "This is still South Africa. Whites and blacks can't be together doing anything, unless the white is in charge."

Danny just shook his head. He understood the reality of that, but he sure hated it. Just as he hated it when people treated him differently, or put him down for his Native American heritage.

"Where are we meeting Bud and Craig?" Ernie asked.

"And how are we getting out of here?"

Danny explained that he had booked them all passage on a British freighter heading for South America, but it didn't leave port until 7 A.M. October 4th.

"That's two nights and a day away," Ernie said.

Danny nodded. He knew that, and was very worried about that as well. This was a very busy port, well-patrolled. Now that the twins had escaped, everyone would be looking for all of them. Hiding was going to be a real problem. Just getting to dock 86-B was going to be a problem. That was a good mile from where they were.

"Here," Ed said, pointing back at the pile of wooden pallets.

Danny, at first, couldn't figure out what Ed meant. This alley clearly wasn't a good hiding place. And it was far too close to those two guards back there.

Then Ed moved to a dolly with four wheels and a handle. There were three of them parked in the alley.

"Pallet movers," Ernie said to his twin brother. "Great thinking."

"Want to clue me in?" Danny asked.

"Watch," Ed said. He grabbed one machine, quickly moved it around like he had handled the thing before. It had two long blades on the front that slipped in under the bottom pallet. With a few quick pumps on a handle, Ed picked up a six foot high stack of empty pallets.

Ernie quickly did the same thing, rolling the pallets out into the open.

"Now, you walk behind us, pretending like you're in charge of what we're doing," Ed said. "We're taking these to dock 86-B."

"You're the boss," Ernie said firmly to Danny, looking him right in the eye. "Remember that and act that way."

"I hate this," Danny said.

Ed smiled. "This is what our parents fought against and died trying to stop."

"Some day it will stop," Ernie said. "But for now, we live with it and get out of this country."

"Can't be fast enough for me," Danny said.

CHAPTER THIRTY-THREE

October 2, 1970
Cape Town, South Africa.

THE THREE OF them got a few odd looks from other workers along the way, but no one stopped them. Danny hated acting like he was in charge of his two friends just because of their skin color. But he tried to, and Ernie and Ed pulled the stacks of pallets carefully, slumping over like they were used to the hard work.

Finally, as they neared the dock where the British freighter would hopefully take them out of this country, Danny heard Bud whisper from a nearby open warehouse door.

"Here."

Danny and the twins glanced over to where Bud was in the dark shadows just inside a warehouse door.

The twins quickly moved the wooden pallets over into an area that held other pallets, then the three of them went inside.

It took a minute for Danny's eyes to adjust. But it soon became clear that the warehouse was stacked completely full of huge crates. Some of the stacks reached clear to the tall ceiling three stories overhead.

The air inside was cooler than out-side, but not by much.

The huge shipping doors of the ware-house were closed, and the only light came from a few high, dirty windows.

"Is Craig all right?" Danny asked as Bud led them deeper into the darkness of the warehouse.

"We heard shots," Ernie said.

"Just fine," Craig said, stepping out of the shadows. "Can't say that I like getting shot at by the police, though."

Danny patted his best friend on the shoulder. "Just think of all the stories we can tell the girls when we get home."

Craig laughed. "Yeah, like they're going to believe us."

Danny laughed as well, very happy to see his best friend alive and well.

"I've found a great place to hide," Bud said.

He led them, single-file, deeper into the giant stacks of crates until they were near the middle-back of the warehouse. Then Bud pointed upward.

"We climb up there and hide on top, or inside those top crates, depending on what's in them. We'll know if workers start moving these things. We'll have time to make a break for it. And guards aren't going to climb every stack in here looking for us."

"Perfect," Ed said, nodding.

"But we're going to need water," Ernie said.

Danny looked up at the tall stacks of wooden crates towering over them. He wasn't real excited about spending the next two nights in here, but at this point, they had no choice.

Or at least none that he could think of.

"The next warehouse over has an office in it," Bud said, pointing to the west wall. "I'm sure we can find water there at night, after everyone's gone. And we have enough food to last us until we get on board the ship."

With that, Bud turned and started up the side of the stack of huge wooden crates like he was climbing the side of a rock mountain. It was as if Bud had spent most of his life climbing wooden crates. He didn't miss a step or a handhold and before Danny realized it, Bud went over the top and disappeared.

A moment later he poked his head back over the edge. "Easy. Everyone take their own stack. But these things are so close together, if we have to, we can run across the top of them."

Danny remembered the terror he had felt jumping from one roof to another over an alley in Cairo. He really didn't like the idea of jumping from crate to crate over a thirty-foot drop.

But so far, in looking for his father, he'd done a lot of things he didn't think he'd ever do. He just hoped crate-jump-ing ahead of guards with guns wouldn't turn out to be one of them.

CHAPTER THIRTY-FOUR

October 3, 1970
Cape Town, South Africa.

THE FIRST NIGHT sleeping on the tops of the tall stacks of crates had been nerve-wracking. The crates were square, and Danny could barely lie side to side without his head or feet being near an edge. So all night he had a constant fear of falling asleep and rolling off.

He had managed to use a few of his clothes from his bag as padding and a pillow, but the rough surface of the wooden crate top still dug into his skin every time he moved. And any noise from outside the huge warehouse made them all sit up and hold their breaths in the dark. The dock was a busy place, day and night, so there were a lot of noises.

It had been a very long night.

After what seemed like an eternity, the sun finally came up, casting bright streams of light through the huge warehouse. From on top of the crates, the place looked more like a giant checkerboard, with the spaces between the crates dark lines. Since the tall stacks weren't much more than four feet apart, all of them had gotten used to jumping over the dark between the crates. It had twisted Danny's stomach the first few times, but now he knew it was nothing more than a really wide step to get from one to another.

Bud had vanished without a word just as the first light of day was starting to color the dirty windows of the warehouse. Now, suddenly, he appeared from out of the dark near Danny's crate.

"The British ship docked last night," Bud said. "They're just finishing unloading it now."

Danny had been worried a lot about how they were going to board tomorrow morning, in the light, with all the dock hands around getting ready for the ship's departure.

"I think," Danny said, "that when it calms down some around the ship, I should go talk with the captain. See if we can board late tonight."

"Good idea," Ernie said. "Better than in the light."

"We can go on separately as well," Ed said. "Less chance of us being noticed that way."

"And I'm going with you to talk to the captain," Craig said. "Less chance of a policeman paying attention if there are two of us."

"I'll make sure there are no police around before you go," Bud said.

"Good," Craig said. "I can't say I was looking forward to another night on top of this wooden mountain."

Everyone agreed to that, then talked softly for a while about what might be the best time to board if the captain of the ship allowed it. They decided that around eleven would be the best, since that appeared to be when there was a shift change of workers and thus the fewest number of people around.

For the rest of the morning, they all tried to sleep some more. Then, just after one in the afternoon, with the twins staying up on their crates, Bud gave the all clear.

Danny and Craig climbed down and strode out into the heat, headed for the ship, pretending to act like they belonged there and knew what they were doing.

There were a few dock workers a good warehouse distance away, but no one seemed to be anywhere near the British ship.

Danny felt really exposed out on the dock beside the huge ship, and even more obvious walking across the long plank way up to the ship's deck.

"Are we supposed to ask for permission to board?" Craig asked as they neared the edge of the ship.

Danny shrugged. "I have no idea, but I would think so."

"I don't see a doorbell," Craig said.

"Or even a place to knock," Danny said, looking both directions along the ship as they hesitated before stepping on board. He had a hunch they would be doing something wrong if they went on board without someone's permission, so he decided they would just stop and wait.

They stood there for a good thirty seconds, both of them looking around, not only for someone on the ship, but for guards with guns to come running in their direction along the dock.

No one seemed to notice them.

"Now I know what a target on a shooting range feels like," Craig said.

"Let's give it another minute, then board and find someone," Danny said. He was sweating in the hot sun and for the second time in two days, his hands were shaking.

At that moment, a voice with a clear British accent echoed down at them from up near the top of what looked like the bridge of the ship. "Permission to come aboard. Come to the top level."

Danny didn't see who shouted, but waved his hand in acknowledgement, then he and Craig boarded the big freighter.

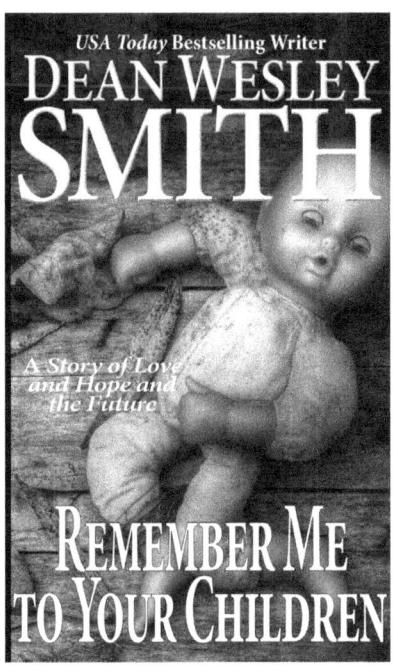
The ship was long, with open holds in the front and back decks, and a three-story center area. Their footsteps echoed on the metal decking and it seemed even hotter on the ship than it had been on the dock, if that was possible.

"You ever get the feeling we're going from the frying pan into the fire?" Craig asked.

"In more ways than one," Danny said. "More ways than one."

CHAPTER THIRTY-FIVE

October 3, 1970
Cape Town, South Africa.

INSIDE THE STEEL-PLATED structure, it wasn't any cooler. In fact, it seemed to be warmer.

"I hope our cabins have air-conditioning," Craig said softly as they climbed the metal staircase.

"Dreaming again," Danny said.

Craig made a snorting sound. "I used to dream of girls and football."

There was nothing Danny could say to that. Because his best friend had come with him, Craig had been shot at more than once, been trapped in a cave, had to jump off a moving ferry, and run from gunmen from the top of one building roof to another. Danny couldn't ask for a better friend, of that he had no doubt.

The upper deck had doors and windows open, and a slight breeze was blowing through the bridge area, cooling it a little.

"Come on in," a man in a blue uniform said from what looked to be the bridge area. The windows were huge along the front, and there was a giant wheel with a chair behind it square in the middle. The panels under the windows were filled with instruments the entire width of the room. And there was another big table along the back wall that held maps and charts. Hundreds of them from what Danny could tell.

"I'm Captain Townsend," the man said in a clear British accent. He smiled and extended his hand. "I assume you are two of my passengers to South America."

Danny and Craig both shook his hand as Danny did the introductions. The captain's hand was firm and calloused. He was shorter than Danny by a few inches and looked stout, as if he hadn't missed a meal in a long time. His uniform jacket was tight, and his tie slightly loose. Danny couldn't even imagine wearing a jacket and tie in this heat, but the captain didn't even seem to be sweating.

"Ya know," Captain Townsend said, smiling, showing a mouthful of really brown and twisted teeth, "I admire a man who has respect for another man's ship. So, what can I do for you boys? You know we don't set sail until tomorrow morning?"

"Yes, sir, we do," Danny said. "But we were hoping we could board later tonight, to stay out of the way tomorrow morning. We'd stay in our cabins and be no problem, I can assure you."

The captain looked first at Danny, then at Craig, no longer smiling. "The ticket master said you American boys were on the run from something. Now that wouldn't be serving your country, would it?"

Danny shook his head. "No, sir. We are both in college and not needed for military service."

Now the captain really frowned. Danny had a hunch he had clearly been ready to give them a long lecture on duty to a country.

"I don't much like taking on trouble on my ship. If not service, then what are you running from?"

Danny glanced at Craig, who just shrugged. Danny had no intention of going through the long story of the Hydra League, but he could tell the captain a little of the truth. Selected parts.

"I'm looking for my father," Danny said. "He disappeared in Cairo a number of months ago. We have information that leads us to believe he was taken to Peru. Four of my friends are helping me on this search."

The captain nodded and just waited for Danny to go on. This man was clearly very smart.

"Craig and I are from Washington State, and while in Cairo, we met Bud and the twins, Ed and Ernie. Bud is from Cairo and Ed and Ernie are from here. They are all about our age."

Now the captain was nodding, as if he was ahead of Danny's story, but still waiting.

"Ed and Ernie are black," Danny said, watching the captain's face. The man didn't seem to have a reaction, so Danny went on. "Their parents were killed by the South African government for protesting against apartheid. The government here is looking for them as well."

"For heaven's sake, son, why did you boys come back here then?"

"We were in Kenya," Danny said, changing the truth of his story a little to make it easier to tell. No point in telling him about a hidden city in the jungles of the Congo. "That was where we discovered we needed to go to Peru in my father's search."

Again, the captain nodded. "And you had to change ships here? Now I see why you want to come on board tonight."

"Sleeping on a wooden crate in a warehouse can get tiring," Craig said, smiling.

The captain laughed. "I can see why it would. But you are putting yourselves and your friends at great risk by telling me this."

He moved over a few feet and picked up a piece of paper. On it in big red letters was the word 'Wanted.'

The captain gave the paper to Danny. "It says there your two friends escaped from a dock jail yesterday, with the help of at least two white boys."

Now the captain was no longer smiling.

Danny felt his stomach clamp up into a knot. He forced himself to try to breathe, but he didn't get much of the warm air.

"Have I said lately how screwed we are?" Craig muttered, staring at the wanted poster.

Danny ignored his friend and squarely faced the captain, looking him in the eye. "Yes, sir, the twins were taken by port security because of their skin color and the fact that our last captain said they looked suspicious. If the government had discovered who they were, they would have been killed without trial. I was the one who broke them out of that cell."

"We all helped," Craig said, smiling a sickly smile.

"As I said, I don't like trouble on my ship," the captain said. He stared at Danny for a minute. Then he nodded. "But I like the policies of this South African government even less. Half my crew is colored, or as they are wanting to be called now, black. My first mate has a dark skin color because he has a father from Pakistan. I hate even docking here."

He took the paper back from Craig and wadded it up into a ball and tossed it into a nearby garbage can. "Come on board tonight at eleven during dock shift changes," the captain said, his voice very serious. "Your cabins are numbered seven and eight on the deck below this one. Stay inside until we are at sea and someone comes for you."

"Thank you, sir," Danny said.

The captain nodded. "Just don't make me sorry I'm doing this."

CHAPTER THIRTY-SIX

October 3, 1970
Cape Town, South Africa.

THAT NIGHT AT eleven, Danny went on board first and alone, greeted by the captain. "I got most of my crew below securing the cargo. Make it quick."

Danny nodded and waved for the rest to come forward. The captain sounded as worried as Danny felt. That wasn't a good sign.

Craig came from the right and was halfway up the gang plank when Ernie appeared out of the shadows and came up the plank behind Craig. Both of them had disappeared with a quick thank you to the captain when Ed appeared and came on board, followed quickly by Bud. It all took less than a minute.

"Stay hidden until we come to get you," the captain said to Danny as he turned away to let Danny follow Bud inside.

The cabins were warm, but not unbearable. Ed and Ernie took one with only two bunks, Craig, Bud, and Danny took the other one that had three.

As Danny closed the door, Bud dropped onto the bunk. "I hope prison beds are this comfortable."

"I don't like this," Bud said, walking around in a circle in the middle of the room like a caged animal would walk.

"We are trapped here, trusting the honor of a British captain."

"If we're going to get out of this country," Danny said, "we don't have a choice."

None of them slept during the next six hours. Danny just sat on a bunk facing the door, expecting it to be opened at any moment by a South African policeman with a big gun.

Bud alternated between pacing and sitting on the floor in the corner. Craig just lay on his bunk staring at the ceiling. They didn't talk. They felt like they didn't dare.

It was still two hours from sailing when the door did burst open, but it wasn't the South African police, but the captain. "Quickly, bring your things. You have to hide."

Danny scrambled to his feet, grabbing the case with the copies of his father's notebooks and his clothes bag, then went out the door behind the captain, a half step ahead of Bud.

The captain said the same thing to the twins, then without waiting to see if he was being followed, went down the hallway to a staircase and then started down.

He didn't stop at the main deck, but kept going down the tight, circular metal staircase.

Danny lost track of how far they went down, but clearly they were going down into the cargo hold.

At the bottom, the captain shoved open a hatch and went through, waiting until all five boys had followed him.

The inside of the freighter's cargo hold was almost as large as the warehouse, and just about as tall. Lights were strung along the ceiling and they gave the place a dim, eerie glow.

Parts of the cargo hold were stacked with the same kind of crates they had spent the night before on. They were all well tied down to the walls and each other. It seemed the big wooden things were standard shipping crates for this area of the world.

The captain pointed to the large stacks of crates secured against a bulkhead. "Climb up on top and stay very silent and out of sight, no matter what you hear. We're done loading this area, but there will be inspectors walking through."

With that, he ducked back through the hatch toward the stairs and slammed the hatch closed.

Thirty seconds later, they were all on top of different crates and had their gear stored on the bulkhead side.

Up that high in the cargo hold, the temperature was higher than it had been outside on the deck. Danny didn't much like the idea of them being trapped down here, but again, he could see no choice.

On the crate beside Danny, Craig stretched out staring at the deck over him, his head resting on a folded up shirt.

"How much did you say you paid for these tickets?"

All Danny could think to say was *Hopefully not with our lives.* So instead, he said nothing.

CHAPTER THIRTY-SEVEN

October 4, 1970
Cape Town, South Africa.

ONE VERY LONG hour later, the hatch below clanged open.

Danny didn't dare glance over the edge, but from the sounds of it, there were three men down there.

They walked around and down the narrow aisle through the middle of the hold between the cargo, then came back.

"Satisfied now, Commander?"

It was the captain's voice.

"They have not yet boarded, and we depart in an hour. As I have said, the ticket agent told them seven, so my guess is that is when you will see them, if they are stupid enough to try to still board after what I understand happened yesterday."

"Thank you, Captain," another man said, his voice low and cold. "We will wait for them on deck. I assume you are correct. These five boys are proving to be very resourceful."

"Yes, very," another man's voice said.

Danny almost choked.

The voice was the same one Danny had heard in Cairo ordering the professor's death. And the same one he had heard before the rope into the cavern was cut.

Somehow, the Hydra League had followed them here.

How was that possible?

And how could the Hydra League be working with South African police?

The sound of movement came from below, then finally the hatch was slammed closed again.

Bud eased silently toward the edge of the crate he was on top of and peeked down.

Danny held his breath and waited.

He was in a cargo hold of a ship in Cape Town, South Africa, and the Hydra League had almost found him. There was going to be nowhere on the planet they could run from these men.

"Clear," Bud whispered.

"Was that who I think it was?" Craig whispered.

Danny nodded, trying to force himself to breathe and calm down.

"Hydra League?" Ernie asked.

"How?" Ed asked.

"At least when we don't get on board, they will stay in South Africa looking for us," Bud said.

"Don't count on it," Danny said.

Craig let out a long breath. "Have I said lately just how screwed we are?"

CHAPTER THIRTY-EIGHT

October 4, 1970
Middle of the South Atlantic.

SEVEN HOURS LATER, no one had come for them.

An hour after their visitors, the ship had clearly left the dock.

For the first few hours, it felt as if the ship was moving slowly through the huge harbor. Then, in the fourth hour, the ship clearly got to rougher open seas.

It got almost impossible to stay on top of the crates with the ship rolling from side to side, so they all climbed down and found hidden areas on the deck surface among the cargo.

"How long does it take to reach international waters?" Craig finally asked after seven hours in the cargo hold.

"We should be well into them by now," Ed said from where he and his brother were hiding between two crates.

"I agree," Ernie said.

"So how come the captain hasn't come for us?" Bud asked.

"I wish I knew," Danny said. "But let's give it more time."

They cracked out what little food they had left and ate that, then talked for a short time about how they were going to get from Brazil to Peru. They needed to get to Machu Picchu, if Dr. Hassett's guess about the meaning of the fourth Hydra Journals entry was correct.

Danny had no doubt that the Hydra League also knew that was where they were heading. Danny had no idea what to do about that. Machu Picchu was an ancient city, but the way it sat on top of those mountain ridges, it just wasn't that big a place for five boys to hide from professional killers.

Suddenly, a series of small bangs echoed through the ship, as if someone was firing guns.

Outside the hatch, a few shouts sent them all scrambling back into the dark shadows between the cargo crates.

Then nothing.

Silence. Just the low rumbling of the ships engines and the creaking of the cargo as it shifted slightly in the rolling waves.

No one came through the cargo hatch, no other sounds could be heard.

"I don't like the sound of that," Craig whispered.

Danny didn't either.

"Maybe I should go see what has happened," Bud said.

"No," Danny said. "We wait. The captain will come for us when he can."

"If he can," Craig said.

They all settled in to wait.

Danny sat with his back against a crate at the end of a dark passage. Craig lay stretched out on the deck between two crates to Danny's right, and the twins and Bud were to his left.

Three more hours wore past. Danny was so tired from not sleeping that he kept wanting to close his eyes, but every time he did, he saw hooded men and giant spiders.

Finally, Bud whispered, "We need to know what is happening. It is after five in the evening."

Danny agreed. He pushed himself to his feet, letting his cramped legs stretch out. "I'll go."

All five of them met in the wider area running down the middle between the high-stacked cargo.

"No," Bud said. "I am better at this sort of thing."

"At this point," Craig said, "what difference does it make? They see one of us, they're going to know we're all here. So I say we all go."

Danny glanced at his best friend. "I agree. And we're going to need water and more food soon. There's no way we can last down here the entire trip to South America. We all go."

They turned and headed toward the hatch into the stairway.

It didn't take them long to find out that something was very wrong.

The hatch seemed almost stuck, which got Danny slightly panicked. If they were locked in here, they would die of thirst and hunger long before they reached South America.

He took a deep breath and stepped back.

"Don't tell me we're locked in here?" Craig said, his voice very worried.

"I don't think so," Danny said. "It doesn't feel locked. But there's something on the other side of it. Help me push."

Danny got down low, and then with Craig to his right and Ernie to his left, the three of them pushed on the hatch. It slid open only part way before stopping.

"There's something on the other side," Craig said.

"I can get through that," Bud said, pointing to the slight opening they had managed. "I'll move it."

Bud barely managed to squeeze through, and it took a little more pushing by Danny and Craig on the door to help him get his head through.

Then he vanished.

A moment later, there was a movement on the other side of the door and the hatch swung open.

"Found the problem," Bud said, pointing to the body of a man on the deck as Danny stepped through.

"Is he dead?" Craig asked as he followed Danny.

"Very," Bud said. "Starting to get cold."

"This can't be good," Craig said.

Danny really hadn't known what he had expected Bud to find, but a body holding the hatch door closed wasn't it. He stared at the man for a moment, trying to understand what he was seeing. If this man had fallen, why hadn't he been discovered before now? Did this have something to do with the bangs and yelling they had heard hours ago?

Then he noticed something.

There was no blood.

And a foam had dried on the dead man's mouth.

"Poisoned," Danny said softly.

CHAPTER THIRTY-NINE

October 4, 1970
Middle of the South Atlantic.

THE FIVE OF them climbed the stairs out of the cargo hold as silently as they could, finally reaching the lower deck of the ship.

Another man's body lay sprawled in the hallway at the top of the stairs, and again, there was no blood. The guy had just fallen there and died.

Some Classic Dean Wesley Smith Stories
Available at your favorite booksellers.

"Any idea how many men were on this ship?" Ernie asked, his voice a whisper.

Danny shook his head. "The captain never said."

"More than likely not more than a dozen," Craig whispered. "Counting the captain."

Danny glanced at his best friend with a puzzled look.

Craig shrugged. "I used to think about crewing on one of these cargo ships to get away from home, see the world."

"We need to find the captain," Bud whispered. He pointed up the stairs and Danny nodded.

Bud went first, then Danny followed.

The ship was silent in a way no ship should ever be silent. The engines were still working, the twisting screws sending a vibration through the decks. But nothing else seemed to be making any noise at all.

At the top of the stairs, Bud went right and then into the bridge of the ship.

Danny was right behind him.

The captain and three other men lay dead in the room. They too had clearly been poisoned.

Out the windows, nothing but dark grayish water could be seen in all directions. The sun was low in the sky, coloring a light cloud cover in pinks and reds.

Danny glanced around at the dead men on the bridge, then turned to his friends, who were all staring out over the water as well.

"We need to search the ship and quickly," he said. "Ernie and Ed, take the main deck, search all the rooms, find out what rooms are on that deck as well. Craig and Bud, you take the deck below this one. Make sure you look in every cabin. I'll search this top deck. We meet back here. Be careful."

All of them nodded and headed out.

Danny stared at the sea in front of the ship. From the looks of it, they were all right for the moment. The sea was fairly calm, and the ship seemed to be on some sort of auto-pilot. But they were going to need to find someone alive.

He did a quick search of the top deck and quickly found the communications room. An explosion had torn it completely apart. There was clearly no contacting anyone for help.

The captain's quarters were beyond that, and then a few smaller rooms, including a wine storage area and a small galley stocked with food.

A man in a white chef's uniform was dead on the floor of that room. He clearly had been working on some sort of salad when he died.

Except for a huge map room behind the bridge, that was it for the top deck. Four dead on the bridge, one in the galley.

A few minutes later Bud and Craig appeared.

"Four dead on the second deck," Craig said, his voice soft. He was clearly affected by seeing all this violence.

Danny was as well, but he was trying to not let it get to him. They had to think, and think fast if what he feared was true.

The twins appeared a few minutes later.

"Four dead in the crew's dining room and one in the galley," Ed said.

"So, no one's alive anywhere?" Danny said after telling them what he had found, including how the communications room had been completely destroyed.

"Signs of small explosion on the second deck," Bud said. "And here as well." He pointed to a place under one panel.

Danny looked closely. Clearly, a small explosion had happened there, leaving black stains spraying out over the polished metal.

"Looks like someone must have set off a lot of gas bombs of some sort," Ernie said.

"Unlucky that everyone was inside," Ed said. "If a couple of crew members had been out in the open air, that wouldn't have worked."

"No reason for them to be outside," Craig said, pointing at the deck three stories below the bridge window. "It was a safe bet everyone would be inside and all the killers had to do was make sure the gas was everywhere."

"But why kill this crew?" Bud asked.

Danny looked at his friends, then said, "Hydra League. They must have suspected we were on board somewhere."

"Why not gas the cargo hold as well?" Bud asked.

"No time to set it?" Craig said. "More than likely it was a second search team that was setting the bombs. The captain was with the one that came into the hold."

"So, you're saying they killed this entire ship's crew to kill us?" Ernie asked.

"Considering what they have done so far, it would seem likely," Danny said. "They think they have to stop us somehow."

"Well," Bud said, "whatever the reason this was done, right now we need to get moving and get these bodies outside and toward the stern of the ship."

"Why?" Craig asked.

"I see you've never been around a dead body in the heat," Bud said, staring at Craig.

Craig's face turned white and Danny felt his stomach lurch at just the thought.

Working together, it took them almost an hour to get all the bodies out and onto the stern cargo area. They covered the bodies in a large canvas tarp and tied it down securely.

That was a job that was going to give Danny nightmares for years, if he survived for years.

They gave the crew a moment of silence in respect, then went back up to the bridge.

"Okay, two really important questions," Craig said, staring out over the ocean and the setting sun in front of them. "First, is the food and water poisoned?"

Ernie shook his head. "This was a gas."

"I doubt it would get into anything that was sealed," Ed said.

"Good," Danny said. At least they wouldn't die from starvation.

"Second question, then," Craig said. "We know we're going west, we know we're somewhere in the southern Atlantic. But can anyone drive this thing?"

Silence as they all stared out at the huge ocean as they rode forward through the rolling waves.

"That's what I was afraid of," Craig said.

Danny looked around and then leaned against the map table. "We're on a ghost ship."

CHAPTER FORTY

October 4, 1970
Middle of the South Atlantic.

DANNY DECIDED AFTER his stomach rumbled loud enough for Craig to comment on it that they all needed to get something to eat and a little rest so that they could think. At the moment they were safe as long as the auto-pilot on the ship stayed on and the Hydra League didn't come back to check on their handiwork.

He mentioned that frightening thought to Bud and they all agreed that they needed to stand watch and stay in the bridge and upper deck for the most part. That way they could see anything approaching.

So Danny sent Bud and Ernie and Ed for food for all of them while he and Craig stayed and stood watch.

The sky had turned from reds and pinks to a dark blue now and the stars had come out.

It was then that Craig said, "We're being followed."

Danny grabbed a pair of binoculars and looked in the direction Craig was pointing. He was right, there was a ship's light there. But it was so far away it was impossible to tell the size of the ship. But it was clearly on the same path they were on.

"Think we could be so lucky and that's another cargo ship?" Craig asked.

Danny shook his head. "Not a chance."

"Think this ship has any weapons on board?" Craig asked.

"Got a feeling we are going to need to find that out right after we eat," Danny said.

"Find out what?" Bud asked as he and Ernie and Ed came back in carrying cans of different food, some plates and silverware, and some jugs of water.

"Weapons?" Craig said. "We are being followed."

"And why does that not surprise me," Bud said.

Danny agreed. Nothing surprised him anymore.

They sat around the big map table eating and talking about options. From what Danny could tell, they had almost none.

Bud came up with the idea of turning off all the ship's lights if they could figure out how to do that.

Danny doubted that would do much good since radar would easily track them.

Craig thought that maybe they could just increase the speed, but none of them were sure that would be a good idea either. Or would serve any real purpose.

So weapons and making the ship their last stand seemed like their only hope. But at least for the moment, the trailing ship didn't seem to be getting any closer. But more than likely by tomorrow morning as the sun gave them light that would change. Danny had no doubt about that.

Absolutely none.

They were on a ghost ship that would soon turn into a battlefield. The five of them would give it a fight, but honestly he didn't give them much hope.

Ed and Ernie took the first watch while Danny, Craig and Bud stretched out in the captain's quarters to sleep for a few hours.

As Danny was falling asleep, all he could think about was his dad. After reading all his notes and such, his dad clearly must have known of the level of pure evil of this Hydra League. Why hadn't he just backed off?

And why were these people so intently set on stopping Danny?

Pieces still didn't make sense and Danny had a hunch they wouldn't until they made it to their next clue.

And more than likely not even then.

CHAPTER FORTY-ONE

October 5, 1970
Middle of the South Atlantic.

THE SUN WAS just starting to show a hint of rising when Craig said, "The ship is getting closer."

It was clear the ship that had been trailing them was small and fast. But that meant it was going to have to get up right against the big cargo ship and the attackers were going to have to climb ropes up the side to get on board.

The five of them had spent hours during the night, after a few hours rest each, either on watch or searching for weapons. They found none. They did find a dozen flare guns in lifeboats and six flares for each gun and some fishing spears of some sort, but that was it. No actual guns at all.

But Danny had no doubt the flare guns could do some real damage, at least at close range. So they each carried one of them. And they stashed the others at specific locations in their defense plan.

They then worked to block or lock all the big metal doors that led up to the top deck. Might as well make it tough for whoever was going to try to kill them to get to them.

Bud had found them an escape route down and out that was mostly a trash chute of some sort, but it would keep them from being trapped up high.

Now all they could do was wait for the other ship to try to board them.

They did have a few lines of attack planned that might slow them down some.

Bud had suggested that they go down on the deck and hide near where someone from the other ship might try to climb up the side and onto the deck. Then when the smaller ship got right below the big ship, the five of them would drop heavy things on the smaller ship.

Danny had liked that idea, even though it got them in the open for gunfire. If they could damage the other boat, it might buy them some time.

Of course, then they would be back to being on a ghost ship. But at the moment that seemed like the best outcome they could hope for.

Craig suggested that once the other smaller boat was close and right against the cargo ship, they could fire some flares into it as well, maybe get lucky and hit something that would catch on fire.

Danny liked that idea as well.

So they had a plan, their fall back final stand in place, their attack set.

Now they just waited as the other ship got closer and closer.

The waiting was pure torture.

They all stayed down and didn't move, expecting the approaching ship to be watching for any signs of life at all.

Within twenty minutes the small craft pulled even with the large cargo ship. Danny and the rest stayed out of sight completely. Anyone near the ship might think they were not on board, so they would have to board to make sure.

The smaller craft fell back and came up the other side, then fell back again and moved in closer to the starboard side.

"Here we go," Danny said to Craig as the ship vanished out of sight down near the waterline of the big cargo ship.

They had figured the boarders would come on board in one of three places with rope ladders affixed to the outside of the tanker and that had been their top pick. So they had stocked everything from heavy footlockers to crates of machine parts and big metal tools that had taken two of them to lift into place.

Bud was the first one to the edge of the ship where the small ship had vanished and peeked over the edge, then quickly scooted back.

"They are tied up against the ship," Bud said. "Right below this point."

He pointed to a spot on the railing.

All of them knew what they had to do.

Danny and Craig grabbed a heavy footlocker and moved it to the edge of the ship and dropped it.

Bud tossed some machine parts over the edge.

The twins picked up a large crate of parts and eased it over the edge.

Bud peeked over and then laughed.

"Direct hits," he said, laughing. "Some big holes in the deck and one guy is down for the count. It's like we kicked a hornet's nest down there."

Danny and Craig quickly eased another footlocker over the edge and gunfire erupted from below, hitting the footlocker just as they released it.

The twins pushed another crate over the edge and Bud cheered.

"Two thugs down."

The gunfire kept coming so they went to just tossing heavy tools over the edge without really exposing themselves.

Then Craig eased up to the edge of the big ship with a flare and fired downward.

"Direct hit," Bud said. "One guy jumped into the water trying to put the flame out."

"How many men are on that thing?" Danny asked, almost afraid to hear the answer.

"Seven more still moving," Bud said.

"Are they going to try to climb up?" Craig asked.

Covering fire opened up from below and Bud ducked back. "I think that is exactly what they are trying right now."

"Craig," Danny said, "move aft and try to get another flare or two into that boat. Ernie, you move toward the stern and do the same."

Both moved quickly, staying low and out of sight of the men below.

"We bomb them with tools," Danny said, grabbing some heavy equipment from some lockers they had found below and sending it over the side.

The three of them kept up a constant rain of heavy metal on the ship and the men trying to climb up.

From both sides both Craig and Ernie fired numbers of flares at the boat and the men.

After the second shot, Danny went ten steps toward the stern and peeked over the edge at the ship going up and down in the rolling waves below.

They had made a mess of the boat, that was for sure.

The small boat was on fire in two places and as he watched, both Ernie and Craig hit it again with more flares. Only two men were left on the small boat still standing, but both were hiding, not even trying to do anything about the fires.

Two men were still on the ropes on the side of the ship, but they seemed to be hanging on for dear life as the rain of metal from above was barely missing them, or clipping them. One looked like he already had a broken shoulder.

Danny took out his flare gun and aimed it at the ropes right above both men.

The flare hit its target and both men went over backwards, one landing in the water and the other hitting the edge of the craft below before bouncing into the water.

The speed of the big cargo ship soon left them behind.

Craig and Ernie again fired into the boat as the two remaining men worked madly to get their boat untied from the larger cargo ship.

Both flares hit targets and both men again ducked for cover.

Two more flares and this time one of the flares hit a gas line and the explosion sent all of them back onto the deck of the cargo ship.

Danny felt like his eyebrows had been singed.

"Wow," Ernie said, shaking his head and trying to clear his ears.

Danny's ears were ringing as well as he scrambled back to the edge to see the small boat below burning.

The small boat was clearly going down.

And fast.

There was no sign of any of the men and most of the boat was on fire.

The five of them watched as after a moment the speed of the cargo ship pushed the nose of the smaller ship under water and then sunk it, ripping it from where it had been tied to the large ship like pulling a loose scab from a wound.

"Holy shit, we did it," Bud shouted.

As Danny stood up, feeling intense relief, a voice behind him laughed and said, "I didn't expect you would need my help."

All five of them spun around, flare guns raised.

The man was smiling, his hands in the air.

It took only a moment for Danny to realize he was staring at his father.

And the next moment he was in his father's arms for the best hug he had ever remembered getting.

And giving.

CHAPTER FORTY-TWO

October 5, 1970
Middle of the South Atlantic.

THE FIVE OF them, plus Danny's father, stood around the big map table on the bridge eating and laughing and talking. Bud and the Twins had scrounged up more food and jugs of water and Danny couldn't remember when canned beans and franks had ever tasted so good.

Danny wasn't so sure who was the happiest seeing his father, him or Craig or the twins. Bud seemed to be just taking it all in stride as he always did.

Danny was stunned when he learned that his father had known where they were most of the time, but hadn't been able to get to them ahead of the Hydra men.

And his father was very happy to hear they had copies of his journals and the originals safely hidden back in Cairo.

It seemed that when Danny's father discovered Hydra was coming after him, he vanished, making it seem as if he had been abducted. He had a number of people helping him along the way and when he realized that Hydra was coming after his family and friends as well, he got his wife and brother to safety as soon as his brother got off the plane in Seattle from Cairo.

"We going to be able to see them?" Danny asked.

Danny's father nodded. "As soon as it is safe. They are protected for now."

Danny was very glad to hear that. He hadn't realized how much deep down he had worried about his mother and his uncle until his father said that. He couldn't do anything, so he had just sort of put them out of his mind as much as possible.

"You two just vanished into Cairo," Danny's father said to Danny and Craig. "It was impressive how you did that."

Danny pointed to Bud. "We had expert help."

Bud bowed slightly.

Danny's father went on. "We just couldn't keep up with you five. We were always a half step behind the Hydra men and a full step behind you. Until you ended up here on this ship."

Danny nodded.

He knew that his father had come in on a small craft with a crew of ten and had approached the cargo ship in the shadow, keeping the big ship between him and the Hydra boat. His father and a few others had boarded, fully armed, while Danny and the others fought the Hydra men.

They ate and talked for a few minutes more about the strange fight they had put up and how it had worked even without real weapons.

"The crew of this ship are under tarps on the aft deck," Bud said, reminding them of the deaths of good people who had tried to help them. "Best we could do."

"We'll take care of them before we go," Danny's father said, nodding sadly.

All Danny could do was nod. The captain had given his life and his crew's lives to help them.

"And professor, where exactly are we headed," Ernie asked.

"I would imagine the same place you five were headed," Danny's father said, smiling. "Machu Picchu. And now that we can all work together, I have a hunch we just might be able to solve this puzzle."

"And you want us all along with you?" Bud asked.

"You five solved four pieces of one of the great puzzles of all time," Danny's father said, looking at Danny. "And survived in the process. Of course I want us all working on this together."

Danny looked at his father and he could tell that he wasn't telling the entire truth.

"But you expect the five of us to go one way while you go another," Danny said. "Am I correct?"

"We will need to do that at times," his father said, smiling. "Sometimes teams are better working together, sometimes apart."

"And safer," Bud said, nodding.

Danny didn't like the sound of that at all, not after finally finding his father, but he nodded, then turned to Craig, his best friend. "Do you want to continue on?"

Craig just laughed. "Doing anything else at this point would sound downright boring. I'm in."

Danny smiled and turned to Bud. "There is still treasure out there. You still in?"

"I wouldn't miss this for half the loose change in Cairo," Bud said.

"You two?" Danny asked, turning to the twins.

"We will be honored to be part of this mission and to continue to work with you and the professor," Ernie said for both of them.

Danny turned back to his father, a large smile on his face. "Seems you have more recruits."

"I am honored and thankful," Danny's father said, putting his arm around Danny. "And damn proud of all of you."

Danny just smiled.

"And I want to thank each of you personally for helping Danny look for me," Danny's father said. "It means more than you know."

All of them nodded and Danny felt better and happier than he had felt in memory.

"So now how do we get off this ghost ship?" Bud asked.

Danny glanced at his father, who was smiling, then turned back to Bud. "We don't. At least not yet."

Danny saw his father nodding.

"Did you forget that none of us can run this thing?" Craig asked, sounding shocked.

Danny turned to his father. "I assume you are going to leave a couple men who can operate this cargo ship?"

Again his father nodded. "And fix the radio equipment?"

"Good idea," Bud said.

"They will pose as two crew members who were out in the open when the gas attack hit and on their own got the ship close to port in Brazil. Help will come from the port at that point to finish taking over the ship."

"So why?" Craig asked.

"Because Hydra needs to think we were never on board this ship," Danny said.

Again his father nodded.

"So they will spend their time in South Africa," Ernie said, nodding.

"We can hope," Danny's father said. "But I doubt it will slow them down by too much. But finally they will be behind and that's where we need them."

"Still leaves the question of how we get off?" Bud asked.

"A boat will pick you up in the middle of the night one day off the coast of Brazil," Danny's father said. "That will get you to shore and from there you need to make your way to Machu Picchu. Money and equipment and supplies will be waiting for you as well as transportation around the tip and up the South American coastline."

"So when will we see you again?" Danny asked.

"I have to get more help for this cause," Danny's father said. "This will be a very long fight ahead of us and we have to be ready to win this before any of us can truly be safe."

Danny just nodded. He felt ready now for anything that might come their way. And knowing his father was out there working toward the same end calmed him more than he wanted to admit.

So two hours later, Danny stood with his best friends on the deck of the cargo ship in the wind and the setting daylight and watched the small ship carrying his father vanish off ahead of them.

The two men from his father's team were already working on the radio and correcting the ship's course to get it back solidly in the shipping lanes.

When the small boat could no longer be seen, Danny turned to his four friends. "Thank you. We set out to find my father and we did. And I can't thank you enough."

"Technically he found us," Bud said and Craig punched him lightly.

They all laughed and to Danny that laugh felt wonderful.

"So what are we supposed to do for the next ten days until we get off this monster?" Bud asked.

"I think we might want to study the journals more," Danny said.

Craig and the twins nodded.

"We might as well be as ready as we can be for what's coming," Craig said.

"Exactly," Danny said. "And whatever it is, I have a hunch it will be exciting."

"And that might be the greatest under-statement of the century," Bud said.

Danny had no doubt that was the truth.

And he found that exciting.

As long as he now knew his father was alive and working with them. That really was all that mattered.

Coming Next Issue in *Smith's Monthly*

NUMBER FORTY-ONE
FEBRUARY, 2017

Original Stories, Novels, and Articles

Smith's MONTHLY

DEAN WESLEY SMITH

TOMBSTONE CANYON
A Thunder Mountain Novel

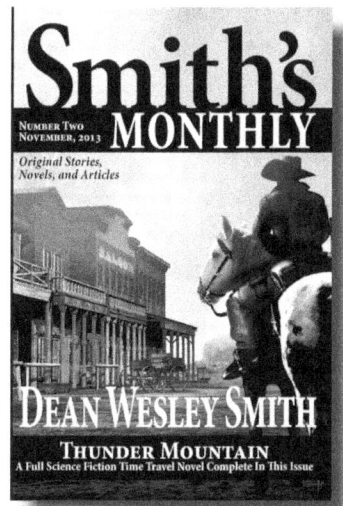

#1...October 2013   *#2...November 2013*   *#3...December 2013*

#4...January 2014   *#5...February 2014*   *#6...March 2014*

#7...April 2014

#8...May 2014

#9...June 2014

#10...July 2014

#11...August 2014

#12...September 2014

#13...October 2014

#14...November 2014

#15...December 2014

#16...January 2015

#17...February 2015

#18...March 2015

#19...April 2015

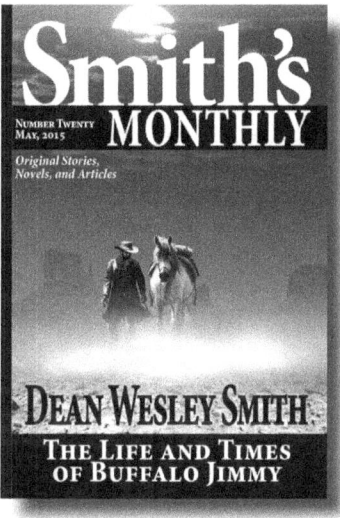

#20...May 2015

#21...June 2015

#22...July 2015

#23...August 2015

#24...September 2015

#25...October 2015

#26...November 2015

#27...December 2015

#28...January 2016

#29...February 2016

#30...March 2016

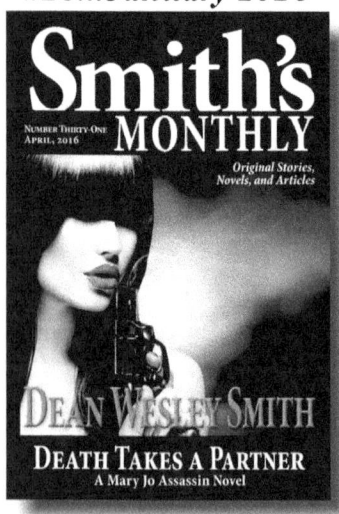

#31...April 2016

#32...May 2016

#33....June 2016

#34...July 2016

#35...August 2016

#36...September 2016

#37...October 2016

#38...November 2016

#39...December 2016

#40...January 2017

Thank You!!

I would like to thank the following wonderful people who support my blog and my work through Patreon. Your support is very important to me. Thanks!

Irette Y Patterson
Kathryn Rooney
Erick Lindman
Christopher Ridge
Raphael Husbands
James Gotaas
milady133
Danica Oakley
Kenny Norris
Kate MacLeod
Leah Cutter
Leigh Anderson
Robert J. McCarter
Jennette Heikes
Jamie Curierre
Albert Lemke
Marsha Kessler
Diane Darcy
Robin Brande
James Husum
Terry Mixon
Shantnu Tiwari
Chong Go
Maria Grace
Gnondpom
David Hendrickson
Fen

Sherman Cox
Miguel Angel Alonso Pulido
Marian Goldeen
Michelle Tatam
J.R. Murdock
Gunnar Gunderson
Jesse P Thurston
coraa
Martin Barkawitz
David Beers
Leslie Claire Walker
Nancy Hendrickson
F.I. Goldhaber
Michael J Lawrence
Barbara G. Tarn
Anthony St. Clair
Ann Tucker
Karl Gallagher
T. Thorn Coyle
Cristof Jones Harrison
Tasha Turner Lennhoff
Brenda Smith
Kari Wolfe
Mary Jo Rabe

And a very special thank you to Betsey Wilcox.